I0744184

GIVE & TAKE

THE LOST & FOUND TRILOGY BOOK ONE

VM RHEAULT

Copyright © 2022 Vania Rheault

Give & Take
The Lost & Found Trilogy Book One

Re-edited and republished November 2023

Published by Coffee & Kisses Press
This is a work of fiction. Names, characters, places, and incidents are the
product of the author's imagination or are used fictitiously. Any resemblance to
actual persons, living or dead, events, or locales is entirely coincidental.

Cover design by Vania Rheault via Canva.com
Pictures purchased and used with permission from depositphotos.com
City Background: Contributor, @ dell640;
Photo ID, 35619901
Handsome man: Contributor, @ PeopleImages.com;
Photo ID, 660838140
Contract vector: Contributor, drsuthee.hotmail.com;
Vector ID, 468487966

Cover fonts: Playfair Display
Author name font: Cinzel Decorative
Interior text font: Fanwood

Coffee & Kisses Press logo designed by
David Willis and Drake Rheault
Coffee & Kisses Press owned and operated by
Vania Rheault.
Printed in the United States of America
All rights reserved.

Paperback ISBN: 978-1-956431-31-5
E-Book ISBN: 978-1-956431-30-8

❀ Created with Vellum

For the readers who gobble up my words as fast as they fall from my fingers. Thank you.

ABOUT THE BOOK

She can't leave if she's already gone.

Jack

My 45th birthday is next week, and I want a baby. I ask Emma Cox, my personal assistant, to surrogate for me.

I've always had feelings for her, but I never wanted to acknowledge them because I'll never get married and risk my wife leaving me and our children the way my mom left my dad, me, and my sister.

I think Emma's crazy when she accepts my terms on the condition we spend time with our friends and families so our child will have a support system without her.

What I didn't understand was she wasn't doing it for our baby. She was doing it to show me what I could have if I put the past behind me.

Something I will never be able to do, no matter how much I love her.

Emma

I've been in love with billionaire Jack Durand since the day I met him. I didn't want to be the office cliché and kept my feelings to myself.

When he asks me to surrogate, against everyone's advice, I say yes. I want to use the time with him to make him fall in love with me.

I didn't realize how deeply his rocky childhood hurt him, and I should break our contract before he breaks my heart.

CHAPTER ONE

Jack

My feet pound the treadmill, and it quakes as perspiration drips off my nose. I stare straight ahead and out the window of the gym Heath and I meet at after work. He's running next to me—the incline steeper than mine, the son of a bitch—and he can't pry his eyes off the little screen attached to his machine. A Rafferty Clark's *Talk of the Town* commercial is playing, hyping up a new and exclusive article on Bridgeport's trendiest gossip e-zine. The web-only magazine doesn't need a commercial to draw in readers. Fresh, and true (what a novelty), gossip about the city's rich and famous does the job well enough.

I hate Rafferty Clark, can't stand his smug smile, and not because he likes to write about me.

"I want to have a baby." I can't stop the words from popping out of my mouth, the desire manifesting into something tangible I can't bottle up.

Heath shoots me a side-eye, slows the speed on his treadmill, and lowers the incline. "You don't have the right parts for that," he says, trotting to a walk for a quick cool down and grabbing his water bottle in the cupholder.

Gratefully, I slow my speed, and with the back of my wrist, brush the sweat off my forehead that's trickling into my eyes. "I don't mean me, specifically. I'm getting old. I want to have a baby."

Heath should understand. Happily married for the past fifteen years, his wife has given him three beautiful little girls, and, from my point of view, he couldn't be luckier.

"I'm not the one you should be talking to, pal." He slams the Stop button on the treadmill and hops off, forcing me to follow if I want to continue the conversation. In an open area behind the treadmills, bikes, and ellipticals, he falls to a mat and starts stretching.

I scowl and sink to the floor next to him, but I don't stretch. "I'm being serious."

"So am I," he says, leaning over to touch his toes. "Talk to Veronica. You've been seeing her for the past two years. Knock her up."

"She doesn't want kids. She's happy with her career." Veronica's the female half of a popular Bridgeport morning program on Channel 7, *Rise and Shine, Bridgeport!* She's on air Monday through Friday from seven in the morning until noon. Along with co-host Felix Rivera, she interviews celebrities, tapes cooking segments, creates crafts for the holidays, and is the apple of Bridgeport's eye. She'd never want a baby to interfere with her professional plans. She wants to be the next Kelly Ripa, and there's nothing standing in her way.

Heath presses the soles of his feet together. "Then what were you thinking? Adoption? Fostering?" He chugs from his water bottle, his eyes never leaving my face.

Uneasily, I shrug. "Surrogacy, maybe."

He nods. "You can afford it, but . . ."

I know how he gets when he's hearing something he doesn't like, and I try not to bristle. I haven't given this a lot of thought, in fact, the issue might not have come up at all except it's my forty-fifth birthday next week, and all my friends have kids nearing the double digits if they aren't already. I'm missing out, in a big way, and I can't wait to find a woman who won't betray me or marry me for my money.

She's not out there.

Veronica and I are a good fit. She makes her own money and uses the fame dating me gives her. I don't want a commitment, and I'm happy to help her career. Ratings for her program are through the roof, month after month. The network is ecstatic, and she wants to keep them that way. A baby isn't part of the deal.

"But what?" I prod. He won't tell me if he thinks I'll lose my cool, and I sit on the mat in a puddle of sweat, desperation, and apprehension, the machines spinning around us.

"Don't you want your son or daughter to grow up with a mother?"

I scoff. "What does that have to do with anything? Claire and I turned out okay."

"That's debatable."

My dad kicked my mother out when I was four, Claire, a toddler. She doesn't remember Mom, but I do, bits and pieces. Scents. Screaming. Crying. That dread, listening to her sobs and denials, still sits in the pit of my stomach, the little boy fear. I won't subject my children to that.

"She can't leave if she's already gone."

That's the closest I'll ever come to admitting how fucking hard it was growing up with that image stuck in my head—

watching from the third floor nursery while the nanny tried to console me as a taxi carried my mother away.

My father didn't give her a chance to say goodbye.

Heath hefts himself to his feet and hauls me off the floor with a strong yank. Spring has sprung, and we'll wait to shower at home.

We retrieve our wallets, keys, and the clothes we wore to work from the locker room, and carrying our bags, we walk to a pub next door. We just ran off a thousand calories, but we'll drink them back quick enough. He chooses a high-top near the window, and our pictures will be all over by the time we're done drinking our glasses of Guinness. Like me sipping a beer should make news.

"So, then what? You're going to look into agencies? Find a woman who has good genes and let a doc with a turkey baster shoot your sperm up there?" Heath picks up where we left off, as if we didn't just have a ten minute intermission.

The waitress sets our glasses of Guinness in front of us and saunters away.

"You don't have to sound so crass," I mutter. "Surrogacy is the only way some people become parents. You could have a little compassion."

"The people you're talking about suffer from infertility or other situations that prevent them from having their own children. There is nothing wrong with you, and Veronica's healthy unless you know something I don't."

His guess is as good as mine. We don't talk about things like that.

I down half my glass. "I thought you'd be on my side."

"I am, but I want more for you than a strange woman popping out a baby that's half you. You should want more than that for yourself. Zoey and I are happy, and I want you to find that, too."

"Aren't you afraid she's going to leave you one day?"

He turns, stares out the window, and hunches his shoulders. Heath and I have been friends for a long time. I'm his daughters' godparent and share the honor with Zoey's sister. We've talked deep before—when his father passed away, when his youngest was born a few weeks too early and she had to spend time in the NICU. A conversation like this isn't anything new. In fact, I'd be surprised if a month didn't go by and we didn't get into something heavy. He's the only one who knows what happened with my mother, the only person I trust to know.

"Sure, but she feels the same way about me. Who isn't having an affair these days? It seems every minute Rafferty Clark is pulling back the sheets on some asshole who can't keep his dick in his pants. Zoey knows I love her, and I show her by being home for dinner, helping the girls with their homework, being present for family movie night. If Zoey leaves, she'll have her own reasons, and it won't be because of me."

"I'm sure my mother had a good reason, too."

"Ron never talks about it."

Heath knows my dad won't say one single thing about my mother. What I know of her leaving is what my little boy heart remembers.

"I wasn't thinking of an agency. I was going to try for something more personal."

Heath raises his eyebrows. "Yeah? One of Emma's friends, maybe? Or your sister?"

"Asking Claire would be a little strange." I try to picture my sister pregnant with my baby and my beer rolls around in my stomach. Nope.

"Not so strange. Siblings carry children for their brothers and sisters, but being that you're more than capable of finding a woman who could give you a baby and you're not shooting blanks, I guess in this case I'd have to agree with you. So, Haisley? Mia?"

Haisley and Mia are my personal assistant's close friends. Emma Cox has been working with me for three years, and she's the best assistant I've ever had. She's pretty, competent, and has a sense of humor that can lift me out of my blackest mood. Best of all, no matter what kind of temper I'm throwing at her, she's not scared of me. She's also Rafferty Clark's girlfriend. She says they're only friends, but you don't look at a friend the way Clark looks at Emma.

"I was thinking more along the lines of Emma," I admit, finishing my beer and waving to the waitress for another round.

Heath whistles. "Clark would never go for it."

"They're only friends."

He laughs. "He's as infamous as the people he gossips about. Emma and Clark are on the gossip sites all the time. You know as well as I do if she's not at work they're together. What makes you think she'd be willing to do that? And what about Veronica? You think she's going to be on board with Emma and a turkey baster?"

"Stop talking about a turkey baster. I'd want to do it naturally."

The waitress sets our beers on the table, her eyes darting between Heath and me, and she scurries away from the tension hanging over us. I'd have better luck bending her over the sink in the men's room than I would talking Emma into bed with me, but I can buy anything. There's got to be a price Emma won't say no to. Everybody has one.

Leaning forward, Heath murmurs, "You want to fuck your PA, knock her up, tell her she won't be a part of her baby's life because you have mommy issues and don't believe your child needs one to grow into a fully-adjusted adult, and you think this *won't* cause any problems? Are you high?"

"Can you focus on what matters? I'm going to be forty-five in a week. I've got a shit-ton of money and nothing else to show for it. I'd like to be a dad, I'd like to carry on the Durand name, despite my mommy issues as you so eloquently called them. I can't commit. Don't want to commit. What I have with Veronica is enough, and she's happy with her career. If Emma won't do it, then I'll look into agencies, but if I can keep it personal, keep a little heart in it, then maybe I can let some of my resentment go that it has to be this way."

Heath shakes his head. "It doesn't have to be this way, but I doubt that's something you'll ever understand. All you're going to do is hurt Emma and she won't want to work for you anymore. If you do convince her to sign a contract, and you do convince her to hand over her baby after it's born, what do you think that will do to her? Surrogates are paid to keep their hearts out of it. You can give Emma all the money in your bank accounts, but she's not built that way. Find someone who is, Jack, or you'll be sorry."

We finish our beer in silence and our glasses empty, he slaps me on the shoulder. "I admire what you're trying to do, but running a business isn't the same as starting a family. One you do with your head, the other you do with your heart. Talk to you tomorrow."

Through the window, I watch him slip into a waiting car, and it melds into the traffic. He'll go home to his fancy brownstone, an adoring wife, and three girls clamoring for his attention the second he steps through the door. He doesn't know what it feels like to be alone, to step inside an empty penthouse and do the same lonely bullshit over and over again. If I had a child, at least I'd have something to look forward to after a long day.

It wouldn't hurt to ask her, and if she expresses any kind of incredulity, I can laugh it off and pretend I was only kidding.

Then I can be discreet, check into a surrogacy agency, and see what comes of it.

I don't want to wait to have a baby.

Maybe I would lose Emma, but what I would gain would be worth the price.

CHAPTER TWO

Emma

I've been in love with Jack Durand since the minute I met him, and I haven't told a single soul, not out loud, though I'm sure there are people who can guess just by looking at me. How cliché is that—an administrative assistant in love with her boss? For the past three years I've come into the office, every day, just like I am now, settle in, set a hot cup of coffee on Jack's desk, and get to work emptying his email and arranging his daily schedule.

Two years ago, he started dating Veronica Chapman. I won't say I can't compete with the glamorous morning talk show host because that would just add to the cliché, and besides, it's not true. I can compete, but Jack's not interested and I'm not the type to lean over his desk and let my boobs fall out of my blouse or sit in a chair and hike up my skirt. He has women throwing themselves at him all the time. The only thing me flirting would do is ruin the professional atmosphere I've managed to create at work. I like my job and he pays me well. We get along, and most of the time, I think we're friends.

It's just difficult to be around him for forty-five hours a week without my heart cracking a tiny bit more each time.

Especially at his birthday party. He's going to ask Veronica to marry him, and I have to be there. I'm in charge of the evening and I'm glad Raff said he'd be my plus one. I'll need the support.

"Good morning, Emma," Jack says, walking past me.

"Good morning. Your nine o'clock is on time, there's coffee on your desk, and your father wants to see you for lunch." I hope he doesn't hear the tremor in my voice. Usually, I can push the heartbreaking thoughts of him and Veronica out of my mind, but with the party, it's going to be a rough few weeks.

He looks good today, maybe a little tired around his golden brown eyes. He didn't bother to shave, and he has that rumpled, sexy look about him. His hair is longer than it should be, and I scribble a mental note to schedule him for a haircut before the party.

"Thanks." He pauses. "Do you have plans after work? Can we meet downstairs for a few minutes?"

"Of course. Whatever you need, Jack."

He lifts a corner of his mouth. "I was hoping you'd say that."

I turn away, and he steps into his office and closes the door.

The first time he asked me to meet him downstairs at the restaurant on the main floor, I thought he was asking me for a date, and I was a flurry of nerves all day. He burst my bubble the second we sat down at the table and he asked me where my tablet was so I could take notes. I'd never been more embarrassed, and I had to go up and retrieve it out of my desk. It was a quick and sharp lesson that Jack only saw me as his secretary and would only ever see me as his secretary.

He's going to want to talk about the party, and I'll be ready. I field calls from both Heath Novak, Jack's good friend, and Veronica, adding their ideas to the list to pass on to the banquet manager at the hotel. Heath thought he was being funny, saying he purchased Jack and me tickets to fly to Cabo on holiday, and for the next hour I daydreamed about us lying in the sun on the beach. Then Veronica called and dumped cold water all over me. She wanted to discuss the flavor of the cake, the guest list, and confirm his appointment with a jeweler.

As his soon-to-be-fiancée, she has a right to weigh in on the party plans, and I don't let it bother me. I'd have no say if I wasn't the one organizing the entire thing, and that's only because no one else wanted the responsibility. I reserved the ballroom at the Bridgeport Hotel six months ago, and I've already placed the order for the cake, a chocolate ganache— everyone knows what a chocoholic Jack is. All the RSVPs came in like I knew they would. People are calling Jack's forty-fifth birthday the event of the year, and no one would miss it. With Veronica's prompting, I entered the appointment with the jeweler into his planner, and after work, I'll apprise him of the progress so far and remind him. Veronica's thorough. She'll have already spoken with the jeweler herself, giving him an idea of what she likes allowing him to steer Jack in the direction of a ring she's picked out for herself.

It's not the way I want a man to propose, but no one asked me.

The rest of the day goes by quickly, and I meet Jack in the corridor outside the elevator at precisely five-thirty. It carries us down to the main floor, and surprisingly, we're the only two inside it.

The floors tick by, and he leans against the wall, his shoulders stiff, his hands shoved into the pockets of his dress pants. I grip my bag and writing tablet. Something feels off about him today, and I wonder if he's heading toward a midlife crisis. His father, Ronald Durand, is in his mid-seventies and is in excellent health, and his grandfather passed away just shy of his one hundredth birthday. Jack comes from good stock, and he has many healthy and happy years to look forward to.

He and Veronica will probably waste no time having a baby, and I swallow past a lump in my throat.

Sometimes life isn't fair.

We reached the lobby, and Jack holds the elevator doors open for me. I step through, murmuring, "Thank you." My heels click against the marble as we cross the lobby toward The Menagerie, an elegant restaurant located in the rear of the building. Patty, the hostess, smiles, used to seeing us. Our meetings downstairs happen at least twice a week. Jack likes the change of scenery, sipping on a whiskey while we tie up loose ends to a deal or hammering out details for a business trip. Sometimes I'll sip a glass of wine, but I'll decline today. Raff and I are going out later, and I texted him earlier and let him know I needed an extra forty-five minutes. He took it in stride—both our schedules are inconsistent at best.

Patty leads us to a table sitting in front of a window that looks out to a lush garden, and I say, "I missed your little's birthday." Jack watches me pull a card out of my bag. "I hope this makes up for it."

Patty smiles. "He'll be delighted you remembered at all."

"I'm sorry I couldn't be there. We'll meet up after Jack's party, okay?"

"Don't worry about it, Emma. I know how busy you are. Let me know, and we'll figure it out." She turns to Jack. "Whiskey, neat?"

He nods.

"Do you want something?" Patty asks me.

"Nothing, thanks."

Her eyes twinkle. "Where are you and Raff going tonight?"

"There's a new club opening downtown. He's covering it for *Talk of the Town*, and I told him I'd tag along."

"Sounds fun. I'll pass your drink order to the bartender," Patty says to Jack, tapping the edge of the card I gave her against her palm. "Have a good night."

"Thanks, you too," I say, slipping into the chair Jack's patiently holding out for me. I sit, and his hand brushes the nape of my neck. His touch sends shivers down my spine, and to cover my nerves, I pull my electronic notepad and stylus out of my bag. I love this thing. It will turn my handwriting into text and send the notes to my email. A cocktail waitress serves Jack's drink, and I wait for her to walk away. "So," I start, "the cake is set to be delivered Wednesday afternoon from Powdered Sugar, your favorite bakery. All the RSVPs have come in, and you have a haircut scheduled on Tuesday . . . you're looking a little scruffy."

He grins wryly. "I thought women liked scruffy."

I love scruff. I could go on for days about how Jack's scruff turns me on, how many evenings I've thought about him and his whiskers scratching the insides of my thighs, how many times he and his scruff have gotten me off. I look down at my notepad. "That would be between you and Veronica. The invitation said seven, but I'll be there early—"

"Do you and your parents get along?" he interrupts me.

I blink. I like to think Jack and I are friends. As good of friends as a CEO and PA can be, but we never get personal. I know Jack's dad because Ron still comes into the office most days, but Jack's never asked me about my family. He'll shoot Raff a dirty stare on the rare occasion Raff waits by my desk until I'm done with my day, but for the most part work is work, personal is personal, and he's never mixed the two.

"Yeah. Well, my father passed away right before I started

working for you. He had a heart attack. My mom and I are close. I see her all the time . . . she's lonely without my dad around. She lives here in Bridgeport. My older brother lives in Seattle with his family, and they fly in for Christmas most years. Why?"

He sips his drink. "Just wondering. Do you think about kids?"

I grip my stylus. "Like, having my own, you mean?"

"Yeah, like that."

I stare at my notepad. I haven't written anything down I don't already have upstairs in my planner. In the three years I've been working for Jack, I haven't dated, haven't tried to meet a man whom I would want to marry because the man I want to spend the rest of my life with is sitting across from me already. Raff and I are good friends, and there's speculation we're more to each other than what we are. Maybe one day if we don't find what we're looking for we'd tie the knot and turn our friendship into something legal, but both of us would have to throw in the towel for that to happen. I don't know what Raff's breaking point is, but the only thing that would make me step over that line is sitting in a church watching Jack and Veronica marry.

Or, you know, maybe listening to him at the party next week asking her to marry him will be enough.

I force out a laugh, and I sound like an asthmatic wheezing. "I'd like to get married first, so, no, I haven't thought much about it. Now, I blocked off half your day tomorrow for the jeweler—"

"Why aren't you married, Emma? You and Clark, right?"

I wish I would have ordered a drink after all. I don't know where Jack's mind is, but it would've been nice to have had a little warning. Talking marriage and babies with a man who has absolutely no interest in how I feel about him is its own kind of hell. I look at the time on my notepad. Our meetings never last longer than forty-five minutes, and I need to stay strong for only twenty more.

"I met someone, a while ago, and he didn't return my feelings. It's difficult to marry someone when they don't feel the same way you do. You try to move on, you know?" I press my lips together and look out the window. Spring is beautiful in Bridgeport, and the trees and flowers are beginning to bloom. I focus on the popping pink and force back my tears.

"I'm sorry."

I shrug. "Part of it's my fault. I see him all the time, and I should cut ties. It would be easier, but I'm not strong enough to do that. The eternal optimist in me, I guess. Now, the jeweler—"

"Do you want me to talk to him?"

"No!" I burst out. For goodness' sake, what is wrong with Jack today? For the past three years he couldn't have cared less about my personal life, and now he wants to speak up on my behalf? "I mean, no, that's fine. He's going to marry someone else, and I'm afraid getting involved would do more harm than good at this point. It's better to leave it alone. I can figure out my own life. Now, *the jeweler*—"

"But I thought you and Clark—"

"Jack! My love life is none of your concern!" He doesn't want it to be his concern, at any rate. He knows how I feel about him. Only a rock would be obtuse enough to miss the vibes I send his way whenever we're together. I try not to, but his eyes, the way a thick lock of his hair falls over his forehead if he goes too long between haircuts, the smooth lines of his fingers and imagining them running over my skin, it creates a chemistry in my body I can't hide. He ignores it because he doesn't want to deal with it, and I understand completely.

Sweat runs from underneath my bra down my ribcage, and my hand gripping the stylus trembles. He rattled me, and I need to finish this meeting and leave. I don't want to say something I'll regret.

"You're right. I'm sorry."

"I know you're trying to be helpful, but if there were any way I could make him see me, I would have, and now it's too late." And that's God's honest truth. If there were any way Jack could see me as more than his secretary, I would do whatever it took, but there's nothing. "Forget it, and let's focus on the task at hand. Your appointment at the jeweler is for two-thirty tomorrow. I blocked out the rest of your day, so feel free to go home if you finish up early."

"Why do I need to go to the jeweler?" He frowns, sincere puzzlement on his face.

My lips part in amazement. "To pick out Veronica's engagement ring. Why else would you need a jeweler?"

He rears back, and water sloshes out of my goblet and onto the tablecloth. "Engagement ring? What engagement ring?"

I'm shocked. There's no other way to describe what I'm feeling. "Are you not an active participant in your own life? Veronica's expecting a proposal at your party. *Next week.* You can't mean to tell me you two haven't discussed it?"

He rubs a finger over his lips, a gesture that never fails to make me squirm. "She might have mentioned something, but I've had other things on my mind."

I try to tamp back the heat in my belly. "Like what? World hunger? Peace for all? This is the rest of your life you're talking about."

He gapes at me.

"Okay, maybe not the rest of your life, but a good ten years or so! Heath and Zoey have been married for over fifteen years. Don't you want a marriage like that? They're so happy together, and I thought you wanted that with Veronica. Get your shit together, Jack. The jeweler, tomorrow, two-thirty. If you love her, why wouldn't you want to marry her? You two are perfect for each other."

They are, that's why the words are so hard to say. I shove the notepad and stylus into my purse. I don't have a coat, the temperatures have been warm enough lately not to need one.

He stands when I do.

Raff chooses that moment to peek into the restaurant to see if I'm finished, and I lift a hand.

"Is there anything else?" I ask stiffly.

Jack glances at me, then to Raff, and then back at me. "No."

"Okay. I'll see you tomorrow. Have a nice night."

"Same to you."

I feel his eyes on me the entire way across the floor, and I don't care if Jack's watching or not. I step into Raff's arms and bury my face into the curve of his shoulder.

"Ah, baby girl," he mutters, his lips pressed against my temple, "why do you make things so hard on yourself?"

"Because I'm stupid."

"Being a hopeless romantic isn't stupid, but he's not capable of giving you what you're looking for."

Raff doesn't have to tell me. When I first started working for Variant International, no one wasted a second telling me not to fall in love with Jack Durand. He has a block of ice where his heart should be and wouldn't marry for love. Maybe he doesn't love Veronica, maybe he does, but all I do is order cake and schedule appointments with the jeweler. Nothing else concerns me.

Raff leads me to the lobby and his car waiting outside, and I look over my shoulder. Jack is still staring at us, his eyes narrowed.

Jack has never felt anything for me, and he never will, I remind myself. Raff's driver opens the door and gratefully, I slide into the backseat of the town car.

"Ready for the VIP treatment?" Raff asks, climbing in next to me.

"Yeah, for sure."

Veronica and Jack's engagement doesn't change anything. I'll always be a nobody in Jack's life.

I settle into the curve of Raff's arm. I don't want Jack.

He kisses the top of my head, and I try with all my heart to believe my own lies.

CHAPTER THREE

Jack

"Let's go out."

From a corner of the couch, I scowl at my sister. "Why?"

"Because everyone's at Cloud 9 tonight."

She's standing in my living room dressed in a jade green cocktail dress, gold high heeled sandals strapped to her feet, and clutching a gold purse.

I sink lower into the cushion. "I'd rather not."

"I'm surprised you're not going with Veronica."

"She's meeting up with people from her show." She did invite me to go, saying the photo ops would be amazing and good for both of us, but I chose to hang back and stay home. The pictures are already starting to clog the social media feeds, and *Talk of the Town* is live streaming the glamorous rooftop event. Clark is there, of course, and every once in a while, I'll catch a glimpse of Emma and her friends. If I'm watching, that is, and I haven't been that often, preferring to sip on a beer and watch the replay of a baseball game instead.

"You're going to make me go alone?" she asks, sulking.

I love my sister. I count Claire as one of my best friends, but I'm not the only one who has had trouble committing. Two times divorced, Claire's one of Bridgeport's richest socialites. She doesn't work, not unless you count fishing for her next husband as a job. Then she works overtime. She's looking for something she's never going to find.

"You won't be alone once you get there." Claire has plenty of rich, snobby friends, and she'll hook up with someone.

"Come on." She shuffles across the carpet, pulls the bottle of beer out of my hand, and guzzles the rest.

I sigh.

"Please," she says, wheedling. She knows I'm close to giving in.

"Fine."

"Hurry up and change your clothes. You can't go like that."

"Give me a second. Christ."

I pull another beer out of the fridge to drink while I dress. Sweats wouldn't make proper attire, not for Cloud 9, but I don't need a tux, either. I decide on black dress pants, black shirt, and no tie. I slip on a black blazer. The rooftop is open, and it will be cool now that the sun has gone down.

"You look great," Claire says, her gaze raking me from head to toe. "Let me see the ring before we go."

I dump my bottle into the recycling bin. "What ring?"

"The ring you're going to propose to Veronica with. I want to see the rock you picked out."

"I don't have it."

Claire pokes out her bottom lip in a faux pout. "When are you going to buy it?"

"Emma made an appointment for me at the jeweler's

tomorrow. How does everyone know I'm proposing to Veronica at my party? *I* didn't know about it until Emma ran through the party's details after work today."

We wait for the lift to bring us down to the building's lobby, and Claire gives me a side-eye. I'm getting a lot of that lately, and I think of Emma's accusation that I'm not participating in my own life. "You're joking, right? Everyone's talking about it. Felix Rivera asked Veronica for details on the show this morning. She pretty much laid it out there that you would be asking her at the party. Don't you guys talk or what? Too busy fucking?"

I shove at her, the way I have since we were kids, and she laughs, stumbling against the elevator's wall.

"Crass. I thought our relationship was more casual than that." *Since when,* I think to myself. We've been exclusive since our first date.

"Since when?" Claire asks. The doors slide open and she steps into the lobby. "You've always seemed content, you've never dated anyone else."

I follow her out of the elevator. "Because she never asks me for anything."

"Oh, God, those pesky females always needing shit," Claire yells, her voice echoing off the walls. The concierge glares, used to, and disliking, my sister's abrasive personality. "It's no wonder I've been divorced twice. Well, Jesus, she can keep on not asking you for anything but with a big rock on her finger. Where are you two going to live? Is she moving into your penthouse?'"

"No," I say, my voice low and dangerous. No women besides Claire, Zoey, and my cleaning lady have ever been in my penthouse, and Veronica will not be the first.

A limo is waiting at the curb, and the driver opens the door allowing my sister to slide onto the bench. I follow, and he shuts the door behind me with a smart snap.

I reach for the bar to pour a whiskey, and Claire stills my hand. "Don't drink here, there's plenty of booze at the club."

"Fine."

Though it's only Thursday, the streets are packed with people already celebrating the weekend. This is Cloud 9's by-invitation-only event—tomorrow night they'll open to the public. Emma's there and she's Clark's plus one. She probably shared her invitation with Haisley or Mia and they plus-oned each other so they could all go. Emma was invited because she works for me. She's always invited to the luncheons, charity dinners, and parties, and she usually attends, saying she doesn't mind representing Variant if I don't feel like going out.

It doesn't hurt that Clark is always by her side, his arm wrapped around her like it belongs there.

Claire nudges me with her foot. "What's the scowl for? Go ahead and drink if you want to."

"It's not that. What do you think of Emma?"

Claire frowns. "What about her? She's nice, actually gives you my messages if you don't answer your cell, unlike the twit before her, and it seems like she knows what she's doing, at least, you've never complained. She has good taste in clothes—I loved the skirt she wore the other day. Why? Did she put in her notice? Is she finally marrying Raff? He's a bowl full of eye candy. They look cute together."

"No. I mean, I don't know. We met at The Menagerie earlier, and she seemed a little sad."

The limo eases to a stop close to the curb in front of the building that houses Cloud 9.

"Did you ask her why?"

"Yeah. She said a long time ago she fell in love with someone who's marrying someone else."

Claire smirks and rolls her eyes. "Maybe she needs to stop seeing him every day."

I look at her sharply. "How did you know that? Do you know who it is?"

The driver opens the door for us.

"God, I need a drink." She's sliding out of the limo before I can press the issue.

She poses on the red carpet for a moment, giving the photographers ample time to catalogue her attendance and which designer she's wearing, and the security guards flanking the doors let her in without asking for her ID or invitation.

I do my thing, too, shutting down the reporters asking me about the impending proposal (Jesus Christ), and follow my sister though she's already to the rooftop and gone by the time the elevator lets me off.

The music is a thrumming base, and the DJ's bouncing in time to the music, one headphone pressed against her ear. She wiggles her fingers at me. I know her name, but we haven't been formally introduced. I raise my hand in return.

I weave around groups, looking for my sister, and I get sucked into several conversations. I don't see Veronica, but it's late and she could have already gone home. She's usually in bed by seven-thirty saying she needs eight to nine hours of sleep to look her best in front of the camera. Every morning she's sitting in the makeup chair by five-thirty, and that's an early start to the day, even for me.

An hour after Claire dumped me, I find my group in the corner, three tables pushed together, the surfaces covered with cream tablecloths, beer bottles, lowball and wine glasses, and candles. Emma's there, Clark's arm wrapped around her, his suit jacket hanging from her shoulders. She's chatting with Haisley and Mia and Clark's laughing at something Heath and Zoey are talking about.

"Hey, what are you two doing here?" I ask Heath.

"Hi, Jack," Zoey says, her pretty blue eyes twinkling in the fairy lights strung up across the rooftop. Heath struck it lucky meeting Zoey, and he knows it, his arm anchored across her shoulders just as firmly as Clark's taking possession of Emma.

"Zoey said she was feeling a little cooped up, so we thought we'd come out. I'm surprised to see you here," Heath says, kicking out a chair for me.

I sit on it backward, not trying to appear badass, simply too lazy to turn it the right way. "Claire forced me." I turn to Clark and hold out my hand. "Clark, Emma."

"Durand," he says, shaking my hand briskly, "you missed Veronica by ten minutes. She must have left through the back while you schmoozed the front."

"That's okay. We didn't plan on meeting up."

"You nervous?" he asks, holding his beer bottle to his lips, a dangerous gleam in his eyes.

"No. Why would I be?" I ask, watching Emma, but she isn't paying attention, she's talking to Haisley and Mia.

Clark lifts a shoulder and chuckles good-naturedly. We aren't enemies, but we aren't friends, and his brittle smile rakes over my skin. "I mean, I don't think I'd propose to my girlfriend in front of a room full of people. I'd keep it between us, you know? Dinner, hot sex. But Veronica's used to an audience, probably what she wants. Don't you think so, Em?"

I've never called Emma, "Em," and the fact that Clark does and how easily it rolls off his tongue tightens my shoulders in the unwelcome and unwanted way I've tried to ignore for three years.

She turns and says, "Hmm?"

Her pupils are dilated either from booze or the dim lighting, and her mahogany hair swirls around her shoulders, the candles on the table catching the strands and setting them on fire.

I swallow.

"That Veronica wants the audience when Durand proposes."

"I suppose some women like that kind of thing." She rests her head on Clark's shoulder. "Right, Zoey?"

"I like proposals that come from a hint of desperation," she says, tamping back a smile.

Emma picks up her wineglass and sips the inch of red. "I haven't heard this story. What happened?"

Heath winces, and I laugh.

Emma catches my eye, a faint smile on her mouth.

Clark glares at me and pulls her closer, and I tear my gaze away from her to look at Zoey.

She starts, "I was going to break up with him. He hadn't seemed interested in weeks. I didn't know what was going on, and he wouldn't talk to me. Do you remember, Jack?"

I nod. It may have been fifteen years ago, but I remember it like it was yesterday. The envy I felt that my best friend found something I never would.

"We were on a walk," Zoey continues, "and I said, 'Heath, I think we've run our course. You haven't seemed happy, and if you're trying to figure out how to let me down gently, it's fine. Let's see other people.'"

Heath picks up the story. "I'd been promoted at work, working sixteen-hour days. I knew she was slipping away, and that day she scared me to death. I didn't want her seeing other people, and I did the only thing I could do. I dropped to my knees right on the pavement in the park. I didn't have a ring or anything, and I said, 'Zoey, I love you so much, I don't know how I'll live without you. Don't break up with me, marry me.'"

"Of course I said yes," Zoey says, laughing and sniffling.

She holds out her hand, her wedding set glittering in the light. "He put it on me, and I haven't taken it off, even through three pregnancies."

"A little fear can go a long way," Heath says, and he nuzzles Zoey's cheek with his lips.

"Is that how you'd want it, Emma?" I ask.

"We know how Emma wants to be proposed to," Haisley says, leaning toward our end of the table.

Emma buries her face in Clark's shoulder. "No, don't," she says, laughing.

"Why?" Mia asks. "It's romantic. Are you taking notes, Raff?" she asks smiling, but her gaze flicks in my direction.

He pours more wine into Emma's glass and smirks at me. "I sure am."

The smug son of a bitch.

"She wants her boyfriend to rent a room at a little B&B, it doesn't matter where, but it has to be winter. They make love in front of the fireplace . . ." Mia fades and Emma lifts her head, her cheeks blazing as hot as the imagined flames.

". . . and he wraps her in a blanket and holds her close," Haisley continues, fluttering her eyelashes. "He says over the crackling of the fire, 'Emma, I'm never happier than when I'm with you. Grow old with me. Marry me and let me love you for the rest of your life.'"

Emma's eyes fill with tears, but not from sentiment or embarrassment. She's laughing, and Clark brushes the wet off her cheeks with the pads of his thumbs. "That's lovely, Em." He kisses her forehead.

She waves a hand. "Oh, well, I've given up on that."

"It's okay," Clark says. "You never know what will happen. Come, dance with me."

She takes another sip of her wine and shrugs out of Clark's jacket. He leads her onto the dance floor, and she steps into his arms as if she's done it a million times before. She probably has.

"They look good together," Heath says, and he pulls from his beer bottle. "That thing we talked about yesterday, you should leave it alone. At least with Emma."

"Yeah," I murmur, watching Clark's fingers slide up and down the exposed skin of her back.

Photographers take pictures of Cloud 9's guests dancing, and I'll be treated to many photos of Clark holding Emma. She may be in love with someone she can't have, but she's moving on, quite easily, from the looks of it.

As long as it doesn't interfere with how she does her job, that's all I care about.

I look at my watch. "I'm out of here," I say to Heath and Zoey. I'm not close to Mia and Haisley and I nod goodbye.

"Gym after work?" Heath confirms, though there's no need. We always meet for a run at the gym Mondays, Wednesdays, and Fridays. I can regal him with tales of picking out an engagement ring for a woman I didn't know I was proposing to, at an appointment made for me by my PA I'm still thinking about asking to have my baby.

From what I've seen of Clark and Emma, she'll tell me no, but I want to ask, or the what-could-have-beens will eat me alive. It shouldn't matter who carries my child, but the graceful curve of Emma's jaw, her elegant posture, and sunny disposition—I want my child to have those things. My child will be half of me, but I want the other half to belong to Emma.

"Same time, same place. Goodnight," I say to the table at large, and I sneak around the dance floor to the elevator. My sister is long gone, perhaps home or with a one-night stand. I don't know why she bothered to drag me with her. She would have been fine without me, but I'm glad she did.

Tonight, I looked at Emma in a way I don't ever let myself.

Not as a boss looking at his PA, but as a man looking at a woman. I understand why Clark is so besotted with her, and I believe she'll have that fireside proposal sooner than she thinks.

I only need nine months of her time first, and the sooner the better.

CHAPTER FOUR

Emma

The next morning, I almost call in to work. It would have been the first time in the three years I've worked for Jack. Generous sick time was a part of my lucrative hire-on package and it's well within my rights to hide for a day, but I know without looking a broken heart isn't on the list of acceptable ailments. I dress for work like I always do, arrive at the office before Jack, set a hot cup of coffee on his desk, and pretend like nothing's wrong.

I do a good job of it until Jack steps out of his office a little before two, smoothing his tie and combing the hair away from his face with his fingers.

"Have a good weekend, Jack." He said he won't be back to the office after the jeweler.

He pauses by my desk. "Plans?"

"Oh, ah," I stumble. He's never asked me that before. "Maybe shopping with Mia and Haisley. I need a new dress for your party, and I always visit my mom on Sundays."

"Seeing Clark tonight? Tomorrow?"

"Yeah, sure." There isn't a weekend that I don't spend part of it with Raff, even if it's going to his place for a small dinner party or him coming to mine and watching a movie. We keep each other company, and the nights don't seem so hard.

Jack rests his fingertips on the surface of my desk. "He's . . . a lucky guy."

I want his words to mean more than they do. He's only being polite, and I take them for the small compliment they are. "Thanks. Veronica, too. Lucky, I mean. I didn't congratulate you yesterday at The Menagerie, and I apologize for that. You two are a great couple. I'm sure you'll be really happy together."

"Thank you." His voice is clipped, and he doesn't say anything more. He strides to the elevator, his shoulders rigid.

I spend the next hour doing little last minute things. Sometimes Jack and Ron are in the middle of an acquisition or merger and he asks me to work through the weekend. I don't mind when he does that, my stupid, foolish heart using every opportunity to be with him. But the weekend before his birthday is clear, and I won't have to think about work or Jack until Monday morning. That won't stop me though, and I wonder what kind of ring Veronica chose for herself. Platinum maybe, to match her trendy silver hair and icy blue eyes.

Ron pokes his head into Jack's office. "Where's Jack?" he asks, scowling.

I don't work with Ron Durand often. He has his own PA, and the only times I've spoken with him have been during work meetings that required my attendance. I don't have a problem with the older man, though he's too acerbic for my taste. Irritable all the time, I don't think I've ever seen him smile. Jack calls his sister, Claire, crabby, and I know exactly where she gets it from.

I sign out of Variant's employee portal and put my computer to sleep. "He's at the jeweler's," I say, and tears burn my throat. I should make plans twenty-four/seven this weekend or I'm going to cry the whole time.

"What the fuck for?" Ron asks, his perpetual frown deepening.

His expletive doesn't faze me. I've heard plenty coming from Jack's mouth when things don't go his way, and Raff, too, can swear like nobody's business if he's drunk and pissed. "To choose an engagement ring for Veronica. I'm about to head home. Was there something you needed me to do for you?" I ask, but I don't know what he could want. Nancy's still here.

"I thought that was gossip."

Ron's content to stand by my desk, crossing his arms over his chest.

"He didn't tell you he was going to propose?" I ask.

Raff and my mom get along great, always have, and he frequently joins me on Sunday afternoons. I would expect my boyfriend to spend a little time with her, too. They wouldn't have to like each other, but she'd at least know he wanted to ask me to marry him before he did.

"That's not something he would have discussed with me."

"Oh, well, he has nothing on his schedule afterward. I don't expect him back until Monday."

He glares at me, and I give up thinking I'll get out of here early.

"What do you think of her?"

"What do I think of Veronica?" I ask to confirm his question. Everyone around here's gone crazy. Jack interested in what my weekend plans are and now his father asking my opinion on his son's fiancée.

"You have a good head on your shoulders. Instincts. You didn't like that Worthington asshole. Could see it on your face, and after that meeting, we checked into him. Found out he was dead broke, and the IRS was hunting him down, the slimy bastard. Saved us millions. So, I'll ask you again, what do you think of that Chapman woman?"

I hadn't any idea my dislike of Victor Worthington had come across on my features or that Ronald Durand cared enough to notice, and not only notice, but do something with it.

He waits.

I haven't spent that much time around Jack and Veronica when they're together. If she visits Jack in his office, she's nice to me and doesn't treat me like a servant, ordering me around, not the way some bosses' girlfriends can. We're not friends, but if she had sat at our table last night and waited for Jack to show, no one would have minded. Raff and Veronica have an easy relationship knowing they help each other out. He reports on her and keeps her relevant, she drives traffic and subscriptions for the premium content to his e-zine.

Whenever I do see Jack and Veronica together, I always think there's something missing, but I've attributed that to my own jealousy and their dislike of PDAs.

Ron's eyes bore into me, still waiting for an answer.

I force the words out. "I think they'll be great together."

He doesn't look happy.

"Don't you want Jack to get married, Mr. Durand?"

His eyes harden. "What I want for Jack and Claire doesn't exist. Claire is finding that out—the hard way. I thought my wife—Never mind. I never remarried. Once was enough. I hoped Jack was smart enough to avoid it, perhaps seeing his sister as an example, but I see he's too weak to avoid his own downfall."

"He's in love." That's the kicker, isn't it? He fell in love, and it wasn't with me.

Ron scoffs. "There's no such thing."

Sometimes I wish there wasn't.

"Is that all you need, Mr. Durand? Jack gave me permission to leave early since he wouldn't be back." He didn't give me permission, but there's nothing left for me to do that would fill up the two hours I have left until five.

"Fine, fine. Do you know when he's doing this proposing? This weekend?"

I open my mouth to tell him that it's none of my business, but he cuts me off. "Don't tell me you don't know. You PAs know everything, and you're sharp. You know more than most."

I could find that flattering, but it sounds like an insult.

Reluctantly, I relent. "At his party."

"Christ. Turning a respectable event into a circus. You couldn't stop him?"

"I only work here, Mr. Durand." Couldn't I stop him? What I wouldn't give to be able to stop him from asking Veronica to marry him in front of five hundred of his nearest and dearest friends.

His eyes narrow. "You have more power than you think you do. Have you ever been married, Emma?"

"No."

He nods, finally happy with something I said. "You'd be smart to keep it that way. Go home."

"Have a good weekend, sir."

"I haven't had a good anything for forty years."

Ron stomps down the corridor, headed toward his own office.

I sigh in relief. Ron Durand is a very intimidating man. I felt I held my own, but I'm glad I don't have to do it often. I feel sorry for Veronica having him for a father-in-law. Ron won't be easy on her, not if he dislikes her, and I don't think my positive prediction of Jack's future with her impressed him.

Before I leave, I press my hand against Jack's office door, and a tear slides down my cheek.

After his party, things will be different.

I just didn't know how different they would be.

CHAPTER FIVE

Jack

I'm pissed.

I'm pissed through the appointment with the jeweler, I'm pissed during my run with Heath. I'm pissed through the weekend, and I prowl around my penthouse, inexplicable anger slithering under my skin.

Saturday and Sunday, there were photos of Emma and Clark all over social media. Regurgitated pictures of them at Cloud 9, them walking down a sidewalk downtown on Friday night, her arms wrapped around one of his. I don't know where they were going or where they'd been, but I could read the picture clear enough. He was protecting her, but I don't understand from what.

I step out of the elevator Monday morning still pissed, but my anger fizzles the moment I see Emma's face. She looks at me with eyes so haunted I wanted to ask her if everything is okay, but I know nothing is okay. I hide in my office most of the day.

Tuesday is more of the same, my father grumbling under

his breath about "godforsaken women." Someone told him I'm supposed to be proposing to Veronica at my party, and the old man didn't take it well.

Emma's changed, her usual sparkle dull and faded. I keep pausing by her desk, wanting to ask if there's anything I can do, but every time I stop, she stiffens and turns away. After the fifth time she does it, I wonder if it's something I did, and my concern turns into a need to apologize.

I catch her walking to the elevator a few minutes after five. I spent another day hiding in my office because I'm in too much of a piss-poor mood to talk to anybody. "Emma."

She turns, her cheeks pale, her eyes luminous with wet.

"What is it?" I finally ask, my arms hanging limply by my sides.

She smiles, and it is so full of hurt, my heart aches all night. "Nothing. I got a little bad news over the weekend."

"Is there anything I can do?"

Imperceptibly, she shakes her head. "No. There's nothing anyone can do. Goodnight, Jack."

"Goodnight."

On Wednesday morning she looks better, though there's still strain pulling at her eyes. The phone keeps her busy, last minute RSVPs, last minute cancellations. It's my birthday and I don't have to be at work, but I declined the breakfast and lunch offers, and instead, I keep my door open and watch Emma work.

I haven't forgotten about asking her to surrogate, but Veronica's want for a proposal came out of left field and hit me smack up against my head harder than a baseball going eighty miles an hour. Emma expressed her astonishment, but I honestly didn't know Veronica wanted me to ask her to marry her. In the two years we've dated, she's always seemed married to her career. There were times we didn't feel more than friends with benefits, and it was only recently she might have mentioned getting married, in an offhanded kind of way I didn't take seriously. Getting married has never been, and will never be, on my radar.

I've been content with the way things were between us, and I thought she was happy, too.

At four, Emma logs off and she pulls her purse out of her desk drawer. Shadows lay underneath her eyes and her skin doesn't shimmer the way it does when she's happy. Leaning against my doorjamb, she says, "I'm going to head home. I have a few things I have to do before the party and I need time to change. I'll be at the hotel at six-thirty to check in with the banquet manager. I've been in touch with her all week. Things should be fine."

I stand from my desk and slowly walk across my office. She looks like a scared kitten, and I think if I move too fast, she'll run away. I grip her shoulders and she looks at me, her eyes wide. I'm taller than Clark is, but Emma and I, we still fit. I mean, I know we would. I've never danced with her, never lay next to her. But I know.

"What is it?"

She brushes her fingers down my tie. She's never touched me, not like this. She's straightened the knot, smoothed the wrinkles out of my jacket, but this is different. There's a feeling in her touch that has never been there before. She meets my eyes and says, "It's nothing. I don't know if we'll have time to talk tonight, so I want to wish you and Veronica the best. I mean that, really."

Her eyes slide away.

She's lying to me.

I release her, and she wastes no time stepping back.

"Thanks."

"You're welcome. I'll see you later."

I want to say more, but I don't know what to say. There's something between us that I've tried like hell to keep buried, but it started to rise to the surface Wednesday after work at The Menagerie and hasn't let up.

Never once glancing my way, she hurries to the elevator and waits for it to reach our floor. She stares at the tile until the doors open and she steps inside.

My phone rings as the doors glide shut, and I pull my phone out of my pocket. Veronica's name flashes, and I grit my teeth. "Hey," I say, willing myself to calm down.

"Hi. Are you still at work? I thought maybe I could stop by your place before the party."

I'm very territorial about my penthouse, and I don't like women there. One night while we were drinking and reminiscing in the maudlin way he sometimes has, Heath speculated it's because I watched my father throw my mother out of our home, and I didn't want to ever have to do that. I might have agreed, but I don't consider the penthouse I live in home. My idea of "home" always flashes memories of the house I grew up in, the halls where my mother's presence lingers because my father didn't move, and where he still lives today.

Maybe it's as simple as not wanting to see the ghosts of past women floating around the rooms, but that would imply I'd been in love with them, and I can honestly say I've never been in love with anyone.

I've never invited Veronica up to the penthouse, and she's bold for asking. I bite out a clipped, "No. I'm going to try to get in a nap. I haven't been sleeping well."

"You always do after . . ." she says amused, her voice fading.

She's right, and I ignore it because she is. "I'll pick you up at 7:15. I can't be too late to my own party. Emma put in a lot of work, and I don't want to cause her any trouble."

Veronica sucks in a breath. She knows there's something

wrong, and she wants to ask me what it is. But even if she did, I wouldn't know what to say. The conversation we need to have should have happened long before now. If we love each other, where we're going to live. The fact she doesn't want children and I do. Couples who are engaged should know those things. "Okay," she says, "I'll be ready."

"I'll see you later." I hang up and slide the phone back into my pocket.

I stop by Emma's desk, watermarks dotting the surface where her tears fell this afternoon. I'd been on a conference call and she didn't think I was watching, but I was. They ran down her cheeks and dripped onto her desk. It was the first time I've ever seen her cry, and she's never been that . . . unprofessional at work before. Something had truly upset her, but by the time the call ended, she'd found some sliver of control and the time to question her had passed.

"Jack! I need a word with you," my father barks down the hallway.

I'm not going to get that nap.

I step inside his office, and he's staring out the window, his hands clenched together at his lower back. "What is it, Dad? I was hoping to hit the sack for an hour before the party."

"It's about that Chapman woman." He doesn't turn around.

"What about her?"

"We never discussed you getting married."

"I don't recall Claire asking permission," I say, helping myself to a drink from his bar.

"It's not the same for you. I didn't teach you how to be a good husband."

"Because you don't know how to be one?" I guess, holding the glass lightly in my hand, but I want nothing more than to throw it across the room. He's never once mentioned my mother in all the years she's been gone, and he has the gall to do this now when I can't stop thinking about Emma crying at her desk.

My father scoffs. "Marriage needs a level of understanding and patience that I never had. Make one mistake, and you don't get a second chance."

"I think," I say mildly, "that it would have to be a pretty big mistake. I don't plan on doing anything that Veronica and I can't talk through." At least, I hope not.

"Do you trust her?" he asks quietly.

I trust very few people in my life. My father, Claire. Heath and Zoey. Emma. Emma earned it by not blabbing her mouth about my personal life to Clark and his e-zine or to the other rag mags. Not once in the three years she's worked for me has anything inappropriate popped in a blogpost.

I finish my drink. "No."

"You'll be wise to keep it that way. A prenup, Jack."

"Of course."

My father's eyes meet mine, and a shiver runs through me. He's beginning to look his age—worn-out, weary. Downtrodden and tired to the bone. "Why didn't you remarry after Mom?"

He shakes his head. "I've never been on board with that. A man marries for life. If he can't handle it, then he has no business trying again. What's the point of vows if you're going to break them with a divorce? There are no do-overs. Not for me." He holds out his hand, and I grasp it, his grip firm. "Happy birthday. The day you were born was the happiest day of my life."

I lift a corner of my mouth at that. "What about Claire?"

"Claire came out crying and never stopped. I don't pretend that's not my fault. She grew up without a mother, and I'll accept the blame for that." He scowls. "Get out of here. I'll stop by to watch this wretched proposal I keep hearing about. Are you sure she's the one?"

"Is any man ever really sure?" I ask.

If I view marriage the way Dad does, no do-overs, until death do us part, I'm looking at the next forty years with Veronica by my side. Emma was a little more flexible, giving me ten years until I could bail on my vows, but I'd like to think I'm like my father, in more than only the business side of life. If I ever give my bride a reason to take off the ring I push onto her finger, I'll never marry again.

My father wilts. "I was sure. It was what happened afterward that destroyed us. It's not the wedding, Jack. It's the marriage. Remember that."

That sounds like advice more geared for a woman fantasizing about the big day than it does for me, but he's right, too. Real life starts after the honeymoon.

"I will. Thanks."

There's plenty of time for me to lie down, but I can't fall asleep. I toss and turn until it's time to dress for the party. I don't know who decided it would be a black-tie event. No one asked me what I wanted. Maybe I wanted a pool party at the country club. That's the kind of party my dad always threw Claire and me when we were kids. Maybe I wanted a bonfire on the beach, coolers full of beer sprinkled liberally on the sand, though it's still too cool to go swimming up at Cavern Lake. Maybe I didn't want a party at all, but no one asked me, and all of a sudden Emma had the ballroom to the Bridgeport Hotel booked, a cake ordered, and invitations sent. Maybe I'm really not participating in my own life if I can't speak up to oppose a black-tie party I don't want to attend, even if it's in my honor.

That will stop tonight.

I step out of the lobby, and the limo is waiting at the curb. Once I'm seated, I help myself to what will be a continuous stream of whiskey. I never use alcohol as a crutch, but for the party, I'll make an exception.

Veronica's waiting on the sidewalk in front of her building drawing the attention of the paparazzi who are enjoying the chance to film her. One of them will belong to Rafferty Clark, live streaming for *Talk of the Town*. She's answering a question someone lobbed at her, but the limo pulls up to the curb and she stops.

I get out to help her in.

The bloggers and reporters shout questions at us, and she lifts her head for a kiss. I've never had a problem with it before now. I know how important her career is to her, and in the two years we've been together, I've understood my role in that. But tonight I stiffen and swiftly rub my lips over hers in a brief kiss that will not look like a man in love kissing his soon-to-be fiancée. Annoyed, I firmly push her toward the limo with a hand to her bare back.

"What was that for?" she asks, disgruntled, swiping at a piece of hair sticking in her lip gloss.

"I'm sorry. Not in the mood for it tonight," I say, letting the driver shut the door.

She snuggles into my side and rubs her thumb over my cheek. "It's only a party."

One I don't want to be at, but I don't admit it, only rest my head against the cushion and close my eyes.

The ride to the hotel doesn't last as long as I want it to, but if I asked the driver to circle the block to give me time I gather my courage (and to have another drink), Veronica will think I want sex. She'd give it to me too, settling in my lap, her dress scrunched up around her waist. Over the past two years, we've had limo sex a few times, but it never stops the inevitable—attendance at a function I couldn't care less about.

Forty-five years old and I'd rather be home in my pajamas watching a movie.

The limo glides to a stop at the curb, and of course the paparazzi are out of control, filming our arrival. The driver opens the door, and I step out first, holding out my hand to help Veronica from the car. She smiles at me, and we pause on the sidewalk in front of the hotel, giving photographers time to take our picture. Reporters shout at us. I wrap my arm around her waist, and leaning into my side, she answers their questions, some about the proposal, some about *Rise and Shine, Bridgeport!*.

I have nothing to say until a reporter asks me about Variant and how my father's health is. He asks if I'm concerned about the future of the company because Claire and I don't have children to pass the family business down to. I reply that I don't have to work if I don't want to, and neither does Claire, obviously. She has family money and money given to her in both divorce settlements. I muse maybe one day we'll sell it, and Dad will chew my head off for planting that idea. Speculation will run rampant. We don't have any plans to sell Variant. Not while I'm healthy enough to run it, with children or without.

I grow bored faster than Veronica does, and finally she breaks away and allows me to escort her into the hotel. Guests linger in the lobby, chatting, and we're held up, shaking hands and accepting congratulations.

Veronica sparkles. She's working just as much as she is having fun. To her, work is fun.

Politely, I disentangle us from the group, and we walk toward the ballroom together. I need a drink, and I won't find it in the lobby.

We pause at the entrance. The ballroom is tinted a blue-silver from the lights running along the ceiling, and a gigantic chandelier rains the iridescent light. Veronica's silver hair and dress fit right in, her skin soaking in the light and reflecting it in return. She's beautiful, and if talk of a proposal hadn't come up, our arrangement could have lasted years.

I'm shallow, and I'm truthful enough to admit it.

Immediately, we're swarmed by guests, and a waiter stops at our group, offering us flutes of champagne. I don't know who was in charge of the guest list. Emma, I suppose, with Claire's help, maybe, and Veronica's, possibly my father's. I look around for Emma. I don't need to search the room for my sister. Her voice carries, and since I don't hear her, I know she hasn't yet arrived. My father won't be here until the last minute. He hates these things as much as I do, but he said he wouldn't miss the proposal, and I believe him.

I catch sight of Emma talking to a server.

The air disappears, and I choke.

It isn't the black dress she's wearing that hugs her every curve or the way she's pinned up her hair revealing the graceful line of her neck. It isn't the dainty sandals strapped to her delicate feet, it isn't the way she tilts her head listening to the waitstaff saying something.

No, it's the utter despair rolling off her body that hits me even from this distance across the room. She's trying not to show it, a small smile playing with her lips coated with a dark red gloss, but it's there in her hunched shoulders, the trembling of her hands.

Wherever Emma is, Clark is never far behind, and I spot him leaning against a column alone sipping on a beer out of the bottle, a hand tucked into the pocket of his pants.

"I'll be right back," I murmur to Veronica. She nods and squeezes my arm.

I stride across the ballroom, ignoring anyone attempting to slow me down.

Clark raises his eyebrows. "Durand. Happy birthday."

"What's wrong with her?" I demand, determined to get to the bottom of this once and for all. "Is she sick?"

"What do you mean?" he asks, confused.

"Emma. Does she have . . ." The word sticks in my throat. "Cancer?"

He squints at me. "What the hell are you talking about? Emma's fine. At least, she hasn't told me anything of the sort, and I think she would have."

Marginally, I relax. I think she would have, too. Told Clark, I mean. A serious diagnosis isn't something someone keeps to themselves. "Then what is it?"

"It's nothing she won't get over in time. Don't worry about it." His lips form a thin line.

"I don't like seeing her like this."

"Like what?" he asks, and we both watch her finish her conversation with the server, or it could be the banquet manager for all I know. I've never met her. Emma moves on to speak to someone else. Everyone knows who she is, and they're probably telling her what a great job she did putting the party together. But I can see it. The strain etched onto her face, the way her smile never reaches her eyes. She never used to be like this.

I sigh. "I don't know."

"Then leave her alone."

"Who *is* she to you?" I ask in frustration. I hear they're only friends, but there has to be more to it than that. He's always with her and he can't keep his hands off her, yet I've never seen them kiss, not on the lips the way lovers kiss.

"She's my friend, Durand. I don't know how many times I have to tell you that for you to believe it. We've been good friends for years. Before she started working for you, before *Talk of the Town* took off. Before any of this mattered so much," he says, waving his bottle around encompassing the entire ballroom.

"You don't sleep together?" I ask skeptically, and I'm fully prepared for him to tell me it's none of my goddamned business, which is exactly what I would tell him if he asked me questions about my sexual partners.

"On Sunday afternoons—"

I tense, preparing for the truth.

"—sometimes I fall asleep on her mother's couch. That's as close as we've ever come, and as close as we ever will."

Running my fingers through my hair (preoccupied, I missed the hair appointment Emma inked into my schedule), I say, "I don't understand."

"There's nothing for you to understand." A waiter passes by, and he swaps his empty beer bottle for a glass of champagne. "We were friends before she met you, and we'll be friends after you marry Veronica. Congratulations, by the way. You two are a good fit." His voice is hard and insincere.

"I think we are, too," she says, stepping up beside me. "You didn't come back."

"I'm sorry. I got caught up," I say, adjusting my arm and allowing her to move closer to me. It's a habit, and Clark doesn't miss it.

"Hi, dollface," he says, and Veronica blushes.

I frown and look between them, but neither gives anything away.

Everyone wants to wish me a happy birthday, and Veronica and I circle the ballroom bouncing from one group to another. Emma didn't arrange for a formal meal, instead, a buffet is set up along the far wall offering everything from caviar to filet mignon. A giant chocolate cake is positioned near the front by the dais, where apparently, I'm expected to ask the big question.

Anger roils through me again, the thought of the proposal and worry for Emma spiking my blood pressure.

She's always disappearing into the back, and it's clear she's here in a work capacity and not as my guest. I didn't ask her to do that. It's a responsibility she took upon herself, and if I had it my way, she'd be sitting at a table with her feet up sipping champagne, not running herself ragged for an event no one will remember a year from now.

My sister finally shows, her voice echoing over the ballroom. I see my father talking to a business acquaintance, and that's my cue. I want to get the singing out of the way, cut the cake, and go home.

I snag a full flute from a passing waiter.

Veronica squeezes my hand, and I keep myself from rudely ripping it from her grasp.

I trot up the short set of stairs, position myself in middle of the dais, and look over the crowd.

Conversation washes over me.

I don't see Emma or Clark, and my heart dips, though it shouldn't. I wanted her to be here when I thanked her for putting the evening together, but the night is almost over. They aren't doing anything wrong leaving early. Everyone has work in the morning.

People notice me standing on the platform, and a murmur travels around the room. I wait until I have everyone's attention and then I begin to speak.

CHAPTER SIX

Emma

I've been hiding, disguising my trips to the back as directing the waitstaff when really, I've been knocking back whiskey and trying not to sob all night.

I can't do this.

I can't be here and listen to him tell everyone he's so in love with Veronica he wants to marry her. I thought I could handle it, but the party crept closer and I couldn't keep my emotions in check. I know Jack caught me crying today, and after he proposes, I'm not going to have a choice. I'm going to have to quit.

My heart won't be able to survive it.

Using the wall as a support, I stand in a dark corner and try to unobtrusively wipe my cheeks. I don't want anyone to know how distraught I am.

Standing in the spotlight and holding a glass of champagne, Jack waits for everyone's attention.

Alcohol swirls in my stomach, my brain a fuzzy mess of booze and despair. I don't know where Raff is, but he'll drive me home, probably spend the night to watch over me. I had a rough weekend, and he was there for every second of it. I didn't even visit Mom on Sunday. I couldn't let her see me like this.

Tears blur my vision, and I feel her rather than see her. Claire stands next to me, her arm brushing against mine. "I'm so sorry," she says, for once not her usual loud and abrasive self.

The lump in my throat expands, and I stare at the floor unable to breathe.

"For what it's worth," she continues, "I think you're a better match for him. Underneath it all, he's a family man, though he tries to deny it. Dad kicked Mom out when Jack was barely old enough to remember it, and that stayed with him. I don't think Veronica is the one to help him lay it to rest."

I rub my nose with the back of my hand. Claire's approval really means a lot to me. "Thanks. I need to find Raff and go. I can't watch this."

"I'm here, baby girl. Come on. Everything will be okay," he says, wrapping an arm around my shoulders.

"Emma," Claire says, and I stop. "There's a lot of time between a proposal and a wedding."

I know what she's getting at, but I lift a shoulder. "He loves her enough to ask."

Her face fills with sympathy. "Yeah."

Raff nudges me forward, and gratefully, I lean into his side. His arm is a comfortable and heavy weight across my shoulders. All my problems would be solved if I could fall in love with him, but we were only destined to be friends.

"Thank you all for coming," Jack starts, and I pause, letting his voice drip over me like warm maple syrup. I swear, there's nothing about the man I don't love. "I don't see her," he continues, "but I want to thank Emma Cox for putting this night together. If she's here, maybe she'll hear you give her a round of applause."

Everyone claps behind my back, some lingering near the door catching my eye.

Raff and I shuffle down the hallway, the light too bright for my eyes. I shouldn't be leaving quite yet—Jack still needs to cut his birthday cake—but the banquet manager has it all under control, and I would insult her if I insisted on micromanaging her every move.

Jack's strong voice carries over the ballroom and down the hotel's corridor. "Growing old isn't fun. Our bodies start falling apart, but if we're lucky, long before our minds do. I've been blessed with good physical and mental health, following in my father's footsteps. Because I've been fortunate, maybe I've put off things I shouldn't have put off. I think with anything in this life, we take time for granted the most."

I stiffen. Raff pauses with me, indulging my sick need to listen to Jack's speech.

"So that being said, thank you all for carving out time in your busy schedules to wish me a happy birthday. It's easy for time to go by, and one day you can look up from an email and realize all the things you've been missing. I know that's what I've done this past week. Stay for more booze and cake. It's chocolate—Emma knows it's my favorite. Thanks again."

Stunned energy zips out of the ballroom and down the hallway to where Raff and I are standing. Everyone was waiting for him to propose to Veronica, and that was when he was supposed to do it.

I meet Raff's gaze, and his expression is as confused as mine is. Gripping his hand, we trot back to the ballroom. Jack's guests are whispering furiously to each other. Veronica's standing alone near the platform, misery on her face as clear as it was on mine for the past few days.

Heath and Zoey join us at the back of the room. Too busy hiding and shooting whiskey, I didn't see them arrive. "Did you know he was going to back out of proposing, Emma?" he asks.

"I had no idea. He left early on Friday. I assumed he'd gone to the jeweler's like he was supposed to. He didn't say anything to you at the gym?"

He shakes his head. "Not a word. He seemed angry, but you know Jack. There's nothing that will get him to talk if he doesn't want to."

"Veronica sure didn't know," Zoey says, looking across the room. Veronica's sitting on the platform, wiping tears off her cheeks.

I sink into a chair and rest my head on the table. I had too much to drink, and it's stuffy in here. My head pounds from the shock.

"I should see if she's all right," Raff says. "I don't want this to blow up online. If she'll talk to me, maybe we can control it. Will you be okay, Em?"

"I'll drive her home," Jack says, suddenly behind my chair. "Don't worry about her."

A shiver runs through me.

"What the fuck was that? Everyone expected you to propose," Heath says, and I don't have the energy to sit up and watch them fight.

"I never said I was going to ask. I never said I wanted to get married. Veronica and I never discussed it, not the way two people in love should talk about something like that. She threw it on me hoping I would fall in line."

"That was a shitty thing to do," Heath snaps.

I turn my head and look out of one eye to see if Heath's as

mad as he sounds, and his face is red. Zoey's chewing on her bottom lip in concern, a hand to her husband's shoulder. I want to tell her I like her dress, but my lips won't work.

"You should have told her before you humiliated her in front of our friends."

"Then maybe she shouldn't have started the rumors," Jack says, clearly surprised someone is blaming him for Veronica's disappointment. "A proposal begins with two people in love who want a future together and who will talk about it in private first. Felix Rivera knew more about the proposal than I did, and I won't put up with that."

Heath scoffs. "You had days. *Days* to get this sorted out."

"That wouldn't have mattered. What was I supposed to do, personally call everyone in Bridgeport and tell them Veronica and I got our wires crossed? And that's only a polite way of putting it. I don't want to get married. I'll never want to get married. She should never have started talking about it without consulting me."

"Jack, are you okay?" Claire asks, rushing up to our table and stopping near my chair.

"Yeah. I'm fine." He blows out a breath.

Heath says, "That's not what I meant, and you know it. You could have told her you weren't going to propose tonight. At least *she* would have known. You told her along with everyone else, and again, that was a really shitty thing to do."

"Maybe it was, but I shouldn't have been put in that position in the first place. Clark was right, what he said at Cloud 9. A proposal is between two people who love each other. That's it. Veronica wanted ratings, not a marriage."

At this, I lift my head and try to ignore the ballroom tilting sideways. I don't believe that. With as miserable as Veronica looked when Raff and I ran back into the ballroom, she wanted the marriage. She wanted the ratings and the marriage, but now she won't have anything. Well, the ratings, but not all publicity is good publicity. *Rise and Shine, Bridgeport!* might take a hit. Raff will do the best he can, but he doesn't control all the social media in the city.

Jack drops to his haunches in front of me. "Hey. You haven't looked good for the past couple of days. Are you okay?"

I hold a hand to my head. "I have a headache."

He smiles. "You smell like a bottle of my favorite whiskey. It's no wonder."

Wincing, I lie. "I might have celebrated a little too much."

Claire huffs. "Right."

Jack looks up from his position on the floor and frowns at her. "What's that supposed to mean?"

"Nothing. You've never been able to see what's right in front of your face."

"Claire," I say. "Please don't."

"Don't what?" Jack asks, and everyone stares at us. "Can someone explain what's going on?"

"It's only a misunderstanding, right, Claire?" I ask, pleading with her not to say anything.

She rolls her eyes. "Sure, that's what it is."

No one believes her, but no one knows what we're talking about, either, and I hope it stays that way.

I don't want her to tell Jack anything. Just because he decided not to propose to Veronica doesn't mean I have a chance. If Jack could feel anything for me, he would have acted on it a long time ago. Besides, even though he didn't propose, that doesn't mean he and Veronica broke up. They could go back to the way things were. He seemed perfectly happy with their arrangement.

"Let's get you to bed. I'm not letting you out of work tomorrow."

"You don't have to. I can—"

"I told Clark I'd see you home. If I don't, he'll write nasty things about me."

"He would not."

"He cares about you, Emma. That's exactly what he'd do. Come on."

I try to stand, and I feel like an animal in the circus, everyone studying me, trying to decipher what Claire was talking about. It's out of character for me to drink too much, and I was supposed to be working, no less. I was hoping to dull the pain, but that kind of pain can't be numbed by anything. The room spins, and gripping the edge of the table, I try to find balance in my heels. Jack swears under his breath.

He sweeps me off my feet, cradling me in his arms, and I'm too tired to be embarrassed that my billionaire boss is carrying me out of his birthday party. I'll worry about saving face tomorrow.

"Do you have a purse?" he asks.

"I left it with the concierge. I didn't want to lose track of it."

"Okay. We'll grab it on the way out. Goodnight, everybody. Thanks for coming."

We leave with a chorus of faint "goodnights" following us out of the ballroom.

My purse dangling from his hand, we wait outside for the limo. The city lights flash, and a cool breeze brushes over my face, cooling my skin. I expect him to put me down, but he never does, and elegantly, he slides into the back of the limo with me still in his arms. He doesn't nudge me to sit on the bench, only hugs me to him. The car gracefully merges into the traffic.

Tears for a different reason trickle down my face. I never thought I would be this close to Jack. I would fantasize about the scent of his cologne, how the soft cotton of his dress shirt would feel against my cheek, his arms and legs strong from all the time he spends in the gym, shielding me from the world.

I wanted it so terribly, and for two years, another woman had it.

I doze against his chest, his arms never loosening their hold. I assume he's dropping me at home but the limo stops, and I look out the window and we're idling in front of his building. "What are we doing?"

"I'm not letting you stay alone. You're not sober. Maybe you haven't had enough to die from alcohol poisoning, but it's not safe for you to be by yourself. I won't hurt you, Emma."

I pull away. We're so close. I can't say we've never been this close because we have. During work meetings when he's wanted me to see his laptop screen, or when I've straightened his tie or leaned over to pour him coffee, always lingering to feel the heat radiating from his body. This is different, and not because I'm sitting in his lap. His eyes are warm, like melted chocolate, and his jaw is covered in whiskers. I could lean only an inch and press my lips to his. I want to, my body trembling with the anticipation of how his kiss would feel. It would be safer for me to insist I go home. He might not think he'll hurt me, but he's hurt me every day for the past three years.

It's not his fault, and I nod.

His driver opens the door for us, and he's able to slide out without putting me down. I keep expecting him to, but he doesn't. I'm tempted to ask if he carried Veronica around like this, but why torture myself if he said yes? I wasn't privy to most of what went on in their relationship, and the less I know of their intimacy, the better. I hope he likes holding me, and he walks through the lobby, never letting me go. He doesn't set me to my feet in the elevator, either, and against every warning I tell myself, I snuggle into his embrace.

The rise and fall of his chest lulls me into an exhausted

haze, and I barely feel him settle me onto a bed, take my heels off, and cover me with a blanket. I want to ask him if I can change out of my dress, but the whiskey and stress from the last few days pull me under and I'm sleeping before I can open my mouth.

CHAPTER SEVEN

Jack

I was stupid and laid her on my bed to sleep.

Oh, you thought I was going to say I was stupid about something else? You're not wrong, but I'm talking about Emma sleeping on my bed. I told her I wouldn't hurt her, and for the first time since I purchased the penthouse, I slept in a guest room.

Christ, last night was a shitshow. Heath getting mad irked me because he wasn't so far off the mark. I *should* have talked to Veronica before my party (not that it would have done much good at that point—I still say I was right about that), but the expectation she shoved onto me without talking to me about it made me angry. I don't like coercion, and that's exactly what it was. She's too used to getting her way. Our arrangement suited me, and imagining sliding a ring onto her finger during a wedding ceremony churned my stomach. Not because it's her —I would feel like that thinking about it with anyone. I don't want to get married.

The sun is starting to come up, I stumble out of the guest room at the same time I always do, needing coffee. I want to be at the office by eight. I told Emma I wouldn't let her skip work, but she'll need an extra hour to go home, shower, and change. I could offer to send someone to her apartment for clothes and tell her she can shower here, but I doubt she'd agree and that's getting a little too close for me. Letting her spend the night was enough. Everyone knows I don't like women in my living space, and I mean it. My relationship with Veronica was how I wanted it, and I occasionally slept at her place. Her work schedule didn't allow her to stay up late, and when she's in bed, she sleeps. She's not a cuddler, and that's actually something I've always appreciated.

I sigh.

How did my life get so fucked up?

I make a pot of coffee and fill a mug for Emma, doctor it with the cream and sugar she favors, and carry it to my bedroom.

She's still sleeping, and she's lovely, lying on top of my comforter, the black lace of her dress swirling around her thighs, a hand tucked under her cheek.

I still want to ask her if she'll have my baby. Now that Veronica and I are no longer together, it may increase my chances of her saying yes. Maybe it's not so much that, but now I know she and Clark aren't a couple. If Clark had truly claimed her last night, I think I would have followed Heath's advice and left it alone. But we're both single, (I don't have any illusions Veronica will forgive me, even after I apologize) and there's nothing stopping us from making a baby together. I don't need her to help me raise it, and I'll buy her off. Heath isn't right about everything. Emma has a price, and I'll find out what it is.

Setting the mug on my nightstand, I sit on the edge of the

mattress and smooth her hair away from her face. It couldn't have been very comfortable sleeping with the pins in her updo, but it doesn't appear she moved at all, so maybe they weren't an issue.

She blinks her eyes open, squinting against the sun poking around the edges of the curtains.

"Good morning," I say, my hand hovering over her temple, my fingers still grazing her hair. "How are you feeling?"

She lifts up onto an elbow and swallows thickly, rubbing her eyes and smearing her mascara. "Like I'll never drink again."

Chuckling, I say, "We all go a little crazy sometimes, but it's not like you. Are you sure you're okay? You've been off for the past few days. I asked Clark about it last night."

Her eyes widen in alarm. "What did he say?"

"That it's none of my business," I say, her reaction surprising me.

She relaxes. "Oh, well, technically, what I was upset over isn't any of my business, either. It was just a thing, you know?"

"No, I don't. It had to be serious. You weren't looking well."

She shrugs but doesn't offer more.

"Here, I fixed you a cup of coffee." I pass her the mug, not letting go until I know she has a firm grasp around the handle.

"Thank you." Closing her eyes, she breathes in the aroma, and my dick twitches. For Christ's sake. If she says she'll surrogate for me, I won't have any trouble doing my part.

She swallows a sip of coffee. "I'm sorry about last night. I don't know much about your relationship, but that couldn't have been an easy decision."

"To tell you the truth, she did me a favor. I was stuck. It wasn't a bad stuck or a good stuck, I was just stuck with no incentive to change. If anything, it made me see I wasn't being fair. She wanted more. She should have talked to me about it instead of trying to trick me, but she wanted more, and I wasn't willing to give it to her. The sting will wear off, we'll both see it's for the best."

She pauses, sucks in a breath to say something, then lets it out slowly. Her hair is coming loose, her dress a cloud of black lace against the teal green and grey of my comforter. She looks right in my bed, though I have no one to compare her to. She feels right, and warning bells go off in my head. I can't get close to her, not if I want her to do what I want her to do.

Surrogacy is a business transaction, and I have to keep my feelings out of it.

She parts her lips and finally asks, "You didn't love her?"

I rest my hand on her bare leg. She's not wearing stockings. "No, Emma. I didn't love her."

She stares at me, her dark blue eyes flecked with green. "I should go."

I press my fingers into her skin. "Wait. There's something I want to ask you."

The bedroom is quiet, so quiet I can hear her breath come out in shallow little puffs. I think of Heath's warning, that I'll hurt her and she won't want to work for me anymore. I've weighed that, calculated the loss against the gain.

I could be heartless and say she's expendable, easily replaceable as any PA is, but Emma's my friend, and her photos flashed all over social media whenever she and Clark went somewhere always rubbed me the wrong way. I care about her, but I want a child, and at this stage of my life, nothing is more important than that, not even our friendship.

"What is it?"

"Will you have my baby?"

CHAPTER EIGHT

Emma

"He asked you to do what?" Raff barks, his body rigid with anger.

When Jack asked me if I would surrogate for him, my mind shut down and went completely blank.

Haisley and Mia, who weren't invited to Jack's birthday party and heard about what happened on social media, lean closer, disbelief written all over their faces.

We're sitting in my living room drinking wine and nibbling from a charcuterie board. I called an emergency meeting of my closest friends, and they were waiting with supplies when I came home from one of the most awkward days of work I have ever had.

"He wants me to surrogate for him," I repeat, choosing an olive from the board so I don't have to make eye contact with anyone.

"I hope you told him off," Raff says, leaning against my fireplace, a glass of red wine in his hand. He hasn't gotten any sleep since Jack's party, staying up all night helping Veronica with the impossible task of heading off bad press. Dark shadows lay under his eyes, and he hasn't shaved. After Haisley and Mia leave, he'll probably crash in my spare room. He and Veronica have done all they can, spreading the story she and Jack decided before the party not to get married after all, which is why he didn't propose. It's a story not everyone will believe considering so many people filmed her and took pictures of her crying after Jack's speech.

"And how does he want . . ." Mia fades, her hands fluttering in the air.

"What?" I have no idea what she's talking about, and neither does anyone else. We gape at her.

"You know," she continues, "How does he want his sperm, to, *you know*. Doctor appointments?"

"Oh," I say, and my cheeks heat. That was one of the things I asked Jack about. "He wants to, umm, do it naturally."

"He's out of his mind." Raff finishes off his wine and pours more. "I suppose he thought he could pay you to do this, too, right? How much did he offer you? Five million? Ten? How much is your baby worth, Emma? Jesus Christ."

"I haven't gotten that far. I couldn't get past, you know. *Sleeping with him*."

And oh, has my mind been stuck on that. Especially since I woke up in his bed, felt the texture of his comforter, the scent of his pillow bombarding my senses. There was nothing my body wanted more than to roll around naked with him while he tells me he loves me.

The latter won't happen, and if I'm smart, the former won't, either.

He wants to pay me to break my heart.

"If he wants a baby, why didn't he marry Veronica? Having

a baby would have been the next natural step," Haisley says, nibbling on a cracker.

Raff scowls.

"She doesn't want kids," I say, though knowing what I know now of their relationship, I would bet he didn't care enough to ask. "He said her career was enough for her."

"I hope you're not considering it," Raff says, pacing my living room. "He can go through an agency if he's that determined. It's ridiculous. All this because he's got a commitment phobia. That child will grow up without a mother, raised by nannies instead of parents. He'd do better to adopt a dog."

"But what if . . ." I stop. What are the chances I could pull it off? Slim to none is my guess.

"Oh, Emma. That's a bad idea," Mia says, on the same page. "That's a huge risk."

"I know, but . . ."

Raff stops in the middle of my living room and pins me with a glare. "Emma Cox! No. You've worked with him for three years. Three years, and two of those years he dated another woman. You think sex will make him fall in love with you? That's the dumbest thing I've ever heard, and I report gossip for a living. I've heard some pretty dumb shit."

"Besides, what if you really did get pregnant? You'd give up your baby?" Mia asks softly, squeezing my hand. "You'd never do that, honey, not for all the money in the world. Especially, *especially*, if that baby belonged to Jack."

"I know, but if there were a chance . . . we'll have to spend time together. Not only the sex part. He'd want to get to know me, right? Medical history, my likes and dislikes. Wouldn't he?" Saying it out loud, it sounds stupid. My favorite color has no bearing on a pregnancy.

"He wants one of your eggs and your uterus, Em. He doesn't care if you choose pancakes instead of waffles at brunch. Tell him to fuck off. The way he treated Veronica was atrocious and heartless, and he deserves it."

"She was in that relationship, too, you know. She must have been happy with the way things were. It wasn't all Jack."

"Maybe, but he was callous and inconsiderate, and he'll treat you the same way."

"What would you do, Emma? Secretly go on birth control?" Haisley asks.

I blanch. "I would never trick him like that."

She shakes her head. "You're healthy, and your periods are regular—"

Raff raises an eyebrow.

"What?" She lifts her hands, palms up. "We're women and we talk about women things." Turning back to me, she says, "He won't need any time at all to knock you up. A month, maybe two, then those nine months after that wouldn't be you and him talking and falling in love, it would be nine months of you trying to figure out a way to say goodbye to that baby because he'll sue you if you try to break a contract."

She's right. Jack always gets what he wants, and if I'm pregnant with his baby, we go to prenatal appointments and he sees that little peanut on the ultrasound screen, he'll stop at nothing until that baby is out of my belly and in his arms. Jack may not be cutthroat and ruthless, but if he sets his eyes on something and he wants it, he doesn't stop until it's his.

But I can't shake the allure of making love with him, and I want it so badly it's a physical yearning deep in my core where my biological clock ticks.

"You'll regret it, Emma," Mia says, and my heart agrees.

We finish the evening talking about the party and what Jack did to Veronica. Raff doesn't contribute, staring stoically into his wineglass. He rushed to her side last night, and I wonder if there was more to it than simply wanting to be the first to post damage control online. If there is, I hope it works out for him. He's been alone too long, and he deserves to be happy.

As I suspected, he chooses to spend the night, and I walk Mia and Haisley to their car, thank them for coming, and tell them goodbye.

I go back inside, and Raff's puttering around in the living room cleaning up wineglasses, napkins, and our empty board. He leaves everything in the kitchen and pours the dregs of a wine bottle into his glass. I haven't had much to drink, still hungover from the party and reeling from Jack's request.

"Em," he says, dropping tiredly onto the couch, "I know you've been in love with Jack for a long time, but if you can't tell him how you feel, you're no better than he and Veronica are. Sex isn't love, baby girl, and you know that. You and he could have sex for the rest of your lives, but that's not where love comes from. I told you, he's not capable of giving you what you want. Of giving any woman that. He proved it last night. I don't want him to break your heart."

"But you know how I feel about him," I say, hoping he has some advice if I really want to go through with it. "If there's a tiny chance that I could show him how much I love him and he could see me as more than a—"

"Baby machine?"

I scowl. "—secretary, then shouldn't I try?"

He sighs and swirls the inch of red in his glass. "I'm not going to talk you out of it, am I? You thought they were going to get married and that your chance was gone. Him jilting her is a big shiny present dropped in your lap, isn't it?"

"You don't have to make him sound so insensitive."

He rakes his hand through his hair in agitation. "You don't get it—he *is* insensitive. And if you let him get you pregnant, you'll see just how insensitive he can be."

That's not the Jack I know, but we've never talked babies before. If I'm going to do this, I need to be smart. "Then what should I do?"

"Haisley knows what she's talking about. He'll have an iron-clad contract drawn up. You'll have to read it and be clear and firm if there are points you don't like. I can put you in touch with a family law attorney if you want to approach this seriously, and you should, but I don't see any scenario where you come out ahead. You don't even know if he'll let you see the kid after it's born. I'm guessing not since that's not how surrogacy works. Research your legal rights and don't accept less than what a real surrogate is offered. Be honest with yourself, Emma. If you get pregnant, you'll want to be a family, and that's not what Jack wants. You'll want a family, and after the baby is born, you won't even have a job."

I lower myself onto a chair. That's it. That's what I was hoping for, and Raff knows me so well, he only needed two seconds to read my heart. If I carried Jack's baby, I would want to be a family.

"I should say no," I whisper.

"You should say no, baby girl. He's got the money to pay for a real surrogate. He doesn't need you. I'm going to check the websites for news and then lie down. I didn't get any sleep last night, and there wasn't time for me to catnap today. Don't be too hard on Veronica. She wanted something she can't have, just like you. Goodnight."

Raff kisses the top of my head and shuffles into my spare room where he keeps a few changes of clothes, pajamas, and a spare laptop.

I won't have a job. I didn't think of that. I like working for Variant, and if I say yes and things go badly, I'll have to quit. If Jack had gone through with his proposal, I would have had to, but giving him a baby, no, not any baby, but *my* baby, would be worse. So, so much worse.

I didn't get much sleep either, but I pull out my laptop and search surrogate agencies. Tomorrow, Jack will want to talk about his offer, and I need to be prepared. I'll need to know what to ask for and what I'm willing to give up for a few nights in bed with a billionaire.

CHAPTER NINE

Jack

I don't blame Veronica for doing all she can to smooth this over as quickly as possible. I wasn't as angry with her as I sounded the night of my party. I'll accept my share of the responsibility for how the evening went simply because I did have some warning of what Veronica wanted, and I could have stopped the whole thing before it got so out of hand. I could have told Claire I had no intention of proposing, and she could have spread that around on my behalf. I could have told my father when he tried to dispense that last minute advice. I could have told Emma to cancel the appointment when she mentioned the jeweler. I should have told Veronica I wasn't going to propose, but I was so pissed off she was trying to push me in a direction I didn't want to go, I wanted to pay her back.

I didn't expect Clark to run to her rescue leaving a drunk Emma behind.

Though, I'm glad he did.

I can't get the image of her in my bed out of my mind.

This morning she came into the office like she always does and I found a cup of coffee on my desk just as I always do, but on the way to my first meeting, I bumped into her in the hallway and she had a guarded look about her that she's never had before.

"Emma," I said, "do you have time after work today to talk?"

She nodded, a frown creasing the smooth skin of her forehead, and the day went by as it always does.

We won't go down to The Menagerie. I want to hammer out a rough draft of the contract, and we don't need an audience. There are things that are dealbreakers, and if she brings up any of them, I'm shutting her down, fast.

At five, I'm about to ask if she's done for the day and ready to talk, but my father strides past her desk and snaps, "They're great for each other, huh?" and barrels into my office, slamming the door shut in Emma's stunned face.

"What the fuck was that?" he asks, not pausing on the way to my minibar.

I managed to avoid this yesterday, hiding, pretending to be on conference calls whenever my father wanted to talk, and over the noon hour, I went out for longer than necessary claiming a business lunch. He knew I was full of shit, but he let me be. We were both legitimately busy today with the beginning stages of a huge acquisition, but it appears on this late Friday afternoon, the business day done, my luck has run out.

"I'm assuming you mean at the party?" I ask irritably, hoping Emma doesn't leave.

"Yes. That's exactly what I'm talking about."

"I had no intention of proposing—"

"For fuck's sake, not that. Emma. You carried her out of there like you were goddamned Prince Charming, and now it's all over that you left that Chapman woman for your PA."

"It is?" In my perusal to see how Veronica put out the fires I started, I didn't see that bit of gossip.

"Yes, it is. Claire high-tailed it over to me specifically to point it out. And you know what? She looked damned good."

"Claire did?" I'm not following.

"No. Emma. I like her."

I wanted to wait until I went home, but I give up and pour a drink. "So do I."

"Then do something with it."

Leaning against the floor-to-ceiling window, I ask, "Like what?"

He points at me, his hand shaking. "I know you think I'm an old coot who comes into the office because I don't have anything better to do, and for the most part, you're right. But I also have a lot of regrets, things I can't run from, things I can't fix. They're my fault, so I hide behind paperwork. You turned forty-five on Wednesday, and your little speech might have been lip service, but there's truth to it, too."

Anger shoots through me, but calmly, I say, "You've never once encouraged me to get married and have always ragged on Claire for her choices. Just because you think Emma looked good in my arms, and she was drunk by the way, or she wouldn't have been there at all, does not mean I will 'do anything' with her. Veronica found out the hard way that I won't marry. I will never put my children through what I felt when I was four."

Sweat beads along Dad's forehead. "I will not—"

"No, you won't. You never talk about it, but I watched her stumble into the back of that yellow taxi crying so hard she couldn't see, and that's seared into my brain for the rest of my life. There's not a day that goes by that I don't think of it. So don't you ever tell me what you think I should do with my life.

You've kept your nose out of it for forty-five years. Do it for another forty-five."

He sets the glass on the tray. "And that, Jack, is one of my biggest regrets. Goodnight." Wearily, he opens my office door revealing Emma, who I pray to God didn't hear much, if any, of that conversation. "Goodnight, Emma," he says, walking by her desk, dragging his fingertips along the surface the same exact way I do every time.

"Goodnight, Mr. Durand," she replies, and I can see why he likes her. She respects him and isn't scared of him. Not like Veronica who would go out of her way to avoid him. It's why he started calling her "that Chapman woman" in the first place. It irked him she would be that weak.

I smile at her. "Sorry about that."

"It's okay. He wasn't happy about what happened at the party." She stands from her desk and smooths the skirt of her dress.

She looks pretty today in a light blue sheath, her hair pulled back into a ponytail fastened with a matching floral scarf.

"Nobody is." I haven't heard from Heath, either. I skipped our run on Wednesday in favor of the nap I wasn't able to take, not after the conversation I had with Dad in his office. Heath chewed me out at the party, and there's been radio silence since. I'll speak with Emma and then go to the gym for our regular Friday run. If he shows, he shows, and if he doesn't, I'll know where I stand. We've survived bumps in the past. This won't be any different.

Emma steps inside my office and I close the door. She looks around like she's never been in here before, her eyes darting from the bookshelves to my bar to the conference table butting against the windows to the conversation area where I'll sit with clients who need to feel like they aren't doing business.

I pull out a chair for her at the conference table. If we treat this like a business transaction, there won't be any room for emotions. She doesn't have any papers with her, she didn't bring her tablet, not even her phone. I hope she's taking this seriously.

She sits and crosses her legs.

I pull a thin pile of paper off my desk and sit across from her, my back to the city.

"Thank you for considering this." She hasn't said she'd do it. Sitting on my bed in a pouf of lace and smeared mascara, her complexion pale, she asked me for a day to think about it. Her time is up, and I'll pressure her for an answer. I want to get this going.

"I don't understand, Jack," she says, twisting her fingers on the tabletop. "You're good looking and rich. You can have any woman in the city, and that's not an exaggeration. You've made the top five on the Bridgeport bachelor lists for years, even when you were dating Veronica. Why don't you get married and have children?"

"I don't want to get married, and I don't believe a child needs a mother to grow into a well-adjusted adult. I'm getting old, and I want to have a baby. I don't want a wife and all the bullshit that goes along with that."

She sucks in a breath. "You think being part of a loving marriage is bullshit?"

"There's no love in marriage, Emma."

"You don't think you'll ever fall in love?"

"No."

She purses her lips and looks away. I give her time for that to sink in. I don't understand why no one can accept marriage isn't in my future.

"Then why should I believe you'll be a good father? Raff says if you're lonely you should adopt a dog."

Of course she would tell her friends about this. I couldn't

expect her to keep it a secret, not when she started to show. Her friends would demand an explanation, least of which, who knocked her up, but there will be details she can keep to herself, especially from the media, and writing an NDA for her to sign just shot up to the top of my list.

"I suppose Clark told you to tell me no."

"Yes, he did. You're asking me to give away a baby, and I want to know why."

I rub my finger over my lips. She won't do it if I'm not honest. "My mother left me and Claire when we were little. She and my father had a huge fight, and I remember hearing her cry. From the third floor nursery, I watched her climb into a taxi, and we didn't see her ever again. I never want my child to go through that, and that's why I want to hire you to be surrogate. You can't leave if you're already gone."

"Jack."

She breathes my name in a gasp of shock and pity, and that's the last thing I need.

I straighten. It's time to get down to business. "These are the main points I want you to consider. There will be no negotiation to these terms. You'll work for me through the pregnancy, and I'll attend all your doctor's appointments. I want to be a part of it. After you have the baby, you can choose to work for Variant in any capacity, though I would imagine remaining my PA would be uncomfortable for us both. You won't have any contact with the child after it's born. You will have no parental rights from the moment the nurse lays that baby in my arms. Everything you need will be paid for. If, for any reason, the child needs medical assistance from a family member such as a blood transfusion or other where a relative is considered the best option, you will be notified and allowed to assist if you so choose."

She nods. Maybe she's more prepared than I think she is.

Nothing I said was a surprise.

"How long are you willing to try?" she asks.

I skim the paper. I thought about this, too. Emma's gorgeous and as my dick proved yesterday morning when she woke up in my bed, I won't have any trouble fulfilling my own side of things. Even now, I'm looking forward to sinking into her, hearing her whimper as she comes, her arms wrapped around my neck—

No. I have to get in there, do my job, and leave. Pull out, zip up, and get the fuck out of there. Turn her over so I can't see the hurt that I know will be on her beautiful face.

"Six months."

Her eyes widen. "You're willing to sleep with me for six months?"

I tamp down my irritation. She sounds like we're going to screw every night for half a year. "A woman's cycle is receptive for a pregnancy six days a month, Emma. You should know that. Buy an ovulation kit, and when the time is right, let me know. I'll want to see the results for myself, of course. Sperm live up to five days in the reproductive tract, and I think we'd only need to have sex twice a month for results. In that time if we don't conceive, I'll reconsider my options. I'm not getting any younger—in fact, I waited far too long for this as it is."

I *should* have thought of this ten years ago.

"So, if I'm broken, you don't want me."

I rear back in my chair. "That's a little extreme. If we don't conceive, you can't fulfill your end of the bargain. It's not personal."

She quirks the corner of her mouth. "What if the problem is you?"

I scowl. "I've already been tested. I have plenty of sperm and their motility is fine, even for someone of my age."

"Then you've thought of everything."

"I have, yes."

"I can't help but think there are better ways for you to do this."

"This isn't for me. It's for the child's future."

"What if I want our baby to have a mother?"

My throat closes and I can't breathe.

Our baby.

"If you want *your* baby to have a mother, then you should follow Clark's advice. I've already outlined my whys, Emma. You won't change my mind. The only other thing we haven't discussed is financial compensation. I'm willing to pay you what you think your time and body are worth—within reason. I understand the physical toll a pregnancy can have, and I wouldn't think it would be easy for a woman to give up a child. Name your price."

Standing from the table, she walks over to the window. Bridgeport is a huge city, and skyscrapers crowd us from every direction. She's beautiful, the sun glowing against her skin, and I wonder who this elusive man is she's in love with. I never did find out, never did press Claire who seemed to know.

She looks at me, and the sad woman she turned into before my party is back, her eyes filled with a bleakness that drops a pit of apprehension the size of the Grand Canyon into my stomach.

"You don't have to pay me. I'll do it for free."

CHAPTER TEN

Emma

I don't know what made me say that. The story about his parents, maybe, or the stupid idea that we won't get that far. If he's kept himself from falling in love because his mother abandoned him when he was a child, I can work with that. I know if Jack and I aren't meant to be I can't truly make him fall in love with me, and if I thought he loved Veronica, I wouldn't try. But he doesn't love her, and if that's all that's standing in our way, I might have a chance.

Raff would call me a naïve fool, and maybe I am, but I love Jack so much and watching him sit there and listening to him spout his coldhearted plans for the future, all I want is to rescue him from a life of loneliness.

"You can't be serious. If you can't come up with a sum, I'll pay you what I think is best."

I shrug, feigning nonchalance.

"Then you agree to my terms?" he asks, tapping a pen against the sheaf of paper.

"Yes. I looked up surrogacy last night, and you're not suggesting anything that isn't the norm, but I have my own terms." If he's scared of commitment, he's not going to like what I have to say.

"What are they?"

"We spend time together. I'm not going to let you fuck me twice a month."

He winces.

Well, what does he expect? If there isn't love when you make a baby, you're fucking. Plain and simple.

"What do you mean, spend time together? I'll see you at work every day."

"That's not enough. I want to hang out with Mia and Haisley, Heath and Zoey and their children. I like Claire and your father. Invite me to family dinners."

He slams his pen onto the table. "Jesus Christ, Emma. We don't do family dinners."

I shove my hands onto my hips. "Then what kind of family are you proposing for our baby?" I'll keep saying it, even if it does turn him white as a sheet. "You already think she doesn't need a mother. If we have a girl, she's going to need some kind of feminine presence in her life, and that won't be a nanny. Claire will be her aunt. Ron will be our child's grandfather. If you're not on speaking terms with him, who will be around for our baby when you're working, or sick, or on a business trip? Strangers aren't going to raise our child, Jack. I hope you'll be a better father than that."

He opens his mouth, but nothing comes out.

I wait.

"Fine," he croaks. "Family dinners. And hanging out with friends? Seriously? We already do that."

"No, we don't. If you need a babysitter, Zoey or her oldest daughter will want to do it, and it sounds like right now Heath is mad at you. It doesn't matter if you cut me out, having a baby creates a family. She's going to need more than only you." I don't know why I keep saying she—maybe because it needles him whenever it comes out of my mouth.

"For fuck's sake." He loosens his tie.

"Mia and Haisley, and Raff, too. If you don't want me to hear news about our child, then you'll have to write into your contract that I can't live in Bridgeport after the baby's born."

Alarmed, his gaze shoots to mine.

"What? You gave me the option to still work here. You don't think I won't see our daughter running through the lobby? Visiting you in your office? Visiting Ron? You think Zoey won't tell me about birthdays? That Raff won't share pictures of you and her with me? I'm not going to simply disappear after I push her out, Jack. So, revisit and revise. Unless you force me to, I'm not going anywhere."

He grits his teeth. "Is that it?"

"No."

I kick off my heels and walk across the thick carpeting. I push on the back of his chair, swiveling him to face me, and step between his legs.

Sitting on his thigh, I wrap my arms around his neck. I can't tell you how many times I've fantasized about doing exactly this, and I revel in the closeness, his body heat and scent, his hard muscles. The past couple of days have been difficult for him, and he looks tired. He hasn't shaved, and he skipped the salon appointment I scheduled for him before the party. I run my fingers through his hair and swallow back a cry. If only he could love me. If only he wanted me here, in his lap. If only he would put his arms around me and hold me close.

I rub my lips against his, his scruff scratching at my skin.

He stiffens, his arms rigid and unmoving on the chair's armrests.

"One more thing," I murmur against his lips. "When we have sex, we'll both be naked, in a bed. Our baby won't be conceived with a wham-bam-thank-you-ma'am five second fuck over a kitchen table. And after we're done, we cuddle and talk. Maybe we won't make a baby with love, but we are friends, at least, and we can act like it."

I press my lips to his, and groaning, he opens his mouth. Our tongues twist together, and he skims his hand under my dress and up thigh. His fingertips dig into my skin and I wiggle closer. Jack isn't the type to screw in his office. I've never seen him do it in the three years I've worked here, and even if it's after hours and no one is in the building, I don't think he'd do me on the loveseat, no matter how much I wanted him to.

He pulls out the elastic in my ponytail and grabs a handful of my hair. He yanks, tilting my head and taking control of our kiss.

"Is that all you want?" he pants, pulling away.

"Two more things," I say, winding his tie around my hand. "I think we should practice."

"Practice what?"

"Having sex. We should make sure we're compatible before we sign anything, don't you think?"

If our kiss is anything to go by, I already know we'll be compatible, but my main goal is to spend as much time with him as possible, dating, seeing friends and family, and showing him what our life would be like if he could put the past behind him.

"What's the other?" he asks, nipping at my bottom lip.

"You're going to have to meet my mother."

Abruptly, he stands, and I topple to the carpet in a heap of desire and bewilderment. "What was that for?"

"I don't think that's necessary. You're not going to tell her about this, are you?" he asks, stepping away from me.

"I think I won't have a choice once it looks like I shoved a basketball up my shirt," I say sarcastically. He might have the technical details down, but he didn't consider what was actually going to happen if I surrogate for him. "If you don't want people to know what we're doing, why did you ask me?"

He stops at the bar and pours a drink, and I sit on the floor and watch him sip. He lifts his glass in offer. It's tempting, but I shake my head. I'm still queasy from his party.

"Because you're kind and intelligent. Because you're beautiful, elegant, and graceful. You're everything I want my child to be. That's why I asked."

I swallow. I had no idea he thought those things about me. The closest he's ever come to hinting at anything like that is whenever Raff and I would meet up around him and he would glare at us. I always thought that it had more to do with Raff's line of work than it did jealousy, but maybe I was wrong. Maybe Jack never wanted to admit he has feelings for me. Maybe I'm in a better position than I thought.

"You can find a surrogate who is all those things," I point out, "and avoid the complications."

"No. I don't want a stranger carrying my baby."

I throw up my hands. "Fine. But that means tolerating a few things while we try to conceive and through the pregnancy, if it happens. That's life. Maybe you can hide in your office, but I won't be able to and it sure would be nice if I had your support going through it."

"I'm sorry. You're right." He sets his empty glass on the tray and standing in front of me, holds out his hand. I place my much smaller one in his and he pulls me to my feet, but instead of releasing me, he wraps his arm around my back.

He lowers his head.

"What are you doing?"

"Practicing."

CHAPTER ELEVEN

Jack

I ... didn't completely think this through. No shit, right? I didn't get past Emma saying yes, but once she did, all the ramifications that weren't legal dumped on me like a bucket of ice water. Family dinners, hanging out with our friends. Meeting her mother. Christ. God only knows how she'll react to Emma giving a baby away.

But she pinned me down like she knew she would. I can't raise a child alone.

Not if I don't want her to have the kind of childhood I did.

Her.

Scowling, I pull the gym's doors open. Emma's got me saying that, and now I can't stop thinking about a little girl who looks like her.

Fuck.

I change and dump my things into a locker.

Heath's already running, and he flicks a glance at me out of the corner of his eye. "I thought you wouldn't show."

I set the treadmill's speed and incline. "I had a meeting with Emma."

Heath's still angry, and he doesn't say anything for two miles. "She agree?"

"Yes. I'm going to her place tonight for dinner."

I don't know what to think of her requests. I see the logic behind expanding our circle for the baby's sake, especially when she pointed out I would need help raising my child. Claire and I were raised by a nanny, and I hadn't thought of it until Emma brought it up that I don't particularly want my son or daughter to have that kind of experience. I was lucky I had Claire, and unless Emma agrees to carry another baby, my child will be an only. It will be important that I do everything I can to ensure she's not alone.

"You're getting down and dirty already? She's ovulating?"

"Hell if I know. She wants to spend time together."

Heath smirks.

"What?" I ask, annoyed.

"Nothing. She's not going to let you bang her over a kitchen table. Good for her."

"What's with people and kitchen tables? I've never been crass enough to bend anyone over a table, whether it's in my kitchen or not, and I'm not about to start."

"When you're in love, you never know when the mood will strike," he says. "Zoey and I—"

"I don't want to know."

"All I'm saying is, good for her. I know you. You think shoving it in and pulling it out is all you're going to have to do, and she wanted better for herself. You have to admire her for that."

I fall into a steady rhythm, and as the miles speed by, I realize that actually, I do. She brought up a lot of points I hadn't considered, and a woman who isn't as sensitive and compassionate as Emma wouldn't have mentioned them, either. She cares about her child, the kind of life I'm going to give her, and she's not even a glimmer in our eyes yet. I respect that, and it validates choosing her.

"What else did she want?"

"Why do you think there's more?"

"She's a woman. There's always more."

I laugh. I'm relieved he's not pissed at me. I don't like being at odds with my friends. "Family dinners."

"With Ron and Claire?"

"Yeah."

"That won't be awkward."

"Possibly less so than meeting her mother."

Heath chokes and slams the Stop button. He hops off the treadmill and bends over, his hands braced above his knees.

I can't tell if he's laughing or dying.

"Emma wants you to meet her mother?" he sputters.

I hit the Stop button, too. I didn't get in as many miles as I wanted, but I don't want to be too late heading over to Emma's.

"I didn't want to, but it's not anything I can avoid once she starts showing."

Chuckling, Heath shuffles to the stretching area and drops onto a mat. "Can I be there?"

"You can be at all the friends' dinners she's dragging me to."

"What's the point to all that?"

"She said because the baby won't grow up with a mother, she wants her to have as many people close to her as possible. I need to talk to you about being a godparent, like I am to your girls."

Heath sobers. "She really said that?"

"Yeah."

"Jack."

I know what's in his tone. "I'm not changing my mind."

"You're going to hurt her. You know that, don't you?"

"I don't care." I get to my feet. I need to shower if I'm going to be on time.

"You might not now, but you will."

———

On the way to Emma's, I stop at a florist's shop and buy a bouquet of pink roses. It's been a long time since I bought a woman flowers, Veronica never needing the romantic gesture. She never told me she did, and since she didn't, I didn't put in any extra energy.

I've never been to Emma's before, and I park in front of her building that's several blocks from Heath and Zoey's. The street is peaceful and kids play outside, and one little girl is drawing a hopscotch using pink chalk. I pull a rose out of the bouquet and give it to her. With an awed smile, she lifts the bloom to her nose the way all women do when given flowers.

Emma fits into the neighborhood, I bet, and knows all her neighbors. I can picture her sitting on the stoop drinking wine and talking to the mothers while their children play.

I knock on her door, and she answers almost immediately, wearing a casual dress I've never seen before. Even after three years, I don't know Emma that well, a fact she was more than quick and happy to point out. If we do bump into each other at events like Cloud 9's opening, she's always with Clark and I was with Veronica. She'd never wear something like this, but the plain cotton dress suits her, as does the headband keeping the hair out of her face.

"Hey," I say, suddenly ill at ease. Our professional dynamic is changing, and it's another thing I didn't think about. "Here. I hope you like pink. I gave one to a little girl drawing on your sidewalk. I think she liked it."

She peers around me. "That's Tessa. I'm sure she loved it. Her dad passed away a few months ago. Some kind of cancer, I think. Her mom's been pretty quiet about it."

"That's too bad."

"You're lucky your father's in good health. Come in. You look nice."

After I showered, I changed into jeans and a cotton button down shirt, and skipped the tie. I wasn't sure a suit would have been appropriate, but now I regret my casual attire. Emma's forcing me to see this as something more than a business trans-action, but it's all I want it to be.

I follow her into a small kitchen and a bottle of wine is breathing on the counter. I walk through and into her living room. A set of French doors lets out into a yard shared by the other apartments, and a patio table and four chairs sit on a slab of cement. Flowers are blooming in planters, and her property management recently cut the grass. "This is a nice little place."

"Thanks. I've lived here a long time. It's not as close to Variant as I would like, but if I moved, I'd lose the yard, and I like sitting outside. Do you want some wine?"

"Sure. You'll have to stop once you're pregnant, you know. In fact, there's a list of things I want to go over with you after we conceive."

Her lips twitching, she pours. "Is that why you want me to keep my job? So you can hound me all the time about eating salad and drinking water? I know how to be healthy, Jack."

"Yeah, but you've never had a baby before, have you?" I'm flippant, but I pause. She could have a hundred kids I don't know about.

She offers me a glass of white, and I curl my hand around the delicate wineglass. She's cooking something that smells wonderful, and my stomach rumbles. I'm always starving after a run.

"No, but I doubt it's that different. I can ask Zoey for tips."

"Paige was born too early and spent five weeks in the NICU," I say, my mouth dry. Zoey's water broke too soon, and I relive the stress and the fear of that afternoon. Heath was a mess until they were able to bring Paige home, and even then he slept on a cot in the nursery for months to be there if she needed him.

Paige is a precocious four year old now, and you'd never know she came into the world causing such chaos.

"Oh, that must have been scary. She's never said anything to me."

"She doesn't like talking about it. She always starts crying." I clear my throat. "We need to talk about stuff like that, what we would do if something like that happened to us."

There are so many contingencies and things that could go wrong.

"Since you said the minute she leaves my body I'm not a consideration, I guess that would be for you to decide. Are you hungry? I made shrimp Alfredo."

"Yeah, sure."

She places the roses in a vase at the edge of the table, and we sit. We don't speak while we eat, and I start to I grow annoyed. I thought we were supposed to be spending time together, and I don't fucking know, *getting to know each other,* but we can't do that if she won't talk to me.

"Do you want me to help you clean up?" I ask, trying to keep the irritation out of my voice.

We're both done, and we didn't speak two words to each other. I want to leave. All her talk about creating a baby in friendship was a load of bullshit.

"No, I can do it later." She finishes the last of the wine in her glass, pushes away from the table, and tugs on my hand.

"What?"

"You said we'd practice."

She swallows and licks her trembling lips.

I understand now why she wasn't talking to me. She's nervous.

"Emma, we don't need to practice," I say, but my cock hardens as I watch the thrum of her blood pulse in her neck. I want her nervous. I want her quivering with anticipation, eager for my hands on her. "You're overthinking this. I'll need two seconds to make a baby—you won't have to do anything."

Her cheeks pink. "It's more for me, if you need to know. I haven't been with anyone for . . . years," she finishes in a whisper.

I pull my head out of my ass. She's not nervous. She's scared. "Emma, I would never hurt you."

"I know, but I need a trial run, okay?"

When a beautiful woman wants to practice having sex because she hasn't been with anyone for a while, you don't say no. "Okay."

She tugs on my hand again, and I follow her down a narrow hallway.

We pass a smaller bedroom and I catch a glimpse of a men's suit hanging from the closet door, but we step into her bedroom and I forget about it.

The room is very feminine, like Emma. The bed is a huge king, and gauzy cream draping hangs from bedposts that reach the ceiling. Heath and Zoey's girls would have a fit over it, exclaiming they would feel like princesses sleeping there, and I bet lying in bed, Emma does look like a princess. The walls are painted a soft cream and every inch of wall space is taken up with shelves, pictures, and a large dresser. I don't know if she's usually organized or messy, but there isn't any clothing heaped on the floor or on a chair that sits in the corner that matches the rose-colored comforter and cream walls. Near a door that looks like it could lead to a bathroom, a mirror frames our reflections. We look good together, and I avert my gaze.

The sun hasn't gone down yet, and the soft light brightens the room. Emma might be more comfortable if we do this in the dark, but we'd have to wait a few more hours for that to happen. I close the blinds to the largest window, darkening the room.

I rub her arms. "Don't be nervous."

"I can't help it. The last man I slept with was four years ago, and since working for Variant, I haven't been interested in dating anyone."

"It's okay. Lie on the bed with me. We'll go slow."

She crawls over the comforter, the skirt of her dress tangling between her legs.

I've tried to never consider Emma as anything more than my assistant, but whenever Clark would wait for her near her desk or the way he would skulk one step behind her, I always wanted to bash his face in. I never let it get the better of me. I had Veronica and there was no reason to be jealous. But as she lies on the bed and looks at me with such absolute faith in her eyes, there is no man I'd trust to do this but me.

I lie on my side next to her, cradle her cheek with my palm, and cover her lips with mine. They're soft and warm, like they were in my office when she sat in my lap. She was braver then, knowing I don't have sex in my office, knowing she was safe and I wouldn't ask for more than passionate kisses. She closes her eyes, and so do I, pushing my tongue past her lips and tasting the sweetness of her mouth. Her breath hitches and my cock feels like it's going to explode. I lean into her and press my dick against her hip.

With a hand to her back, I encourage her to roll against my chest, and I wedge my leg between hers. She pulls the hem of my shirt up and presses her hand against my skin.

She might not think so, but this is a new experience for me, too.

There's never been a reason I've had sex except for pleasure. I've never used it to deepen a relationship, never used it to show someone how I feel. While we do this, I want to try to tell Emma that her baby will be safe with me, that I'll take care of her no matter the cost. I want her to believe I'll be a good dad.

I move my lips from hers and trail kisses along her cheek, across her jaw, and down her neck. Her dress is low-cut, and I brush my lips across the tops of her breasts. I don't want to wait any longer; I've had enough foreplay. We can still go slowly, but I want to explore without clothes on.

"Are you comfortable getting undressed?" I ask.

The sun has gone down a bit more, but the room is still light enough I can see her blink. I rub my thumb over her lips.

"We don't have to, Emma."

"I want to, but I'm nervous."

"You don't have to be. We'll take our time, enjoy each other, and if you want me to stop, I will."

She pauses. "All right."

Quickly, I kiss her and roll off the side of the bed. She scoots off the opposite side, steps out of her dress, and stands in only her bra and panties. She's gorgeous in white lace, the hazy light disguising any imperfections. If she has any. At forty-five, I have my share, only regular workouts keeping any excess fat from accumulating over the years. I don't know if Emma works out, but during her pregnancy, I'll need to see to it she exercises. We can go on long walks, and I'll ask Heath about prenatal yoga. If I recall correctly, he and Zoey liked doing that together.

She says, "I'm ahead of you."

"I'm thinking about how beautiful you are." It's not

completely true, but better than admitting I was picturing us getting sweaty during a yoga class.

"You don't have to say things like that. I haven't signed anything, but after tonight, you can assume my signature is on the dotted line."

"That's not why I said it. I'm only telling you the truth."

She smiles and reaches behind her back for her bra strap. "Then hurry up."

I unbutton my shirt, but next time, I'd like her to do it. There's something about being undressed by a woman I've always appreciated, and I want to have that experience with Emma. For now, I undress myself and remove my briefs. Her eyes widen. I suppose my size would be a bit apprehensive to a woman who hasn't had sex for a few years, but I've never had an over-blown opinion of myself and if Veronica was impressed, she never said.

Emma pulls back the sheets and comforter, and I do the same on my side.

We slide in and meet in the middle. I don't give her a second to be afraid of me. I pull her to my chest and bury my face in the sweet curve of her neck. My whiskers scratch her skin, and she giggles. I smile, and lifting my head, I say, "I like that sound."

"It's not very romantic."

"It's perfect, Emma. Let me touch you."

She pauses. "Okay."

I skim my hand down her flat belly, across her hip, and over her thigh. She stiffens for a moment, but she relaxes and opens her legs. Fluttering my fingers over her delicate skin, I find what I'm looking for and gently, so gently, push one of my fingers inside her.

She sucks in a breath, but I know I'm not hurting her. She's so soft and wet, there isn't any resistance, but she's tight and this will be one of the most memorable experiences of my life.

"Are you doing okay?" I ask, checking in.

"Yeah. Will you kiss me?"

I lower my head and cover her lips with mine. I slowly move my finger in and out of her, and she wraps her arms around my neck, pressing her breasts against my chest. Her skin is on fire, or maybe that's mine. I add another finger, encouraging her to relax and loosen up. I'm not going to be able to wait much longer, and she'll understand that when I said I could make a baby in two seconds, I wasn't kidding.

"Will you touch me?" I whisper in her ear.

Tentatively, she reaches between our bodies and cups her hand around my cock. It surges, and already an orgasm is building. Maybe asking her to touch me wasn't the smartest idea, but I want to be inside her and I wanted her to feel what exactly I'm going to be pushing into her.

I find her clit with my thumb, and she tilts her hips. There's not a better indicator she's enjoying this than her body instinctively asking for more.

"Jack," she whimpers, and Christ, is it sexy.

"I want to be inside you when you come. I want to feel that."

Widening her legs, she gives me her consent without words. I settle between her thighs, the tip of my cock nudging where my fingers had been moments ago. "I'm going to go as slow as I can, sweetheart, but you're so wet, it won't hurt. I promise."

Her gaze is unwavering. "I trust you."

"I won't break it." I slide into her, and my cock is already spurting. I stop and count to ten. Pausing was probably good for her, too, her shallow panting echoing through the darkening bedroom. "Are you okay?"

"Yeah. It's not as uncomfortable as I thought it would be."

I slide in deeper, and her fingers dig into my biceps.

"Emma?"

"I'm okay."

"All right. I need a minute." I settle my weight on top of her, and I inhale a much-needed breath.

Tugging my head down, she shoves her tongue into my mouth, licking at me as her hips rock and her heels dig into the mattress. I give her my full weight and slide my cock into her the rest of the way, my tip hitting her center.

She gasps against my lips.

"I'm sorry, was that too much?" I pull out a little bit.

"No. I mean, I didn't expect that."

"I'll be more careful." Gritting my teeth in control, I glide back and forth.

I don't want to come before she does, and anchoring on a knee, I partially pull out and find her clit.

"Jack."

"Come for me, Emma. I want to feel you."

A moan whines from the back of her throat, and I know it won't be long. Her skin is so smooth and slippery, and she glows with perspiration. I can only see her outline now, but she's beautiful, full of passion and desire.

Her orgasm crests and her muscles clench at my cock. It's been a while for me, too, and unable to hold back any longer, I fill her with everything I have.

I don't know how much time goes by until my dick finally stops twitching, and I relax on top of her, my arms keeping me from crushing her. I rest my forehead against her temple. "Christ."

She laughs. "That's good, right?"

"Better than good. Was it good for you, too? I tried to be gentle."

She kisses my cheek, but she drags her lips over my jaw and licks at my neck, turning the kiss turns into something else. "I love how you taste," she murmurs. She does it again, her tongue leaving a wet trail across my skin, her fingers tangling in my hair. There's something more peaceful about her now that we've had sex, maybe because she knows it won't hurt and there's nothing to be scared of.

She nibbles, and her teeth graze my jaw. I lean into her kisses and my cock stiffens.

"Emma." I sigh her name. I don't want to enjoy this. Don't want to enjoy being here in her bed, in her arms.

"Don't go," she whispers. "Please."

I can't stay here. There's nothing to be gained by spending the night. I can't get close to her emotionally, and that's what cuddling after sex is. There's a reason why men leave the second they're done, and I should do the same. She wanted sex in a bed, and I gave her that.

"Please," she murmurs against my skin, and even though I'm hard and want to have her again, I pull out. After a moment's pause, I reluctantly relent and hug her to my side.

She rests her head on my shoulder and I try to appreciate the affection for the friendship it represents. There isn't a sound in her little apartment apart from a clock ticking somewhere and her soft inhales and exhales, her delicate breath floating across my skin.

I don't know if I could have made her pregnant tonight. If there was a chance, I think she would have mentioned it, but I don't want to shatter the peace with an insensitive question.

The second I think she's sleeping, I untangle our limbs and slide out of bed. Finding my clothes on the floor is easy enough, and I'm dressed and out the door five minutes later. If she asks why I didn't stay, I'll say I had to do something for work. It's the only thing she'll believe. Short of an emergency, there's no reason for me not to spend the night.

The cool spring air is refreshing, and I stop for a moment on the sidewalk.

This is going to be more difficult than I thought.

I have to keep myself from wanting more. Picturing a yellow taxi carrying my mother away is all I need, and I repeat the mantra that has become life and death.

She can't leave if she's already gone.

CHAPTER TWELVE

Emma

I felt him crawl out of bed, but I pretended to be asleep. Giving him the benefit of the doubt, I hoped he was only running to grab something out of his truck. He didn't come back, but I didn't let my disappointment get the best of me.

While he was dressing, I could have called him out on it, but I can't expect him to give me everything I want the second I want it. The fact that he came over, ate dinner with me, and had sex in my bed is an absolute win as far as I'm concerned. Maybe I was too nervous to try to convey everything I was feeling, but I think I'm off to a good start the way he said my name before he left.

Jack and I didn't plan anything for today, and usually on Saturdays I spend most, if not all, day with Raff going to some kind of event for *Talk of the Town*, but I'm not worried. Jack won't back out of his promises, and we have plenty of time to figure out when we'll spend time with family and friends during the months of trying and nine months of pregnancy. If he can't fall in love with me, then it won't matter how much time I have.

It's something I'll need to face, but I'm not giving up hope yet.

Last night I didn't run water into the saucepan to soak, and I do that now before attempting to scrub it clean. I toss the empty wine bottle into the recycling and load our dishes into the dishwasher. I start a pot of coffee, wash the saucepan, and carry a mug of coffee outside to the patio. I settle into a chair and sigh, enjoying the peaceful morning.

My phone chimes, and I read Raff's text: *Dinner tonight?*

Always, I reply. I'll never turn down one of Raff's invitations.

I have tickets for the opening of that play. I'm interviewing the two leads for the 'zine. Do you want to go?

Of course. What time?

I'll send a limo for you at seven.

Perfect, I reply. I'm about to set my phone down but my mother texts. *Missed you last weekend. Are you visiting me tomorrow?*

I couldn't pretend everything was normal when I thought Jack was going to propose to Veronica. My mother knows I'm in love with him, and she also knows he'd been dating Veronica for the past couple of years. Whenever I would visit, we never spoke much about it, or my job, preferring to shop, go out to lunch, and chit chat about lighter things. I always appreciated that. Now she'll want to talk about Jack's birthday party, why he didn't propose to Veronica, and why he carried me out of the hotel.

I don't scroll through social media often, but I didn't miss the blog gossip and the pictures of me in Jack's arms or the numerous pictures of Veronica crying, who, by the looks of it, watched him carry me out.

Yes, I'll be there. We can go to brunch.

Perfect.

We always have brunch at a little restaurant not far from our house. Normally, I ask Raff if he wants to go, but I have a feeling it would be better if I spoke to my mother alone. She's going to react to my news like everyone else, and her disapproval will sting. Jack's lucky my brother doesn't live in Bridgeport. I wouldn't have been able to say yes. I value my life too much . . . and Jack's.

I'm still wet with Jack's semen, and his scent saturates my skin. I burrow into the patio chair and relive the moments of him in my bed. His fingers inside me, his scruff rubbing my cheeks raw as he kissed me. It wasn't the sex that made the time with him special. I was nervous, maybe a little apprehensive. I hadn't been with anyone for a long time (and while we were eating, it struck me just how long it had been), and he handled me exactly the way I wanted him to. I wouldn't have changed anything about last night, well, except him leaving, but like I said, I need to lose a couple of battles to win the war.

I don't want to shower yet, and I sip coffee, spin dreams, and listen to the squirrels and birds play in the trees.

———

At exactly seven o'clock, a limo glides to a stop at the curb in front of my apartment. The driver opens the door for me and I climb in, arrange my poufy skirt on the bench, and set my purse aside.

"Someone plugged you in, and I can probably guess who," Raff says, catching on to my mood. Unable to help myself, I floated through the day. I might have done other things like vacuum my floors, laundry, and taken a bath, but in my mind, I spent the day with Jack in bed.

I laugh, startled. "I've never heard it put quite that way before."

His lips twist with amusement. "You're lit up brighter than a brand new lightbulb. You're going through with it, huh? I didn't think I'd be able to talk you out of it."

Lifting a shoulder, I say, "I could blame you, you know. You ran after Veronica at Jack's party and left me all alone. He only stepped in because he saw I was too tipsy to go home by myself."

"She's not having an easy time."

Raff fills a lowball with an inch of whiskey and offers me the glass.

I shake my head.

"Pregnant already?"

My cycle isn't good for me to get pregnant, and I'm surprised Jack didn't ask. Next weekend will be better timing, and maybe if we go to his place instead of mine, he'll let me spend the night.

"No. I want wine with dinner. And what do you mean, she's having a hard time?" I blink. "Does she love him? I never got that vibe when I saw them together."

"You don't want to marry a man if you don't love him, Em."

I lean back against the cushion, my dress's tulle scratching my skin. Play openings are always a big deal, and this one stars two brilliant actors who have both won EGOTs. I dressed up a little more than what the occasion calls for, and I look like I'll belong standing next to Raff in his crisp tux. "Sure, you do. You're not a woman and you have family money, and your own, for that matter. Do you know her history? Have you ever dug up anything about her, I mean, personally? Maybe she needed him."

Raff frowns. He's not in the dirt business. It's why actors like the two we'll watch tonight gave him permission to interview them. "No, and I'm not going to start."

"Then you have no idea if she wanted to marry Jack for love. She could have wanted his money. We already know she liked and used the attention." I don't really think of Veronica like that, even though I've spent the past two years envious of her relationship with Jack. I'm playing devil's advocate because, well, for a public figure, no one knows that much about her.

"She makes her own money. Durand has said on the record it's why he was in a relationship with her in the first place."

"Then I guess I'm out of the running," I say, and suddenly my throat is burning. I don't have money, family or otherwise. Well, not much of it—I have a nest egg I'm proud of, but that's all. I live the lifestyle I do because of the people I hang out with. Jack pays me well, but I would never be invited to the events I am if it weren't for my position as his assistant and Raff's friendship.

"Durand would never think you want him for his money. He knows you better than that. I think Veronica is really in love with the schmuck, and she thinks he left her for you. Him knocking you up will only confirm the rumors."

"I don't understand why they weren't talking to each other," I say, reaching over and pulling the glass out of Raff's hand. I need a drink after all. "The night you picked me up at The Menagerie, we were talking about his party and his engagement, and he acted like it was the first he'd heard of it. If they were communicating during their relationship, she would have known Jack doesn't have feelings for me."

"Emma, it's not words, it's actions. You haven't looked at the pictures of him carrying you out of the Bridgeport Hotel, have you?"

I press the smooth glass against my lips. "Not really, but

you know I don't bother with that. My mother wants to have brunch tomorrow, and I'm sure she saw them. It would be to my own detriment if I didn't know what she was talking about. You know how she is."

"I do, and I'm sure she saw this." He pulls his phone out of his pocket, opens the *Talk of the Town* app, and glides his finger across the screen to scroll. He stops, and zooms in on a picture, and tosses the phone to me. I let it land in my lap and pick it up.

The photographer was standing across the street when he took the photo, capturing us waiting outside on the sidewalk for the limo. I admire the way my dress's skirt drips over my legs, my sandals peeking out from the hem, and my head tucked into the divot of his shoulder. The hotel's lights shine behind us, casting us in a glow that looks almost heavenly. My little black purse hangs from his hand.

But that's not what anyone will be talking about.

Jack's pressing his lips to my forehead, his eyes closed.

We look like lovers going home after a romantic evening together.

"I don't remember him doing that," I say softly.

"I'm surprised you remember anything. You never drink that much." He pulls the phone from my hand, swipes, and shoves it back to me. The photo is of us getting into the limo. "He never put you down, not once, I bet. He carried you all the way up to his penthouse, didn't he? He's never had a woman up there. Did you know that? Veronica told me they always stayed at her place. In two years, she's never even seen the inside. Yet, he let you sleep in his bed. What does that tell you?"

I put his phone to sleep and toss it back to him. "All it tells me is he wanted to ask me to surrogate, and he used the opportunity to get me alone. I was barely awake when he asked, and I had to tell him I needed to think about it. You can read into these pictures all you want, but there's nothing to them. I've been right under his nose for three years, and he's not interested. I should follow your advice before I do something stupid like get pregnant. He's never going to fall in love with me."

Raff moves to my side of the bench and pulls me close. "That's what I was trying to tell you, baby girl, but that was before I saw these pictures. Whether he wants to admit it or not, there's something there. It's up to you if you want to take that risk."

I don't have a chance to respond. The limo stops in front of the restaurant, and eagerly, I step onto the sidewalk and drag in a lungful of air. Raff is telling me my heart's desire, but with every bit of evidence in my favor, two bits stack against me.

With a hand to my back, Raff escorts me into the building, a paparazzo thinking he's stealthy peering around a corner and snapping our picture.

We eat a lovely meal, and afterward, we're treated to more of the same at the theatre, the paparazzi wasting no time taking our photos as we pose on the red carpet, Raff's arm wrapped possessively around my waist. We're common fixtures at events like this, and our presence should have been an everyday occurrence, but Jack's party changed everything.

"Emma! Over here."

A reporter who looks vaguely familiar flashes me a dazzling smile, and the reporters near him eavesdrop, hoping for news.

Raff scowls. "Bryce."

"Clark. It's always entertaining to see you on the other side. How do you like sharing Emma with Jack Durand?"

Raff swears under his breath, and my lips part in stunned confusion. "What? What are you talking about?"

"Come on, Emma, don't do me like that. You can tell me the truth. You left Durand's birthday party with him. A party where he was supposed to propose to Veronica Chapman,

Bridgeport's princess. Now you're here with Clark? He can't like that unless you have an agreement."

"Yes, we have an agreement—"

Bryce smirks.

"—it's called an employer/employee relationship. I'm nothing to Jack but his secretary."

Bryce tips his head. He knows before Jack's party we were rarely seen together at social events.

"Then you and Clark? You've been friends for years, amirite? Friends with benefits, perhaps?"

Raff chuckles. "It must be a slow news night for you. You know Em and I are only friends, and if we were more to each other, I would have announced it myself, not let some two-bit blogger make a dime and a few thousand hits off my life. Back off."

"Have a good night, you two," Bryce says, giving up and focusing his attention behind us, hunting for juicier gossip.

"Oh, we will," Raff says, rubbing his lips over my temple.

I elbow him in the side. "That's the last thing we need."

He laughs. "It's all fun and games."

"Until someone gets hurt," I finish, and he drops his smile.

We're both thinking of Veronica.

CHAPTER THIRTEEN

Jack

Veronica and I would have attended the opening night of the most anticipated play of the summer, and I admit, it's odd to be home. I could have found a different date, but I'm reluctant to do so if I'm going to commit at least the next ten to eleven months to Emma. She wants to do everything she can to ensure our baby will have a bright future without her, and it would be in poor taste to hook up.

Heath and I haven't exactly mended all our fences, either, and that leaves me feeling out of sorts. It will be a relief to have dinner with them, or whatever Emma has planned. I need to fix our friendship—I'll need their help and support after the baby's born.

Claire, bless her, has been quiet. She texted and asked if I'm all right, and that's the last I've heard from her. She's usually a more tenacious gossip, but she's seen all the photos online and displaying an act of sensitivity that is unlike her, is letting me have some space. I could have asked her to go to the play, but it's not her style, and the fact she didn't ask me to go first is a good indicator she doesn't care about attending.

My father is giving me the cold shoulder, ignoring me after I told him off. Granted, I've never spoken to him much over the weekends, but Monday will be interesting. We usually spend the day in back-to-back meetings together, and I'll need to speak to him about a family dinner. He'll think I've lost my mind.

The house phone rings, and I hope it's Emma downstairs wanting to talk. I grab the phone and say, "Durand."

"Mr. Durand, this is Diego in the lobby. Miss Chapman is here to see you. Shall I send her up?"

"No. I'll come down." He knows better than to ask. "Thank you."

He hangs up on me.

A talk with Veronica is overdue. I never apologized, never spoke to the press. If I didn't want to apologize privately, I should have apologized publicly and given Clark my side of the story in an exclusive. I was too caught up asking Emma to surrogate, and practice sex is all I've been able to think about since I snuck out of her apartment last night. She didn't mention meeting her mother this weekend, and I desperately appreciate the time to think of what in the hell I'm going to say.

It would be wise to hire a surrogate, but I want Emma and no number of consequences will change my mind.

The elevator carries me down to the lobby, and Veronica's attracting attention, the building's tenants walking by curiously casting her furtive glances. She looks normal, wearing a blouse, summer pants, and heels, but she turns in my direction, sensing me behind her, and I frown. She looks as bad as Emma did the night of my party. Bruises are smudged beneath her eyes, and she's dropped a couple of pounds, something she'd be happy with if it wasn't due to stress and unhappiness.

I pause, uncertain. She couldn't have loved me. Never once in the two years we saw each other did we say the words.

"Veronica," I say, approaching her. "What are you doing here?"

"I deserve an explanation, Jack."

I tense. "I don't have an explanation other than the fact I don't want to get married. You would have known that if you had bothered to speak to me about it like an adult instead of trying to coerce me into a proposal. No one tells me what to do. Not even you."

Her lips tremble. "Then this has nothing to do with Emma. Absolutely nothing. There's no reason whatsoever for you carrying her out of the hotel the way you did."

"I was worried about her. She drank too much and couldn't be alone."

Veronica gasps. "You brought her upstairs."

I purse my lips. I've never invited Veronica to spend the night, eat dinner, or anything else, and I do not want to admit I brought Emma up to my penthouse. And I'm especially not going to tell her Emma slept on my bed.

She steps closer and rests her hand against the thin cotton of my t-shirt. "What does she have that I don't?"

I resist grabbing her wrist and shoving her hand off me. We used to be lovers, but after what she did, we're little more than acquaintances. "Nothing. We're not together. I gave you two years of my life, but in the end, I wanted something different." This is going to turn into a huge shitshow no matter what I do. *Fuck.* I give in and say, "I asked Emma to surrogate for me."

Licking her lips, she steps closer and tilts her head. "I can give you babies. All you had to do was say you wanted them. You don't need to ask Emma to surrogate. I'll give you whatever you want."

It's what everyone expected, too. That Veronica and I

would marry, and that we would have kids. "You never said you wanted children. I assumed your career was enough."

"It is, but if you want a family, I can give you one. Please, Jack."

I should accept. A wise man would accept, but I can't. My mother's pleas echo through my head, her denials ping around my heart. I don't know what she and my father were fighting about that day. Even if I'd heard what they were saying, my four-year-old mind wouldn't have understood. All I know is my father loved my mother, desperately, passionately, and she did something so terrible he threw her out. She left Claire and me behind, and I will not give a woman the same chance to do that to my child.

"No. I'm sorry I hurt you, but it wouldn't have happened if you had talked to me. You would have understood without a doubt that I'm not getting married. Not all rumors are true, but some are, and this one is. After two years, I assumed you knew that, and that was my mistake. Emma is doing me a favor and she'll be compensated. She signed a contract."

Well, she hasn't yet, but based on our conversation yesterday afternoon, my attorney is drawing one up over the weekend. I had to choose what I thought was an appropriate fee considering Emma displayed an unusual lack of shrewdness and self-preservation that's not like her. She'd do it for free. She's not innocent enough to believe anything in this life comes free.

It's the contingencies that worry me. The baby born too early, like Paige, or if there are other complications with the pregnancy and something happens to Emma. If the baby will have special needs. I will love that baby no matter what, but there are some things that are easier faced with two parents who can support each other, and the prospect of raising a child alone who requires specialized care scares me.

"Then I hope you can keep it business as usual with her like you have with me," she says.

I scowl. "What's that supposed to mean?"

"Where do you think she is tonight? And *who* do you think she's with? Is it written into your tidy contract that she can't screw other men while she's doing this for you? How *are* you going to get her pregnant? A fertility specialist? That doesn't sound like you. You avoid your own yearly physicals, and at your age, your preventative care list is a mile long. I can't imagine you asking Emma to spread her legs on an exam table. You'll want to sleep with her, but you'll have to take turns."

I don't need any time at all to put two and two together. Emma and Clark attended the play tonight. "He said they aren't sleeping together."

Veronica's eyes widen. "And you believed him? Why would he tell you? What he does with Emma is none of your business."

"It is if she's carrying my baby."

She laughs. "Last I heard, pregnant women still have sex, and if she's already knocked up, your part is done. Admit you want her, and you're manipulating her into a relationship because you're too scared to tell her how you feel. And you accused me of coercion? Please. All you had to do was tell me you're in love with her. I would have understood. I'm not heartless." Narrowing her eyes, she continues, "You know, I always defended you whenever someone would call you cruel and unfeeling. I would say, you don't know him. Don't know the kind of man he is underneath. But you know what? I think they did. Good luck."

I watch her walk away, but that's not what I see. What I see is Clark undressing Emma while she's growing with my child inside her, and I shake with anger.

Paparazzi take Veronica's photo on the sidewalk and yell

questions at her, but I don't care what she tells them. She can pin me with all the blame. I deserve it for being obtuse, but I never thought she wanted more than what I was giving her. I was wrong, and it's not the first time.

In my penthouse, I find my phone and open *Talk of the Town*'s website. Because it's Clark, he's the top news story on his own site, and I watch the clip of him and Emma chatting with a reporter. She's stunning in a blue and silver dress, and she's wearing a glittery headband that sits on her head like a tiara. Clark's arm is glued around her waist. I turn on the audio and listen to her deny a relationship with me. "I'm nothing to Jack but his secretary."

My heart plummets at the same time I nod. That's right. She's nothing to me but my secretary. She and Clark walk away and he nuzzles her temple with his lips. I grit my teeth. I hate seeing them together. She jabs him with her elbow, and he laughs.

I toss and turn all night.

Rage fuels me through the rest of the weekend, and by Monday morning, my blood pressure is through the roof and I'm spoiling for a fight.

A cup of steaming coffee is sitting on my desk when I enter my office. Emma's already here, but I didn't see her. I drape my suit jacket over the back of my chair, wake up my computer, and I stomp into the hallway. Yes, I stomp. My anger hasn't abated one bit since Veronica's accusations, and I won't calm down until I confront Emma.

She rounds the corner with my father's PA, a sheaf of paper in her hands. She's gorgeous dressed in high heels, a deep blue skirt, and a white sleeveless blouse covered in polka-dots the color of her skirt. Her hair is free today, bouncing around her shoulders as she walks. She catches sight of me and stumbles.

Nancy glances at my expression and swiftly does a one-eighty turning the way she came, leaving Emma to face me alone. Coward.

Emma's not, and she clicks toward me. "What's wrong with you?"

I snap.

I grab her arm, and in shock, she drops the papers she's holding. They flutter to the floor. I drag her into my office, slamming the door behind us. Crowding her against the wall, I brace one arm above her head, and with my other hand, grip her throat. I'm not into kink, but her pulse fluttering under my fingertips could change my mind.

"Did Clark stay with you after the play?" I growl.

Her breath comes out in panicked little puffs, and my cock stiffens. I could fuck her right here . . . there's a first time for everything.

"Wh-what are you talking about?"

"You heard me, Emma. Did Clark stay at your apartment after the play?"

She understands what I'm after now, and her fear dissipates. "Yes, as a matter of fact, he did."

"Did you sleep with him?"

She wraps her arms around my wrist and attempts to pull my hand away from her neck. "What do you care?"

I tighten my hold. "I care because I don't want the mother of my child fucking other men."

"Ever? That's not what I signed up for."

I gnash my teeth together. "That didn't come out right."

"Get your hands off me."

I tighten my grip, and she swallows, her delicate Adam's apple gliding under my palm.

"I can't go out with a good friend, but you can have Veronica at your penthouse," she rasps. "Hypocrite."

"We spoke in the lobby."

Emma stares at me. "Seriously? You think I'm going to believe that?"

"I don't give a fuck what you believe. I don't want you sleeping with Clark."

A flutter passes over her eyes, and her clasp on my wrist turns into a caress. "Let me go."

I loosen my hand, and she sucks in a ragged breath. Bruises are already forming beneath her ear, purple shadows exactly where my fingertips sank into her skin. I look away, ashamed.

She doesn't move. "Jack."

I stare at the floor. I don't know what got into me. I could have seriously hurt her.

"Jack."

I meet her eyes.

She steps forward and murmurs, "I will be yours, and only yours, for as long as you want me. Come home with me after work. I'll cook dinner, you can relax, and we'll go to bed early."

It sounds like something I need, but I've avoided an evening like that with a woman my entire life. I don't need reminders of what I've lost and what I've kept from myself, too scared to grow attached to anyone who could leave like my mother did. "Thank you."

She rests her cheek against my chest and wraps her arms around my waist. I can't remember the last time someone hugged me.

I give in to the need and hug her back, kissing the top of her head.

"Raff sleeps in my second bedroom," she says, pulling away. "There's nothing between us except friendship. You have to believe that, or this surrogacy won't work. I'm not going to defend myself every second because you don't trust me, and if you *ever* manhandle me that way again, I'll break our contract *and* I'll quit. You might be inspecting me under a microscope searching for all my little flaws that won't make me a good mother, but you will be raising our child, and everything you do from this day forward will tell me if you'll be a good father. Remember that. Your nine o'clock is on time."

She steps into the hallway leaving my door open, and I watch her crouch and pick up the papers she dropped when I grabbed her.

Christ. If I can't prove to her I can be a good dad, she'll have every right to break our contract. And if I do try to sue her, she'll have plenty of evidence to prove herself a more competent parent.

I need to do better.

She sits behind her desk and glares.

Yeah, I need to do better.

Without another word, I walk by her and meet my father in the conference room where we hold the majority of our meetings.

He glances at me from the window. "Jack, I'm sorry about Friday—"

I cut him off. "Don't worry about it. What do you think about a family dinner Saturday night?"

What he says sums up the past week.

"What the fuck is a family dinner?"

CHAPTER FOURTEEN

Emma

He stood me up.

It's not a surprise. I pushed him too hard. I thought I could use his jealousy of my friendship with Raff to manipulate him into dinner and sex, and it didn't work. I'll never be able to get him to do anything he doesn't want to do, and if he doesn't come to his own conclusion he wants me in his life, and our baby's, then nothing I do will make a difference. He needs to lead, or think that he is, but I've never played relationship chess, and I don't know what to do.

I made dinner and waited for him to show. Two hours and a bottle of wine later, I stored leftovers in the fridge and ran a hot bath.

I'm stupid and kept hoping he would turn up, but I went to bed alone, and I sure as hell woke up alone. I locked the door and Jack doesn't have any reason to have a key.

The bruises along my throat aren't that bad, but they're bright enough I tie a scarf that matches the skirt I'm wearing to work around my neck. I tried covering them with makeup, but the blouse I'm wearing has a collar and it would have rubbed off throughout the day. A scarf is easier, and I wear them sometimes, so no one will suspect anything.

I've never seen Jack violent before, and if I didn't know without a shadow of a doubt it was in reaction to Raff staying at my apartment, I would back out of our contract. He would let me, too. He has no excuse for treating me like that, and I meant what I said. I will quit if he ever does it again. I don't care how much I love him.

I arrive at the office before him, and like I normally do, set a cup of coffee on his desk. I check his email and flag the important items he needs to look at today.

The elevator doors open, and I stiffen.

He walks down the hallway toward my desk, and he looks handsome dressed in a sharp black suit. His eyes land on my scarf, and he averts his guilty gaze. "I'm sorry about last night. I got caught up here."

I let my hurt bubble over. "Fine. Whatever. But you could have had the common courtesy to text me. Call me. Email me—you know I keep my notifications on. I don't know how you treated Veronica, and I don't know how you think you can treat me, but your daughter's nanny is going to need to know where you are every second of your day, and when she's older, *she's* going to want to know where you are and she'll deserve to know. Sometimes there are emergencies, and you can't do whatever you want whenever you want to do it. If you think you can, then you need to rethink having a baby because she is going to change your whole life."

"You're right. I'm sorry. This is all new to me, Emma."

I frown. "Manners are new to you? You know what? After working for you for three years, I believe that." I turn my attention to my computer.

He sighs. "I talked to my father. We're going over to the house Saturday evening for dinner."

"I called Zoey yesterday. She said they'd host a barbecue Friday night and invite Mia and Haisley, Raff, and some of their neighbors. It sounds fun." I flick a glance at Jack, and his expression says he thinks it will be anything but fun.

"Then I guess we'll see your mother Sunday. Full weekend." He forces a smile.

"I've decided not to tell my mother until the last minute." She badgered me with questions all through brunch, and I barely had time to eat. I realized what a mistake it would be to tell her the truth, and what even more of a mistake it would be to let her meet Jack.

He leans against my desk and crosses his arms over his chest. "Why?"

"Because my baby won't be her grandchild, and my pregnancy is going to break her heart. It's fine to tell your dad and Claire, but I have five, six, if I'm lucky seven, months before I have to tell her the truth. I'm going to wait as long as I can."

"If you think that's best."

"I do."

"Okay. Do you have plans after work?"

"No. Why?"

He rams his fingers through his hair in frustration. He still needs a haircut. "Emma, why are you mad? I made a mistake, okay? I'll text you the next time plans change."

"I don't think you're telling me the truth, that's why I'm mad. You avoided me last night. You weren't here or I would have been with you. If you stay late, I stay late. That's how it's been for the three years I've worked for you. If you didn't want to spend the evening at my place, you should have said so, instead, you blew me off."

"I don't want a relationship. I don't want dinners and relaxing evenings. I want to stick to the plan."

I read between the lines. *I don't want a relationship with you.* His words shouldn't hurt me, but they do. He's not telling me anything I didn't already know. Lifting my chin, I say, "Good to know. We'll skip Zoey and Heath's place and you can give your dad and Claire my regrets. I'll be ovulating this weekend. I've always been on time and don't need a test. Come over sometime on Saturday. We'll do what we need to do and you can leave."

"No. I still want to go to Zoey and Heath's, and my dad, for some crazy reason, is looking forward to dinner on Saturday. What you said makes sense. My baby is going to need family around her."

I nod and turn toward the computer.

"The courier sent over the contract. Can you sign it after work?"

Oh. That's what he wanted to ask me. Nothing about dinner, or even going downstairs to The Menagerie to order a drink and talk.

"Yeah, sure." My voice trembles, and I couldn't stop it.

"Hey." He turns my chair and kneels in front of me. He's scruffy, his hair flopping over his forehead from the aggressive way he shoved his hand through it. His eyes are deep brown, exuding a concern he didn't hint at flinging that fake apology at me, and his suit hugs his shoulders perfectly. He's everything I want, and slowly, so slowly, I am now beginning to understand, that it won't matter how many babies I have for him, he's everything I'll never have.

Gently, he unties my scarf and pulls it from around my neck. He winces. "I'm sorry. I am so sorry."

A tear runs down my cheek. "What are you so scared of? I

would never hurt you, Jack." *I love you.* I think the words, but I'll never say them.

I'll never say them because he'll never want to hear them.

He frames my face in his hands and leans forward.

He's going to kiss me, and I want him to, so terribly, but he freezes and I jerk my gaze to look over his shoulder.

His father is standing in the middle of the hallway watching us, and unconsciously, I cover my throat with my hand. Jack staggers to his feet, my scarf falling from his fingers into my lap.

Ron clears his throat. "We've got a meeting in ten."

Jack nods. "I'll be there."

Ron turns toward his office, and Jack steps into his, softly closing the door behind him.

We don't talk for the rest of the day.

———

At five after five, I knock on his door before opening it without permission. Usually he keeps it open, but today he shut me out, and I better get used to it. He's fighting a war I know hardly anything about. What I know is what he told me, and he summed up forty-one years of heartache into two sentences.

"It's on the table," he says, watching me cautiously.

The sheaf of paper is thicker than I thought it would be, and I should read it, ask for a copy for the family law attorney Raff referred me to, but I'm already in too deep, and I flip to the last page and sign my name by the hot pink arrow.

He frowns. "You're not going to read it? There are points in there I think you should know."

I push down the pain. "It's thirty pages of you telling me you don't want me to be our child's mother. I don't need to know any more than that."

"Fair enough, but I added everything we talked about, like family and emergencies. If the baby needs something that you can provide, I'll tell you immediately."

"I think you should go to parenting classes. Is that in there?" I ask, tapping the pen on the top page. "If it's not, you should add that. You have no idea what you're doing."

"That's ridiculous. What would I learn in a class like that?" he asks, pushing away from his desk.

"Oh, I don't know. Infant CPR? How to perform the Heimlich if she decides to swallow a Lego? Discipline? Child development? How will you know if she's behind? Maybe she'll be autistic. You'll have a head start if you take a class before she's born."

He pales. "If I'm going, then I'm not going alone. You'll have to come with me."

"Why would I go? I won't be her mother! Going to stupid Lamaze classes with you will be enough, thank you very much." My stomach pitches. I don't want to learn how to labor with Jack as a support. I swipe the pile of paper off the table. "On second thought, I'm going to read these after all. I don't want you in the room while I'm delivering her. I'll hire a doula."

"Of course I'm going to be there while you're in labor. Don't be an idiot. What the fuck is a doula?"

"She's a support person who communicates with the doctors and nurses on the laboring woman's behalf. She'll be all I need."

"I want to be there."

The more I think of him holding my hand and breathing through a contraction with me, feeding me ice chips, encouraging me to push, the more sweat accumulates on my skin, and my heart is pounding a mile a minute. I can't have him there. I can't.

"No."

"Why? I want to see her be born."

"Because we'll feel like a family, and we won't be one! I'll labor with a doula, and when I push her out, the nurse will take her away." I finish with a whisper.

Jack's still, his eyes on me. "Add what you need to the contract, and I'll have my attorney revise it."

"Thank you," I say to the floor, and with the paper's sharp edges biting into my skin, I run from his office. I snag my purse that's sitting on top of my desk and don't stop until I'm at home lying on my bed, screaming into my pillow.

————

I sit up for most of the night, skimming the contract and adding my own notes. There are a few more things besides him laboring with me I want to change. I add the parenting classes he'll go to alone, and because he won't be in the delivery room, my mother will attend Lamaze classes with me and be present if she chooses. I don't want her to be. This is my mess, and when the nurse carries my baby away, I want to be able to break down in private. I'll search for a doula that specializes in surrogacy and find a therapist. After giving away my daughter, I'm going to need one.

I also add that I won't live in Bridgeport after the delivery. I was being glib the day I poked at Jack about my job and watching our daughter visit her father at the Variant building, but I can't do that. I can't be in the same city they are—I'll look for them everywhere. Jack will want to know where I'm going, and it's his right to know, so I write I'll move to Seattle to live near my brother once I'm healed enough to do so. Jack's being very generous considering I said I would do this for free, and I'll have plenty of money until I find a place to live and a new job.

I'll even have enough to help my mother move if she wants to be near us.

The next morning, I know the minute he's read through all my changes. His door flies open. "Emma."

I swallow and turn away. "Don't."

He pauses, then says quietly, "I'll send the papers to my attorney for the revision."

I don't have anything to say, and I continue to empty his email inbox the way I always do.

He disappears into his office.

I find the composure to finish out the rest of the week. I still haven't given up on the small chance that maybe Jack will fall in love with me. It's evident now, that he has feelings for me, but I have to figure out how to unlock them. He doesn't want his child to have a mother. He doesn't trust her not to leave like his own mother did, but I want to know why she left.

Jack approaches me Friday afternoon, and I try like hell to keep my feelings hidden.

We haven't spoken all week, even forgoing drinks at The Menagerie when I know he could have used the extra time. He and Ron are negotiating an important acquisition, and I've always helped him. He didn't ask and that hurts.

Raff, too, has been suspiciously absent, and the social media sites haven't reported on his whereabouts. That left me restless and out of sorts, and to distract me, Mia and Haisley invited me out for shopping and drinks. My mother also suspected something was wrong and invited me to dinner. We talked a lot about Dad, her intention to steer me toward a man more emotionally available, and I left her house feeling worse than before. I miss my dad, and I miss being able to ask his advice. In this situation, I know he would have agreed with Mom. "Jack's a blind fool if he can't see what's right in front of him. Find someone who appreciates you. There are plenty of fish in the sea," he'd say, then wink. "I caught your mom on my fourth try." Which I know would be a load of bull. My parents had been together since high school.

The point is, anyone who knows what I'm doing and what I'm hoping to accomplish thinks it's a hopeless cause, and how can I disagree with *everyone?*

It's when I look into Jack's eyes, how I feel when I'm in his arms . . . that's what keeps me from abandoning him.

"Do you still want to go to Heath and Zoey's?" he asks, his fingertips resting against the surface of my desk.

"If you want me there."

"It would be nice if you were. We may not agree on some things, but I can't raise our baby alone."

I want to point out he doesn't have to at all, that I would be very willing to share in raising her with him, with or without a ring on my finger, but marriage isn't Jack's issue—it's my entire existence after the baby's born.

"Okay. I need to go home and change. Did Heath give you a time at the gym on Wednesday?"

"Six o'clock."

"I'll meet you there."

He frowns. "No. I'll go home and change and pick you up." He pauses. "You said this was a good weekend."

I nod.

"After Heath and Zoey's then?"

"All right."

He walks away.

I'm still getting what I want. I wanted to make love with him, and I'll be getting that this weekend. I should be concentrating on now, not thinking so far ahead. I have to shake off this gloom, look forward to the evening with friends, and enjoy being with him.

Because if he has his way, I have less than a year, and if I can't get him to change his mind, I'll never see him or our baby again.

———

The bruises around my throat faded enough I don't bother with anything but a few dabs of concealer. The scarf worked fine this week, except for Ron catching Jack kneeling at my feet and apologizing for putting them on me. I know Ron saw them, but Jack never said if his father mentioned it.

I change into a frothy blue and white floral sundress, cinch my waist with a matching belt, and leave my hair down. I've never been to Heath and Zoey's—they're more Jack's friends than mine—and if we do meet up, it's always somewhere else, like Cloud 9.

Jack knocks on my door precisely at six. He looks good dressed in casual summer khaki pants and a white and blue striped cotton button down shirt.

"Ready?"

"Yeah. I need shoes." I strap white wedges onto my feet just in case I have to walk across their yard, and he helps me to his car, his arm around my shoulders.

Heath and Zoey don't live that far from me, only far enough for several income tax brackets to go by. Heath does very well as a financial advisor, and Jack trusts Heath with millions of his dollars. I have a small sum invested, but only with thoughts to retirement. Their brownstone isn't something I would ever be able to afford, heavily investing or not. "Do you think our daughter should have a yard?" I muse.

Jack parks on the tree-lined street. "It's something to consider," he says, killing the engine. "I'll give her everything she needs, Emma. You know I will."

"I know."

I let him open the truck's door for me, and his hand never leaves mine as we mount the steps and he rings the doorbell.

A little girl dressed similarly to me opens the door, her blond hair pulled back into a ponytail, and pink-framed glasses sit on her nose. "Hi." She grins. "We're having a party."

"Hello, Miss Paige," Jack says, hefting the little girl into his arms, rubbing his scruff over her cheeks.

She giggles. "Stop! Daddy does that to me."

"And you love it," Heath says, stepping into the hallway. "Emma. Jack. Come in and grab a drink."

"Put me down now," Paige says, wiggling, and Jack sets her to her feet.

"Gracie and Hilary and a few of the neighborhood munchkins are running around," Heath says, tilting his head down the hallway. His daughter gleefully scampers away. "We don't have parties very often. The girls are thrilled."

"Glad to help," Jack mumbles, knowing full well this party is for us because of us.

"Your home is beautiful," I say, looking around. Framed photos of their family are everywhere, and I tear my gaze away. This is going to be hard, a lot harder than I thought. Heath and Zoey are happily married with three gorgeous and intelligent daughters. My heart isn't going to survive this party.

"The girls will show you around later—everyone who comes through has to see their rooms. But first, the kitchen," Heath says, leading us down the hallway that opens on one side to a large, airy kitchen. Jack rests his hand on the nape of my neck under my hair, and I lean into his side.

Zoey's pouring wine, and she hands me a glass full of rosé. Haisley and Mia are standing in a group of women near a door that lets out onto a patio, and they wave at me. Outside, a grill is already set up, and children are playing in the grass. A firepit sits off to the side, and two little boys run around it, chasing each other swinging lightsabers, capes flying.

"There's beer outside in a cooler, or something stronger in the bar in the living room," Heath says to Jack. "None of this sissy stuff."

"Hey," Zoey says, laughing. "We don't need that kind of attitude in here. Go on."

Heath pulls Zoey into his arms and covers her mouth with his. Paige and another little girl who looks identical to her, but older and sans glasses, run in and yell, "They're doing it again. Gross!" They dart off to a chorus of laughter.

I don't laugh, and neither does Jack.

It's evident how much Heath loves his wife. It's there in his touch, the way he holds her in place allowing him to devour her mouth.

I want that, God, do I want that, and I chug my wine hoping to dull what is turning out to be a very big mistake. Jack and I should have kept to ourselves.

Heath pulls away and rubs his thumb over Zoey's cheek. Turning to Jack, he says, "I'll get you a drink. Come on."

"Will you be okay?" Jack asks, sliding his hand from my neck down my back, stopping right above my butt.

"I'll be fine. Have fun."

"We're not going to hurt her, Jack," Zoey says. "Maybe get her drunk, but that's what a party's for."

"Ah, I think I had enough of that at Jack's birthday," I say, and everyone who heard me quiets. They're thinking about that photo the paparazzo took of him holding me and kissing my forehead outside the hotel while we waited for the limo.

"Okay, I'll see you later," he says tersely, undoubtedly thinking the same, and probably regretting he gave the paparazzi a chance to take our pictures at all. He follows Heath into a room I can't see from here.

Zoey leans in, clutching the bottle of rosé to her chest. "Now tell us all about this arrangement you have with Jack. Heath told me, and I couldn't believe it. I'm so glad you suggested getting together. I've been wanting to talk to you, but I didn't know how to ask."

"Some stupid idea," I say as Mia and Haisley join us.

I fill them in on the contract, the negotiations and last-minute addendums, hoping I could get him to fall in love with me, but I know he won't and I explain about having to move after the baby's born because I won't be able to stay here. I don't leave anything out, and after I'm done, my heart is a shattered mess and I can't see through all the tears in my eyes.

"I need more to drink, Zoey." I hold out my empty wineglass.

"Honey, after a story like that, we all do," she says, but no one laughs.

Everyone is as sad as I am.

CHAPTER FIFTEEN

Jack

I like this. It feels right. Driving here together, catching Emma's eye from time to time across the floor and communicating in smiles and slight shakes of the head. Veronica and I were more social publicly, and we didn't hang out with friends like this. Casual. Men outside or in the living room drinking beer and shooting the shit, women gossiping in the kitchen, kids playing.

I like it, and I push it back.

The addition Emma made to the contract spooked me. There's no way in hell I'm letting her move to Seattle. I don't give a damn if she has family there or not. She's not leaving Bridgeport, not even if I have to waste money suing her to stay. I have no legal right to keep her in Minnesota, and any sane judge will throw the case out of court, if by some miracle it even made it that far. According to the contract, she gives up any parental rights the moment I assume possession of the baby, and she'll be free to do whatever she likes. Move to Seattle, find a husband, have more children. Nope. My daughter is not going to have half-siblings she'll never meet. I'll sue Emma over that, too.

"Why are you frowning? Aren't you having a good time?" Heath asks, lifting the lid to the grill. The scent of charcoal fills the air, and heat bursts with the crackle of embers. I love grilling, but for obvious reasons, I don't do it at the penthouse.

"Emma says she's moving to Seattle after she has the baby," I say, tightening my grip on my beer bottle. Heath turns the steaks over, and Clark pulls another beer out of the cooler near our feet, ice clinking against the sides.

I don't know why he was invited. He's Emma's friend, but he's not mine, and as far as I know, he's not Heath's either. But Clark's more a part of our group than I thought. He knows everyone here, and I caught him chatting with Heath's neighbor earlier, his arm wrapped around Emma's shoulders like he has the fucking right to touch my—

Twisting the cap, Clark says, "What did you expect her to do? Did you think she'd still be your PA? Maybe reassign her and hope that would be enough? You know, for a smart guy who runs a multi-billion dollar company, you're sure stupid."

"Hey," Heath says, closing the lid. "Calm down."

"I don't want to calm down. Emma is my best friend, and Durand's running her out of town."

Glaring, I say, "I am not. It's her choice to go." I'm not taking responsibility for this.

"If you call that a choice. Did you ask her why she's doing this for you?"

I freeze. I thought it was to help me because we're friends, or maybe for the money, but it couldn't be about money. She said she'd do it for free.

"No, you didn't, and the simple reason is you don't care. Once you decide you want something, that's all you can think about until you have it. I've reported shit on you for years, Durand, so don't bother to deny it. Companies, property, cars, women. You don't stop, and then the second it's yours, you don't give a shit anymore. We all remember the way you pursued Veronica. You had her for as long as you wanted her, and when you were done, you threw her out. Is that how you're going to treat Emma?"

"That's not what happened. We used each other." That's the truth. We enjoyed each other's company and we used each other to have built-in dates for social obligations. We slept together when we felt like it, but I rarely wanted to spend the night and she rarely asked me to stay. She never wanted more until everyone started talking engagement rings, and the one person she neglected to inform was me.

Clark scoffs. "Sure, even if I buy that, what is Emma getting out of this arrangement with you? If you're using her, and she's using you?" He narrows his eyes. "What exactly are you getting from Emma that you couldn't get from any other surrogate in this whole goddamned world? You can afford to hire the fucking Queen of England to have your baby, but you chose Emma. Why?"

I tell him what I told her. "Because she's beautiful and considerate and kind. She has qualities I want my child to have."

"And you're only too happy to smash all of them into the ground, aren't you? You're like a little kid. You don't want her, but no one else can have her either."

"She can move on when this is done," I say, despite the fact that five seconds ago in my head I was suing her if she tried.

"She'll be too broken. And if you knew her, cared about her, you would understand that. I'm going inside."

Through the glass, I watch him whisper something into

Emma's ear, and he strides toward the front door. Emma hurries after him, and I grit my teeth.

"He's right, you know, and he didn't say anything I didn't tell you before you asked her." Heath whistles sharply across the grass. "Graciela, tell your mother the meat's done. Can you help her set the tables?"

"Yeah, Dad," Heath's oldest says, already running toward the patio.

"I want what you have. A *sliver* of what you have."

"The sliver starts with a partner you love who loves you back. Ask any happily married man here, and he'll tell you. Do you love her, Jack?"

I feel something for Emma, but I can't call it love. I got scared when she added the Seattle addendum, I get pissed off when I think about her with another man. But then I remember that taxi driving away with my mother inside it, and all I can think about is her leaving me and how I can't survive another loss like that one.

"I don't know."

"Then you shouldn't be asking her what you did. Why *is* she doing this for you?"

"I'm giving her three million dollars."

Heath shakes his head and reaches for the platter Graciela is holding out for him. "Thanks, sweetie," he says to her and then to me, "that's not why she's doing it. If you don't know, maybe you should ask. What she says might surprise you."

I don't get a chance to talk to her alone for the rest of the night, not that I would ask her something like that at a time like this. We eat, scattered around the yard in various chairs, picnic tables, and even sitting on the grass with the kids. Mia and Haisley don't leave her side, and I grow irritated watching them. They see her almost every day, they don't have to occupy all her time.

Somehow, I end up sitting next to Paige at a picnic table, cutting her steak into little bite-sized pieces and stabbing her corn on the cob with skewers that look like more corn on the cob. Zoey grins at me, and I wonder if it was by design. I'm slowly beginning to understand that being a single parent is going to be a lot harder than it initially seemed. Not if I want to be a good father, and I do.

The evening is perfect for eating outdoors. Heath and Zoey strung fairy lights from the pergola, and they twinkle against the setting sun. In true sexist fashion, after the meal, the women help Zoey set her kitchen to rights, drinking more wine and gossiping about the gossip already shared. Us men do the manly thing and set up the firepit. I search for Emma to see if she wants to sit with me and steal a quiet moment, but I can't find her.

She wouldn't leave without telling me, though I did have a sharp moment of, I wouldn't call it fear, but irritation isn't the right word either, hesitation, maybe, or apprehension, that she left with Clark after I pissed him off. But a few minutes later she came back into the living room and reclaimed her seat on the couch.

"Have you seen Emma?" I ask Zoey who's putting together an ice cream sundae buffet.

She looks over at me from an open gallon of vanilla. "I think the girls corralled her and she's upstairs. It's past Paige's bedtime, but Sheila can let her sleep in tomorrow morning."

Sheila is the girls' nanny, and that's another thing I'll have to ask Zoey about. How she shares responsibility of the girls with a stranger. I dislike the idea, but Sheila has been their nanny for many years and she probably doesn't feel like a stranger anymore. Even if my daughter had a mother, she would still need a sitter.

I shake off those concerns. Emma isn't pregnant yet.

"Thanks."

I trot up the stairway, family pictures hanging on the walls guiding my way to the top. When you've spend fifteen years with someone, you accumulate a lot of history. I'm already forty-five. Fifteen years puts me at sixty. I don't know how old Emma is. She looks young enough to get pregnant and that's all I cared about. Monday I'll call down to HR and ask what her birthdate is. She's been my PA for three years, I should know her birthday.

"What about this one?" I hear Emma say, and I peer around the doorjamb of Paige's room.

Emma's sitting on the floor letting Paige paint her fingernails. The question, I see, referred to a tiny sticker, and Paige fastens it onto Emma's forefinger. Gabriela, and Heath and Zoey's middle daughter, Hilary, are there too, painting each other's nails. Playing beauty salon, Emma looks right at home surrounded by little girls, nail polish, stickers, and glitter.

They don't notice me, and I watch them for a lot longer than I should.

Paige finishes painting Emma's nails, and in fatigue, she crawls into Emma's lap, rests her head on her shoulders, and closes her eyes.

"I'll go tell Mom Paige is ready for bed," Graciela says quietly.

Emma hugs Paige, and a lump forms in my throat. "In a minute, okay, Gracie?" she asks. "My nails are still wet."

Gracie smiles. "Okay."

I go back downstairs to find Heath propositioning Zoey with a can of whipped cream. She parts her lips and he sprays some into her mouth. He kisses her, licking at the cream, and she laughs.

"How do you keep the spark?" I'm not a stranger to the way they love each other, but I've never been this envious.

He comes up for air and says, "Sometimes it's hard. Paige's birth scared the shit out of both of us, but instead of turning on each other, we leaned into each other. We make time to go out. We don't use sex as a weapon. We talk, never go to bed mad at each other. It's little things. If I'm going to be late, I text—" I wince— "if she has plans, she writes them in my planner. We're on the same page, always. Three kids, two full time jobs . . . it's work, and we know it is." He tips Zoey's face up with a finger under her chin. "But there is so much joy and love in this house."

Zoey hugs Heath, resting her head against his chest. She asks me, "Did you find Emma?"

I clear my throat. "She's playing beauty school or something with the girls. Paige looked down for the count."

"I better go up there and rescue Emma, then. When she's tired, Paige will crawl into any available lap."

"They looked like they were doing okay."

"Emma's a guest. If you two want to babysit, we'll take you up on it, anytime. I'll detach Paige and send her outside." Zoey kisses Heath on the cheek and walks out of the kitchen.

I stand hopelessly in the middle of the room.

"I don't know, Jack. I don't know who this is harder on. Emma or you. Not all women leave, and even if they do, most women don't leave their children behind. Your father kept your mother from bringing you and Claire with her. You understand that, don't you? If Zoey came down here right now and asked me for a divorce and packed her bags, she would bring the girls with her and I would let her because children need their mothers. Ron kept you and Claire, and she had no choice. It's not all her fault."

I sit outside and stare into the fire, the other guests who haven't gone home chatting in low murmurs around me, Mia and Haisley among them. I didn't consider that my mother wanted to keep us and my father wouldn't let her. The taxi drove away, and that was the last I saw of her. I never once thought my father wanted it that way.

Emma steps onto the patio and searches the group, looking for an empty chair. There isn't one, and Haisley half-rises in an invitation to move and scrunch with Mia, but I hold out my hand. Emma rounds the firepit, settles in my lap, and rests her head against my shoulder, much like I saw Paige do upstairs.

I wrap my arms around her, and she melts into me.

Heath and Zoey do the same in a chair across from us, and the evening ends on a perfect note.

———

We drive to her place in silence, and I resist holding her hand or rehashing the evening. I'm curious what Clark said to her before he left, but I don't want to mention his name and ask.

Emma's residential street is quiet, a couple walking close together, a dog leading them down the sidewalk. Everything I see I could turn into an experience with Emma, never mind she's never said she wanted a dog.

I find an open space a block from her apartment and kill the engine. She sits, waiting for me to open my door, get out, and open hers, but I don't move fast enough. She's out of the truck and stepping onto the sidewalk before I can unlatch my seatbelt.

Veronica goaded me with ideas of Emma and a doctor's office, but this is worse. Dates to have sex . . . I'd rather drop her off at a clinic.

Even a bed isn't going to help, and I let my anger simmer. It's the only way I'm going to get hard. Rough, because this situation is my fucking fault and I won't do anything to change it.

She unlocks the door with an unsteady hand. I'm on her

the second we're standing in her little foyer and she shuts the door. She drops her purse, her keys landing on the carpet without a sound. I back her against the wall, tangle my fingers in her hair and slant my lips over hers, our teeth crashing together. She cries out, but that spurs me on, and I reach for the hem of her dress. I yank it up just far enough for me to find her panties, and I shove my hand between her legs. I push two fingers inside her, and my shoulder muffles another one of her cries.

I can take her hard, but if I don't get her off first, this will be nothing but a quick fuck and I don't want my child conceived like that. I tear away from her, drop to my knees, and rip the delicate scrap of lace.

"Jack," Emma says, her legs trembling.

I grip her dress in my hands and lick her seam. Her scent gets me high, and her flavor is so sweet. I'll never forget how she tastes. Not in a month, not in a year, not in ten.

My tongue finds its way through her delicate folds and nudges her clit.

Whimpering now, she tugs at my hair.

She hasn't told me to stop, that she doesn't want to do it this way, and I push two fingers into her again. I eat her out more viciously than I have ever taken a woman. Her wetness runs down my wrist, and her muscles clench around my fingers. She's about to come, and I dig my fingers into her thigh as she presses her pussy against my mouth.

A sob bursts from her throat, and she comes, her muscles clenching around me. I add a third finger, stretching her, and her clit quivers under my tongue.

I lick at her until she jerks away, and I stand, wiping my mouth with the back of my hand. Emma's sagging against the wall, and if I were a gentleman, I would carry her to bed, but we're having this out right here. I unbuckle my belt and she watches with hooded eyes. Her gaze doesn't tear away from mine even when I shove my briefs down just far enough to release my cock. I'm ready, and I lift her up by her ass, anchor her to the wall, and drive into her, the skirt of her dress tangled around her waist.

She's so tight, so wet, and she mews into my ear, setting my blood on fire. I'm still so angry, I could fuck her, come, drop her to the ground, and leave without a hint of remorse, but I count to ten, nibble at her neck, and give her time to adjust to me inside her. Only then do I lift her up and down, creating the delicious friction I need to come.

I hit her center and she gasps, but this time I don't retreat. I go at her harder, slamming into her.

I come and push inside her as far as I can go. She clings to me, her face pressed into my neck.

I groan.

Sweat slicks my skin, and my throat's raw.

I shudder, my cock twitching.

We're still attached, and I carry her to her bedroom and gently lay her on the bed.

She looks sexy as sin. Her hair is spread over the comforter, her dress is tangled around her waist, and her shoes are still strapped to her feet.

I pull out and immediately tuck my cock into my briefs and pull up my pants.

"Stay with me, Jack," she whispers.

"No."

It's all I say, and I walk out of her bedroom without looking back.

The only indication I hurt her is the tiny, thin sob that comes from her room that haunts me all the way home.

CHAPTER SIXTEEN

Emma

I'm getting to him.

I woke to a long text from Zoey explaining the guys gave Jack a hard time last night about our arrangement, and that he was quizzing Heath on how to keep a relationship stable and the passion in a marriage alive.

He's thinking about those things, and that gives me hope.

Raff said something similar on his way out the door, too angry to stay. "I tried, baby girl, and I think he was listening."

I don't know when Jack is picking me up to go to his dad's, but he answers that question while I'm still lying in bed, reliving our love making in the hall. I've never had sex like that before, and trust Jack to not only be angry enough, but strong enough, to lift me up and screw me that way.

Three fingers inside me, his teeth scraping at my clit. Even angry, he didn't forget about my needs. The man has manners after all.

I find my clit with my fingers. I'm still wet with Jack's

semen and I use it as a lube, slicking my skin. Jack's ignored my breasts. He hasn't sucked on my nipples or even touched them much at all. With all this baby talk, I wonder if he has a hang up with women's boobs. Maybe he only sees them as a food source, but tonight, when we make love, I'll ask him to touch me. Unless I don't get pregnant, tonight will be the last night we have sex. I won't know until the end of next month, and Jack is too smart and too shrewd to agree if I asked to have sex without knowing if I'm pregnant or not.

No, he's going to make this as difficult as it can be for everyone.

I'm calming, stretching languidly in bed after my orgasm when my cell chimes. I dry my fingers on a tissue from the box sitting on my nightstand and pick up my phone.

I read Jack's text: *I'll pick you up at 6:30. Drinks at 6:45. Dinner at 7:15. I don't know what to tell you to wear. We've never done this before.*

I'll be ready, I reply, but what I really want to ask is, you've never done what before? Had dinner as a family? I don't swear often, but what the fuck? Even after Dad passed away, *especially* after Dad passed away, Mom and I and sometimes Raff would have dinner together. Jack has never once had a family dinner?

Claire's been married twice, and they never had either of her husbands over for dinner?

Ron's always been gruff. The first time I met him he said, "Welcome to Variant. Don't get too comfortable," and I blinked, not sure if I heard correctly. The HR assistant giving me a tour of the company laughed nervously. I thought he was only a wounded old man bitter in public but in private he'd drop his abrasive nature.

I guess not.

He couldn't show his own kids affection by listening about their day at the dinner table.

And Jack wants to raise a child in that kind of family.

Maybe we should have done this family stuff *before* we started trying.

I do what I always do on a Saturday: laundry, clean, vacuum, put together a dry-cleaning pile. Living alone doesn't create much work, and when Raff texts and asks if I want to meet him for lunch at a rooftop restaurant that recently opened, I accept. Jack will get mad, especially if someone takes our picture, but what do I care. If he'd spent the night, we could have had the day together, a fact I'll be more than happy to point out if he has the nerve to needle me about it.

Raff and I have a lovely time chatting with the owner during our meal—he needs the notes for an article he's writing for the e-zine. By coincidence, Mia and Haisley join us for dessert. It's a beautiful day, and we linger over coffee and gossip about the party last night and how great Zoey and Heath are together.

"Seeing Jack tonight?" Raff asks, walking me to my door.

"Yes. We're having dinner with Ron and Claire."

He whistles. "You're a masochist."

"I'm in love."

"That's what I said. You're a masochist. Call me tomorrow if you survive." He kisses my cheek and waits until I open my apartment door before walking to his truck.

"Be good tonight," I call after him, almost wishing I were free to do whatever it is he's doing. He'll definitely have more fun than I will be.

He waves in response.

Mom texts and asks if I'm going to her place for lunch tomorrow, and I say I will. I'm not going to tell her I'm surrogating, but she'll want to know more about Jack, and maybe I can tell her we're dating. We *will* be spending a lot of time together for the next little while, and half of the truth is better than none.

At six o'clock, I stand in front of my closet. What does one wear to a first family dinner? I've never been to their house before. Ron doesn't host parties for his employees, and I'm not friends with Claire, though I suspect that neither Jack nor Claire visit their childhood home on a regular basis.

I choose a plain black lace dress, twist my hair into a knot at the back of my head and add a pair of real diamond studs my dad bought me as a graduation present from the U of M.

I look boring. I look like a *surrogate*.

I look like I'm going to work, but I don't have time to change.

The only thing I have time for is a glass of wine before Jack picks me up, and I bet after this dinner he won't let me drink anymore. At least, not until we find out if this weekend worked or not. I better enjoy it while it lasts, and I gulp the Moscato as if my sanity depends on it.

Jack's on time, and he helps me into his truck, a steady hand to my waist. He latches his seatbelt and glides away from the curb. "Do you want me to apologize for last night?" he asks, looking at me out of the corners of his eyes.

I think of him kneeling at my feet, licking me while I bear down on his fingers, and I press my legs together. "No."

"Fine."

He's dressed in black dress pants, a white dress shirt, and a black and silver tie. Great. We both look like we're going to work. I can be a restaurant hostess and he can be a waiter.

"Is your dad going to be dressed like that?" I ask.

"Fuck if I know."

"Your family life doesn't seem like a good atmosphere for raising a child."

"I already know I don't want her raised the way I was. I'll handle it."

"Ah-huh."

"What? Like your family is much better."

I twist in my seat. "You're insulting my mother, and you've never even met her. She's not a lush, or a shopaholic, and she's not a hoarder. If you want to meet her tomorrow, say so."

He purses his lips and turns onto a tree-lined street. "I want to meet your mother."

"Fine."

"Fine."

Jack parks in the driveway of a gorgeous three-story white Queen Anne sitting on a large corner lot. "You grew up here?"

His gaze is pulled to a window on the third floor. "Yes."

"Why didn't your dad move?"

He shrugs. "If you're brave enough, ask him yourself."

"No thanks."

He turns in his seat, resting his wrist on the steering wheel, his lips quirking in amusement. "You look nice."

I click my tongue against the roof of my mouth. "Yeah. Let's go."

I don't give him a chance to open the door for me. He's like a sloth, as if moving at a snail's pace will put off the inevitable. Scowling, he leads me up the driveway, a hand hovering over my lower back. Instead of going through the front door, he pushes a side door open revealing a laundry room.

"This is where the guests come in?" I ask, confused, inhaling the scent of detergent and bleach.

"We're not guests."

"You certainly know how to put a girl in her place."

Gripping my hand, he says, "I included myself."

"This is your home, Jack, of course you're not a guest."

He stops in a hallway that goes only God knows where and lifts my chin with a finger. "This has never been my home."

I want to hug him, but I don't think now would be a good time for sympathy. He'd read it as pity. "Well, that might be problematic."

"Christ, you two, stop making out. I thought I was here for dinner, not a show."

"Claire, shut up," Jack says, but he's smiling. He loves his sister, and I breathe a sigh of relief. If he and Claire didn't get along, I would have serious, *serious* doubts about this whole thing.

We continue down the hallway.

"What are we doing?" Claire asks.

"You just said it. We're having a family dinner," Jack says, the floorboards creaking under his feet.

"And I'll ask again, what are we doing?" She catches my eye. "I guess he didn't, huh?"

I sniff. "Everyone thought he did."

"You two are talking, literally, behind my back. It's rude," Jack says good-naturedly, but before either of us can respond, the hallway opens into a bright kitchen filled with stainless steel appliances and a gorgeous white marble island. An older woman is stirring something on the stove, but she stops when we enter the room.

"Jack, Claire! Aren't you a sight for sore eyes! And look at you," she exclaims, her eyes landing on me. "You are absolutely beautiful. You know, your father has been looking forward to this all day."

"I find that extremely hard to believe," Jack says, kissing the woman's cheek. "This is Irene. She's been with Dad for a while now. Can't remember how long?"

Irene swats his shoulder. "There's no need for math on a

Saturday night. He would never admit it, of course, but he kept wandering in here, asking what time it was. You're late."

"Fashionably," Claire says, leaning over and hugging Irene. "Where is he?"

"In the library. What are you drinking?"

"What he's got in there will be fine. Thanks, Irene." Jack tugs on my arm. "Come on."

I resist and hold my hand out to Irene. "My name is Emma. Nice to meet you, Irene."

"Same. This house needs some new blood," she says.

Jack yanks me away.

"I hope she meant that figuratively," I say, stumbling into his side.

"This was your idea. Whatever happens will be your fault," he says, steadying me with an arm around my shoulders.

"Why are we here again?" Claire asks.

We step into a gorgeous room full of books and wood.

"Can't stomach your old man on a Saturday night?" Ron asks, looking up from pouring a glass of something that looks like whiskey, though it could have been bourbon or brandy. It all looks the same to me.

To my amusement, he's dressed the same as Jack, even down to the same colored tie. Like father like son.

"Oh, look, we're all dressed for a funeral," Claire says, heading toward the bar near the window wearing her black dress.

I bite back a smile.

"Claire," Ron says and kisses her pro-offered cheek. "You look beautiful as always."

"Thanks, Dad."

"Dad," Jack says, approaching his father, his arm stretched out for a handshake. "You know Emma."

He nods. "What are you drinking?"

"Whatever you're having is fine, Mr. Durand. Thank you for the dinner invitation."

Ron pours me a lowball glass of, hell, I'm not going to know unless I ask, and I don't dare. "I don't believe I issued it, and call me Ron, at least. We're not at the office. You took my advice, then," he says to Jack.

"You could say that."

"What advice?" I ask. Maybe the surrogacy idea wasn't Jack's.

"That you and he . . ." Ron twirls his finger in the air.

"After his party, one thing led to another," I say, lifting my face toward Jack's for a kiss.

He scowls but brushes his lips against mine while Claire looks on.

Irene calls us for dinner, and we're saved from further uncomfortable chitchat. Jack's hand brushes the nape of my neck as we follow Ron and Claire into a beautiful dining room and to a table that seats twelve. Jack holds out a chair for me, and the four of us are dwarfed by the space. I wonder if there's a smaller table where they ate more casual meals, but if Ron didn't eat dinner with his children, I'm guessing he didn't eat breakfast or lunch with them, either.

Another woman comes out of nowhere and helps Irene serve us plates of Cornish game hens, new potatoes, asparagus, and dinner rolls. It looks delicious, and after waiting for Claire to taste the first bite, I enjoy the meal.

Sitting across from me and next to Claire, Ron asks about various projects at work, my opinions on some of the businessmen, and what I think about the newest negotiations. I would know more and have more to contribute if Jack hadn't shut me out all week, but I'm still able to offer my opinion and Ron nods, actually listening to me.

Jack narrows his eyes at us, and Claire picks at her food, out of place. She doesn't work for Variant and probably has no idea what we're talking about.

"At some point, we should discuss promoting Emma," Ron says, dabbing his lips with a white cloth napkin. "I've been thinking about it for some time, and since you and she are moving forward in your personal lives, I think it would benefit the company if you and she moved forward professionally."

I never thought I would be more to Variant than Jack's PA, and I'm not sure how I feel about a promotion. I like my job, but it would be nice to earn more money, be included in a more meaningful way, and I would spend a lot more time with Jack. On the other hand, I don't know if I want more responsibility. Jack and Ron work hard, and that's something he'll need to change after our daughter is born.

"That won't be possible," Jack snaps.

Ron sits back, surprised. "Why? You can always hire another PA but finding executives who won't sell you out is practically impossible."

"I think what Jack is trying to say is that he and Emma are going to get married," Claire says, lifting a glass of wine to her lips.

"That shouldn't matter," Ron says, frowning.

"No, that's not what I'm saying. I asked Emma to surrogate for me, and she said yes."

Claire chokes on her wine.

"What the fuck is that supposed to mean?" Ron asks, clutching his napkin in his fist.

"I think you know what it means," Jack says irritably. "She gets pregnant, she gives the baby to me, and afterward, she's moving to Seattle to be near her brother. I'm compensating her quite well, and we're both in agreement. That's why she wanted us to have this dinner. So we could tell you."

I kick Jack under the table, the toe of my heel connecting with his ankle. That is *not* why.

"Ow," he growls, leaning over to rub his leg. "And she wanted to see the kind of family our daughter will grow up in," he adds.

"You already know you're having a girl?" Claire asks, her eyes wide.

"No. She's not pregnant yet. She only signed a contract a couple of days ago."

Ron bows his head and loosens his grip on the napkin. Running his hand over his face, he says, "I'm sorry, Jack. I'm sorry I raised you the way I did, without your mother, and that you think this is an acceptable way to start a family." He meets my eyes over the table. "My grandchild shouldn't be born this way. I'm sorry, Emma. I know you're only trying to help, but you shouldn't do this." Wearily, he pushes away from the table, and his footsteps heavy, walks out of the dining room abandoning his half-eaten dinner.

"Then you two aren't together," Claire asks, looking between us.

I smile sadly. "No, we're not."

"You should go talk to Dad," she says to Jack.

He frowns, clearly not wanting to leave us alone, but says, "I suppose I should." He rests his hand on my shoulder and kisses my temple. "I'll be back in a few minutes."

"Take your time. I want to show Emma the house."

Jack sharply glares at his sister, presses his lips together, and strides out of the room.

"He didn't like that," I say.

"He hates this house," she says, rising from her chair.

"Was it difficult for him to come here? For dinner, I mean," I ask, placing my napkin that I had laying in my lap onto the table and standing from my chair, too. My appetite vanished with Ron's apology, and I'm not interested in what Irene made for dessert.

"I don't think he would have arranged for a family dinner for anyone but you. He never brought Veronica here."

I follow her up two flights of stairs to the third floor, and the walls are severely different from Heath and Zoey's. Family pictures filled their brownstone, and here, only artwork displayed in ornate frames hangs on the walls. There's not a photo of Ron, Claire, and Jack anywhere.

She opens a door to a room that could have only belonged to Jack when he was a teen. "This was his room until he moved away to go to school. After he graduated, he lived in the city and has ever since. Dad didn't touch it."

A small desk with an old desktop computer is positioned under a window, and baseball trophies are stored in a glass cabinet standing in a corner of the room. A navy and grey comforter is pulled tightly across a queen bed. There isn't a speck of dust anywhere. "Is your room the same, too?"

"Yeah. I stayed here a little longer. I didn't want Dad living by himself." She steps into the hallway, and I have no choice but to follow. I want to stay in his room, get to know the boy he was before he turned so jaded, but he's always been like that, and that's another lesson I've ignored.

I think she's going to show me her bedroom but instead steps into a room with hardwood floors, the walls painted a butter yellow. A white wooden rocker sits in one corner next to a huge dollhouse I would have loved to play with when I was a child. A toybox sits against the opposite wall near a white antique crib. "It's like stepping back in time," I whisper.

"Dad hasn't remodeled since Mom left." She pauses. "I know you love my brother, Emma, but I don't understand the surrogacy thing."

I wander around the room, my glance touching on framed

watercolors inspired by *Alice in Wonderland.* "I thought if we spent time together, if we started sleeping together, that maybe I could get him to love me back. It's obviously not working, and I'm afraid I've gotten myself into a big mess. Why didn't you have kids? When you were married?"

She sinks onto a window seat and rests her head against the glass. "My first husband wanted them, but I said I didn't. He called me selfish, and I divorced him soon after. He didn't want a divorce. I think he actually loved me," she says, shaking her head in disbelief, "but I knew if I stayed married to him, I would keep hurting him. My second husband already had children who lived with their mother, and he said he didn't want more. Our marriage existed on paper rather than in real life, and when we divorced, nothing changed but my bank account balance."

"I'm sorry." It sounds inadequate.

"I want to tell you not to give up, Emma. I like you, and I think Dad does, too. I've never heard him talk about promoting anyone, and that's a real compliment. But I think, if I'm truly honest with you, you should cut your losses. Jack's like me. Unable to commit, scared to love. He'll never marry, and simply dating wouldn't be enough for you. It wouldn't be enough for any woman who loves him. Not forever."

My heart sinks. I wanted someone to be on my side. Someone to help me believe that if I hung in there, everything would work out. But out of anyone, Claire would know him best, and if I listened to anyone, I should listen to her.

"Because of what happened between Ron and your mother. What was her name?"

Claire smiles. "Elizabeth. He called her Bess, from the stories I've managed to drag out of people. Jack sat here on this window seat and watched her leave. The minute he was old enough, he moved out of the nursery and into his own room. He never stepped foot in here again."

"Is she still alive?"

Claire's lips part. "I don't know."

"And you don't know why she left?"

"When I was a little girl, I crawled into Dad's lap and asked him why I didn't have a mommy like all my friends. I made him cry, and to a little girl, her daddy's tears are the scariest thing in the world. I never asked again."

I sit on the seat with her. "Then there's no hope."

"I wish there were. He has feelings for you, I can see that. He might even love you, but what good is it if he won't let himself?" She reaches for my hand. "The Durands are broken. We're broken as individuals, and we're broken as a family. I won't let myself marry again. I'm better off single so I can't hurt anyone else. I might have hurt him, but I'm glad I didn't let Roman convince me to have a baby. Jack and I were collateral damage, and my children would have been the same. I got my tubes tied a few years ago, and I'm too old now, regardless, thank God. Find a man who will love you. From what I've seen, Rafferty Clark already does. You two looked sweet eating lunch today, and you deserve that. We better go downstairs. I doubt Dad had much to say that Jack would listen to."

"Thank you, for being honest. Everyone has told me the same thing, but I didn't want to hear it. I think, if you would have told me to keep trying, that I had a chance, I would have. So, thank you."

We stand from the window seat, and Claire looks down at me. We're both in heels, but she's two or three inches taller than I am. "I don't like speaking poorly of Jack. He was my lifeline growing up. Ron has never been easy to live with, and I won't lie. Our nannies raised us. Jack was always more self-reliant, but that feeds into the way he is. He doesn't want to need anyone. He doesn't want to be vulnerable, and that's exactly what we are when we fall in love."

I follow Claire downstairs. Ron's absent, and Jack's sitting alone in the library sipping on a drink staring outside. The sun slowly sinks beyond the horizon, bathing the yard in an orange glow.

"Ready to go?" he asks, setting his drink aside.

"Yeah," I whisper.

He narrows his eyes at me but says, "Claire? Can we drop you at home?"

"No. I think I'll stay here and chat with Irene for a minute."

"Okay. If you need anything, call." Jack busses her cheek with a quick, hard kiss, and she pats his shoulder, years of unhappiness flooding her eyes.

"I will. Goodnight."

"Goodnight, Claire. Thanks again," I say, following Jack out of the library.

Silently, we walk outside, and he holds the truck's door open for me. Sliding behind the wheel, he glances at me before buckling his seatbelt and turning the key in the ignition. "To your place?" he asks, his jaw rigid.

"That's fine." I look out the window.

"What did you and Claire talk about?"

"Nothing much. Girl stuff. A little about her marriages." I talk to the scenery going by in a blur out my window.

It's much more difficult being around Jack now that I've added intimacy to what used to be a professional relationship. Knowing where I stood, thinking he was going to propose to Veronica, it made it bearable, but pushing myself onto him, tasting little bits and pieces of what our life could be like if he would only let me in, it hurts me on a level I wasn't prepared for. Raff, Mia, and Haisley warned me, though Mia and Haisley were more concerned with what would happen if Jack made me pregnant. If I am, I'll pay for that, too.

"Emma? Are you okay?" he asks, threading my fingers with his. I don't want to hold his hand, like we're a real couple heading home from a dinner with his family, but it would be childish to pull away. There's no one to blame for this situation but me.

I turn from the window and paste a smile onto my face. "Yeah. I'm sorry dinner didn't go as expected."

"I don't know what *you* expected, but it went about as well as I thought it would."

"What did your dad have to say?"

"That he hoped for better for my kids than what he'd given Claire and me. I called him a hypocrite. That if the way Claire and I grew up was good enough for us, then it would be good enough for my child. He mumbled something about mistakes, but by that point, I was too angry to listen to anything. My mom did something so terrible he threw her out. My daughter will have a better start in life than I ever had."

"You think I would do something like that? Whatever 'that' is? You wouldn't consider raising her together?"

"I'm not getting married, Emma."

"I know that, but we don't have to be married to be her parents. I could still be part of her life."

"No." He lets go of my hand.

There's a free parking spot in front of my apartment, and I wait for him to round the truck and open my door. He helps me from my seat, and we don't say anything until we're inside.

"Do you want a drink?" I ask.

"No. I drank enough at Dad's."

"All right." Quick and dirty then, like last night. Maybe it's better he doesn't want to go slow, that it doesn't feel like making love when it's anything but.

I kick off my heels and lead him to the bedroom. The sun is barely a glimmer in the sky, and my room is dark. That soothes me, and I turn toward him and lick my lips. One last time, whether I get pregnant or not.

Silently, he turns me around and unzips the zipper. The rasp sends shivers down my spine, and I hope in the dark he doesn't see. The lace is form-fitting, and he pushes the top from my shoulders and down my body until the dress is tangled around my calves. I step out of it and face him. I don't wear fancy lingerie, a black bra and panties suiting my needs for an evening like this. He stares at me, and without breaking eye contact, pulls the pins from my bun. Instead of dropping them onto my dresser, he pockets them, one by one, until my hair is a mess of waves around my shoulders.

When the last pin is tucked into his pocket, I reach for his tie. Slowly, I unknot it, his Adam's apple working as my fingers graze his neck. I let it hang undone and unbutton his dress shirt. He's wearing a white ribbed tank underneath, and I want to sigh in frustration. Impatiently, I tug the dress shirt from his shoulders. At some point, he rolled his sleeves up, revealing his strong forearms, and that saves us a few seconds. The cotton flutters to the floor. I push up the hem of his tank, rubbing my lips over his chest until he pulls it off the rest of the way giving me access to more skin. I want him to feel how much I love him. That had been my intention all along, and if he's not going to bend me over, bang me, and leave, I'll take full advantage of the time he's giving me. I run my hands along his sides, and my kisses turn into little licks.

He sucks in a breath, but he doesn't stop me, and standing on my toes, I nibble his neck, scraping my teeth along the curve of his shoulder.

Like I hoped he would, he unhooks my bra and fills his

hands with my breasts. I shudder, and his name slips out of my mouth. "Jack."

"Do you like that?" he asks, squeezing my nipples.

"Yes," I whimper, lowering my arms and letting my bra fall to the floor next to my dress. My panties are soaked. "I love it when you touch me. You don't know how many days I've sat at my desk daydreaming about this."

He rolls my nipples between his fingers. "Have you?" he mumbles against my lips, and I open my mouth.

He slips his tongue against mine, never letting my nipples go, and my belly stirs with an orgasm.

I reach for his belt and undo the buckle. Quickly, I unbutton his pants, slide down the zipper, and push my hands inside his briefs. He's so hard, and his cock surges under my touch. The tip is wet, and I swirl my fingertips in it. He continues the assault on my nipples, and my breasts are heavy and engorged. Between my legs, I'm aching and swollen. I want him inside me now, even if it will cut our evening short. I've been wanting him, needing this for years, and there's only so much foreplay I can stand.

"I need you, Jack," I whisper.

"I need you, too, but I can't," he says, resting his forehead against mine.

"I know." That might be the closest thing to the truth he'll ever say, and I'll hold it close to my heart, always.

He finishes undressing and I pull off my panties. I'm faster than he is and I draw the comforter and sheets back and crawl into bed. He wrestles with his socks, pulling them off his feet, and he slides in on the opposite side. He reaches for me, his hand immediately finding my slit.

I plaster myself to his chest, propping a knee onto his hip to give him access. He pushes two fingers inside me, and I moan, my lips pressed against his shoulder.

"Christ, Emma, you're so wet. Like this, okay?"

"Yeah."

We're both on our sides, my leg parallel against his, and he pushes his cock inside me, his hand on my butt pulling me closer. "Kiss me," he says, and I do, gliding my lips over his and taking him as far as he can go.

He moves his hand from my ass to my hair, tangling his fingers in it and yanking, positioning my head the way he wants, devouring my mouth.

It might not be love, but this baby will be conceived in passion, and I won't regret that.

Jack lets go of my hair, and I drag in a breath. He wedges his fingers between our bodies and finds my clit. "Come for me," he orders, and I grind against him, needing him to fill me up.

"Jack, I need more," I gasp.

He chuckles. "Greedy."

Nudging me onto my back, he gives it to me, nibbling on my nipple, his finger circling my clit, his cock buried deep inside me.

I come with a cry, the orgasm sparking every inch of my skin. He doesn't give me a moment to settle and starts to move, bracing my arms above my head, his hand locked around my wrists. He pounds into me, and I lift my hips, wanting more, needing it, my stomach quivering, sweat covering my skin.

He lets go and comes with a moan, burying his face in my hair, a hand under my butt keeping me in place.

"It will be okay," I lie, mumbling against his cheek.

To protect my heart, I need to listen to Claire. I didn't listen to anyone else, but I need to listen to her. Jack can't give me what I want.

He settles the rest of his weight on top of me, and I accept it, gladly. He's still inside me and doesn't seem in any hurry to leave. Maybe he knows too, that this is a goodbye of sorts and wants to draw it out for as long as possible. He dozes, and I play with his hair, his scruff scratching at my skin.

I fall asleep, only to waken with him gliding in and out of me in smooth steady strokes, already inside me because he fell asleep that way.

He falls into a deeper sleep after he comes, and I lie still, both hoping and dreading that what we did tonight created a flicker. What will the consequences for me be if we did? What will they be for him if we didn't?

Cuddled into his side, I don't wake up until sunlight is streaming through the window.

CHAPTER SEVENTEEN

Jack

I spent the night. I didn't mean to, but I haven't been sleeping well lately, and Emma was so soft in my arms. I wake up with her head resting against my shoulder.

I could have this, every morning, if she didn't leave me.

And that threat will always keep me from marrying anyone, not only Emma.

She can't leave if she's already gone.

Her face is peaceful as she ekes out the last bit of sleep of the day, her hair a tangle on her pillowcase.

You could have this, my heart reminds me, and yeah, I could have this, for as long as she wanted to give it to me, and I won't surrender myself to anyone.

I succumb to her soft skin and touch her, rubbing my thumb over her cheek. Her eyes flutter open, and I catch the green flecks in the blue. Maybe our daughter will have her eyes. I would like that.

A sad smile plays with her mouth. "You stayed." She rests

her hand against my jaw, and I rub my whiskers against her palm.

"I did."

She whispers, "I'm glad."

The melancholy tone of her voice makes me hard, and I slide into her needing the comfort.

We rock, her arms around my neck, our lips fused together, and I do the one thing I said I would never do. We're not making love to have a baby, we're making love because I'm falling in love with Emma, and there's nothing I can do to stop it.

———

I dress to leave, and she's sitting in a robe on the bed sipping coffee and watching me. Her hair is a jumble of knots, and her lips are swollen. She's never looked more beautiful.

"I need to shower and change. What time do you go to your mom's?"

Her gaze slides away, and I feel her emotionally withdraw. It's so blatant, I swear I can see the change in her even if she looks the same as she did five seconds ago.

I swallow hard.

"I don't think it's a good idea for you to meet her after all."

"Why not? We agreed yesterday." I tense, balling up my tie and shoving it into my pants pocket.

"I know we did, but all we'll get is more of the same from her that we got from Claire and your dad. They thought me being a surrogate is a terrible idea, and my mother will think so too. You get to keep our baby, Jack, and we won't even have access to her for a short visit, a playdate. How do you think she'll feel? It's better if we do what I wanted in the first place.

We can pretend we're friends, and when I can't hide I'm pregnant anymore, I'll tell her then."

I can't argue. I don't know why I wanted to meet Emma's mother, except I thought if she was spending time with my family in an environment that wasn't work related, then I could meet her mom. But we're not married, or engaged, or even dating, and I would have no idea what to say if Mrs. Cox asked me what my intentions are.

I have no intentions but trading a baby for a wad of cash Emma doesn't want.

"Okay. She's your mother. If you think that's best, then I can't say anything."

"Thank you. I'll see you at work tomorrow, okay?"

Why does that sound so impossibly far away?

"Yeah."

I lean over to kiss her cheek, but she dodges me, reminding me of what our true relationship is. I tell her goodbye, and her eyes are blank, her face a mask. She closes the door, not watching me walk to my car.

Emma's finally understanding what I'll give her and what I won't, and I should be grateful breaking it off after the baby's born will be easy. But if I did get her pregnant this weekend, I won't have an excuse to touch her, and I already miss her cute little whimpers when she comes.

The sun on the drive to my building does little to lift my spirits, and the emptiness of my penthouse sets me on edge. I used to like coming home to the quiet after a long day at work, but ever since I decided to have a baby, the empty rooms only emphasize how empty my life is, too.

I shower, daydreaming about Emma and what I would do to her if we stood under the hot stream together, and I get myself off to the faint echo of her whispers this morning when we made love.

I dress in jeans and a t-shirt, not having anywhere to go, and on a whim, I text Claire. *Breakfast, brunch, lunch. Throw me a bone.* Besides her choking on her wine, I don't know what she thinks about Emma surrogating for me, plus I want to know what she and Emma really talked about upstairs while Dad was trying to explain away the last forty-one years of my life.

Claire mentions a time and the rooftop restaurant where Emma, Clark, Mia, and Haisley ate lunch yesterday. I saw the photos, Emma's head resting against his shoulder in that familiar way they have, but I didn't bring it up. I didn't want to start a fight, and I didn't want her to know the real reason I was upset. She didn't invite me to go. I wanted to be in Clark's chair, my fingers playing with the ends of her hair as she leaned into me. I wanted to be there, but after the way I walked out on her after fucking her against the hallway wall, I had no right to want anything, and I kept my mouth shut.

I swap out my t-shirt for a dress shirt, hang a pair of sunglasses from the pocket, and push deck shoes onto my bare feet.

Claire's late as usual, and I sit and drink half a bottle of beer before she shows up, sunglasses perched on the top of her head and her dress's skirt blowing in the breeze. Every man who's eating lunch watches her glide across the rooftop, vainly wishing she would look their way. She's oblivious to all of it, not in the mood to husband-hunt today.

I'm seated near a planter of bright pink flowers, and occasionally, the pungent scent of the soil and fertilizer catch my nose. She approaches the table, and I stand and kiss her cheek. She doesn't evade me, and she kisses me back.

"What's up? Twice in a weekend? You really like this family stuff now."

"Trying to get into the habit. Emma says I can't raise the baby alone." Her idea that we raise our daughter together without getting married sticks in my chest. I don't want Emma in my life halfway. I don't want to fight over weekends and holidays. I don't want to live the life of a divorcé when I'm not divorced.

All or nothing, and I chose nothing.

"No, a nanny will raise her, exactly like we were raised. She'll see you for an hour after you get home from work before she has to go to bed, and it will be like that until she's a teen and she spends more time at her friends' houses than she does at her own. You know how it works, Jack. You know what it was like growing up without Mom around, and your kid will have it the same way."

I grit my teeth. "It would still be that way if Emma and I were together—she likes her job and would want to keep working."

"Yeah, but not right away. I bet if you asked her, she'd love to spend the first three or four years at home. Zoey did until her girls started preschool, if I remember right." She flicks a glance at my beer bottle. "Do I want wine?"

"Yes, you do. I have a very difficult discussion planned for us, and I want the alcohol to grease your tongue."

She grimaces. "That sounds gross coming from my brother."

"Get your mind out of the gutter."

"What? I haven't had sex in months. You got some last night, so don't gloat."

Lifting my beer bottle halfway to my mouth, I pause. "What about Cloud 9? You disappeared before I even made it upstairs. Where did you go?"

"I saw Zeke and didn't want to deal with it, so I left."

"I'm sorry." Claire doesn't talk about her ex-husbands, and it must have been bad for her to mention one of them now.

She lifts a shoulder. "That's what I get for being stupid."

A server stops at our table and asks Claire if she wants a drink. He returns with a glass of red and another bottle of beer and stands with a pencil poised over a notepad. I wasn't looking at the menu, too relieved Claire showed up and I didn't have to spend all of Sunday alone to bother choosing something to eat, and for lack of anything better, I order a Cobb salad like she does.

She sips her wine and waits for the young server to walk out of earshot. "Do you ever think about finding Mom?"

I rear back, distaste souring my mouth. "No. Why the fuck would I want to do that?"

She frowns, my reaction not what she expected. "To ask her why she left us so completely. No visits, no birthday cards. No Christmas presents."

I lift a shoulder. "Maybe she did try to visit, and Dad wouldn't let her. Maybe she did send mail, and Dad didn't let us have it."

"Okay, if you think that, then why wouldn't you want to find her?"

"Because she was weak, that's why. Their divorce involved two little children, and she could have fought harder. She could have followed our nanny to the park. Stopped by the house on the weekends when he was on business trips. She could have visited us at school when Dad wasn't around. If she had really loved us, she would have found a way to be in our lives."

The waiter chooses that moment to serve our salads and refresh our waters. We tell him we don't need anything else, and he hurries away, the popular and trendy rooftop crowded with people who want to be in the right place at the right time.

"Like I assume Emma would want to be for her baby if you gave her the chance?" she asks, stabbing at her lettuce.

"That's different. What we're doing is a business arrangement."

"Divorce is a business arrangement, too. Attorneys, billable hours. Sign on the dotted line. A monetary transfer. It's not so different, Jack. You hate Mom for not fighting for us? One day you'll hate Emma just as much for letting you have your way. You'll be rocking your daughter in the middle of the night through an ear infection, and you'll hate her for not fighting to be there. As much as I wanted out of our marriage to keep from hurting Roman anymore, I hated him for a long time for letting me leave. It told me he didn't love me enough to keep me, but the reality is, he loved me enough to let me have my way. That's stupid, isn't it? Hating someone for giving you what you want?" She ends with a crack in her voice, and she looks into her huge salad bowl, nudging a tomato wedge with her fork.

"Do you regret getting divorced? Do you want him back?"

She wipes a tear off her cheek. "What good would that do? I walked away when we were happy. He'd never trust me to stick by him when times were bad. I married Zeke and hoped he would stop me, run into the church like in those crazy movies, but he didn't. I tried to fill the hole I made in my heart when I divorced Roman by marrying a man who pretended to love me because . . . God, I don't even know why Zeke wanted to marry me. How pathetic is that?"

"It's not pathetic, Claire. You were looking for love."

"I had it, and I threw it in the trash. Hey," she says, and I meet her eyes. "I have to tell you something. You might hear it from someone else, and I don't want it coming back at me."

"What?"

"When I talked to Emma yesterday . . ."

"What?" I ask again, and I wait for Claire to say she warned Emma off me because I'm a heartless son of a bitch from a dysfunctional family who doesn't deserve to raise a child.

Claire sucks in a breath. "I told her . . . I told her she was really brave and thanked her for giving me a niece or nephew. I promised I would do my best to help that baby grow up happy."

I laugh, relieved. "Why did I think you were going to tell me something bad?"

"I don't agree with what you're doing, but I'll be there for you when you realize what you asked Emma to do was a mistake. If you wanted babies that badly, Veronica would have given them to you."

"Claire, I'll tell you what I keep telling everyone, what I told Dad last night at the house. She can't leave if she's already gone."

"You chant that like it's a lifeline, but if you married Veronica, she would have given you a couple of kids, and maybe a few years later you would have gotten a divorce. If you didn't love her, what would it have mattered? 'She can't leave if she's already gone.' That's what you say when you're scared someone you love is going to leave you. You don't want to be with Emma because you're afraid one day you'll come home from work and she won't be there. I don't understand how what you're doing is any different. If you give her a chance, she might not go anywhere, and you could love her for the rest of your life."

"I won't risk it. What I'm doing is right for me, and it will be right for our child. I'll do whatever I need to do to give her a happy life. I'll work as hard as I can to be a good dad."

"She's going to want to know where her mama is, like we did. She'll turn into me, too afraid to hold on to a husband who loves her because she grew up thinking that if her own mother couldn't love her, no one else can, either."

"Claire," I say, appalled.

"What's worse is Emma will move on, marry, and have more children. And your daughter will wonder what was so wrong with her Emma didn't want to be her mother. Is that why you don't want to find Mom? You're afraid after Dad threw her out, she left us behind and started another family? She would have had every right, and so will Emma. What will that do to your daughter? If you find out that's what Mom did, what will it do to you? I have to go. I love you, Jack. Thanks you to, I survived my childhood, and I never want you to forget that."

She leans over the table and kisses my scruffy cheek. I don't shave anymore—I know Emma likes it.

My sister hurries away, eliciting the same stares she did when she arrived, her shoulders hunched and trembling.

The place is so busy, I pay our bill and leave, too, not wanting to hog the table.

At the penthouse, I change into workout clothes and go for a run outside. I could have asked Heath to go, but Sundays are a family day for him and Zoey, and I already wasted some of their weekend asking them to host a party that didn't do anything but ruffle feathers.

Running ten miles doesn't block the conversation with Claire from my mind. She usually keeps to herself, pushing people away and hiding behind a loud and crass personality. She surprised me by being so forthcoming. Mom leaving did more damage than I thought, but never once until Claire mentioned it did I think to look for her. That I could have half siblings chills me, and I make the split-second decision that if I have any, I don't want to meet them. Claire is the only sister who matters to me.

I don't want to spend the rest of Sunday home alone, and instead of flipping the TV on and watching a baseball game like I normally would, I go to the office.

The executive floor is quiet and dark, the cleaners already having done their jobs Friday night. My office is locked, and I let myself in.

Emma's everywhere—sitting at the table reading the contract, poking her head into my office to tell me if a client is running late, leaning against my desk and scribbling notes onto her electronic pad.

Dad wants to promote her.

I should let him.

Pregnant women work, and now I see her round with my child, resting a hand on her bump as she talks to me. In my mind, there's a contract, but not the kind she signed. It's in the form of a ring glittering on her finger. The contract *I* signed, promising to love her forever.

Because I do. She emotionally blocked me out this morning and it scared the fuck out of me.

She's slipping away.

My heart might be cracking, but my brain says it's better to let her go, and I listen.

CHAPTER EIGHTEEN

Emma

There's nothing I want more than for Jack to meet my mother, but not under these circumstances. Raff texts and asks if I'm visiting her, and I say yes and invite him along. At lunch with Mia and Haisley yesterday, he didn't mention where he's been, and I'm going to ask him about it.

Things are changing, but not in the way I'd hoped.

Raff picks me up dressed in khakis and a button down shirt. Mom doesn't mind if we don't dress up, but a t-shirt is too casual for Raff, even if we're only eating lunch on her patio. I'm wearing the skimpiest dress I have. The sun's blazing and the temperature is unusually hot for this time of year. I pulled my hair back into a low ponytail and I'm barefoot. I brought sandals in case there's a change of plan and Mom wants to go to lunch at a restaurant instead, but the full weekend wiped me out and all I want to do is lie on a patio lounger, doze in the sun, and wish I didn't have to do what I have to do in the morning.

"You're looking particularly earthy today," Raff says, stopping at a read light, studying me. "Pregnancy will suit you."

I lift a corner of my mouth. "It's called exhaustion."

"Too much hot sex?" he teases. "You are supposed to sleep, too."

"Ha. Ha. No. Meeting Jack's father outside of work was particularly grueling, and on a tour of their house, all Claire could tell me was how defective Jack was and to stay away because I wouldn't get all my money back on a return."

"At least she's honest. Two failed marriages would do that."

"You'll be happy to know you were right all along. I'm going to tell him tomorrow. In fact, after he left this morning, I sent an email to HR and asked if I could trade places with Nancy. Ron was talking about promoting me and he'll approve the transfer." I squeeze his fingers. "I'm not moving to Seattle."

He lifts my hand to his lips. "You will if this goes south, but Em, I wouldn't blame you. Only miss you."

Raff parks in front of my mother's house, the same one I grew up in. It's smaller (much smaller) than the Durand's home, but I wouldn't trade the square footage for happiness. My parents were never strict, giving me and my brother space to make mistakes, supporting us when we attempted to fix them. Before his heart attack, Dad was planning to retire from the engineering firm where he worked, and after his death, Mom stopped teaching, too sad to keep going.

Martha, Marti to my dad when he was still alive and to her friends she meets on Tuesdays for Canasta, greets us at the door. The first time I dragged Raff home after school sensing he needed more people in his life who cared about him than only his aunt, she immediately welcomed him with open arms and a pan of fudge brownies. Ever since, she's considered him part of our family.

I'm sure she'd do the same for Jack once she found out

about his history, brownies and all. After the initial shock wore off that he could afford to buy his own private island the size of Hawaii, of course.

"Raff," she says, opening the door, "you need some sun. You're looking a little peaked. Did you have a rough week? I saw you and Emma attended the play. You looked gorgeous, Emma. Where did you buy that dress?"

She ushers us in, and I toss my sandals onto the floor. Raff toes off his shoes and we follow her gratefully into the air-conditioned living room. The French doors showcase the table outside already set for lunch, and she lowered the sunshade.

"On clearance last year, I think. It was the first time I wore it. I don't know why you didn't come with us. You could have met the actors. Raff interviewed them and I asked for their autographs."

"I'm too old for that. You two are still young enough to have fun. Raff," she says, already in babying mode and nudging him toward the glass doors, "sit down and I'll bring out a pitcher of sangria. I put a little extra in it for you."

"Thank you, Mrs. Cox."

He trudges out to the patio and lowers himself onto a padded chair. He tilts his head back and closes his eyes.

"Is something going on with him?" Mom asks, leading me into the kitchen.

"I don't know. I haven't seen much of him this week. I was going to ask while we were eating lunch."

"Help me carry out the sandwiches and the chips and dip. Nothing fancy today, I'm afraid. My arthritis has been acting up."

"We don't come out here so you can feed us. Raff has always enjoyed hanging out with you, and you're my mom. I'll always visit because I love you." My voice cracks at the last, and she folds me into her arms.

"This has to do with Jack."

"How do you know?" I ask, sniffling into her shoulder.

"Ever since you started working at Variant, if you cry, it's over Jack Durand. I wish you would quit. He makes you so miserable. Nothing ever came of him carrying you out of the Bridgeport Hotel?"

"Nothing good."

"I'm sorry, baby." She brushes my cheek with the backs of her fingers. "All I want is for you to be happy the way I was happy with your father. You can't do that loving a man who won't love you back. Summer's here, and we both need a vacation. How much time do you have? A couple of weeks? Let's go visit your brother. He's been asking why you haven't flown out, but I never tell him you don't want to miss Jack."

I try to smile. I won't be going anywhere if I'm pregnant. Jack will keep me under lock and key until the baby's born. It's what I wanted, more time to try to get him to fall in love with me, but now I'll see it as nine months of hell waiting to give away a little baby to a man who doesn't know how to love. "That sounds good. We better bring Raff his drink. He's looking peaked *and* parched."

We settle around the table, a light breeze keeping the heat at bay. There's an emptiness with my father gone, and I sag into the chair next to Raff, missing him. My father would have cut quickly to the heart of the matter. He and Raff bonded over chess the first afternoon I brought him home, and he'd have Raff spilling his guts and a solution besides. Now it's up to me to puzzle out how to help. I pour him a glass of the sangria my mother liberally peppered with blueberries, raspberries, and booze. "Are you okay?"

Gratefully, he sips and rubs his eyes. "Things with Veronica aren't going well. Jack caused a lot of problems."

"Is the show giving her a hard time?" I've been too preoccupied with Jack and his request to focus on anything else, not even turning on *Rise and Shine, Bridgeport!* as background noise while I dress for work. I used to watch it every morning, wondering why Jack would choose her over me.

It's nice to know he didn't.

He didn't choose anybody.

"Yeah. They were hoping to do a huge wedding segment, from picking out engagement rings, to wedding venues, to honeymoon destinations. She said the producers threw weeks of planning into the garbage."

"That's not her fault," I say, dragging a chip through a quivering lump of ranch dip. "What are they doing instead?"

"They've been focusing on relationship maintenance, self-care after a breakup, that kind of thing."

I curl my lip in disgust as my mother avidly listens to us. She loves *Rise and Shine, Bridgeport!,* and though she would never tell me to my face, she's one of Veronica Chapman's biggest fans. I'm ashamed I haven't used my connections to introduce her. Jack could have set it up for me without a problem, but that time's come and gone. "That's cruel."

"Yeah. She's doing the best she can, but when something like that happens, you know who your true friends are."

That explains where he's been all week. Helping her dust off her pants. Maybe not literally, but damage control is as important, maybe even more so, than covering the actual event if it had gone well. It sounds as if her career is riding on it. Raff's kind and would do it anyway, but they've helped each other in the past. He wouldn't drop her now when her reputation is at stake.

"Maybe you should have taken her to the play. What's the next big thing to attend in Bridgeport?" I ask.

"You wouldn't mind?" He swirls the sangria in his glass, the berries sinking to the bottom. "We go to things like that together."

"Things change, Raff," I say softly, and Mom rubs my shoulder.

"Thanks, baby girl."

"Go inside and rest. Tomorrow is another day of sweeping dirt under the rug."

"I think I will. Wake me when you want to go."

"Yeah."

We watch him go into the house. He slides the door closed, and I turn back to my plate and crumble a chip between my fingers. I'm not hungry anymore. "How do you know when it's time to give up?"

Mom brushes her fingers over my hair. "You've given Jack three years of your life. How many more do you want to give him without anything in return? You'll be thirty-five this year, Emma. Are you wasting the prime years of your life? You loved him when he dated Veronica Chapman, you loved him when you thought he was going to propose to her. Was that time wasted, or were you using that time to build something? Do you have a foundation waiting for him now that he's single? Does he talk to you?"

All those questions and no answers. It would be easy to think of them as a waste. Loving someone who doesn't love you back usually is, isn't it? And it's not so much that I don't think he can't love me. He was jealous of Raff and has been for a long time (I had the bruises to prove it), but he refuses to fall in love because of something that happened between his parents when he was a child. I can't fix that. I wouldn't even know where to start. "What if his baggage is more than I can carry?"

"Then if you love him enough, you find a cart."

———

Mom and I use the time Raff is napping to video chat with my brother, his wife, and their two kids. He asks if I'm dating anyone, and if we'll visit soon. Mom wants to go, but she'd never fly alone. She and Dad used to fly out all the time, but she says she isn't brave enough to travel by herself. Jack would let us use Variant's private jet, but our relationship isn't on good enough terms for me to ask. Once, or rather, if, I fulfill my surrogate duties, he'll fly me to the west coast to get me out of Minnesota that much faster.

Our call ends on a somber note, and maybe Raff is right. If things go badly, I'll move, Mom will come with me, and things will have turned out how they're supposed to.

It's a depressing thought.

I help Mom clean up the patio table and the kitchen and find Raff sleeping on my bed. He's spent so much time in this room that it feels as much his as it does mine.

I lower myself next to him and brush my fingers over his cheek.

His eyes flutter open.

"Things would be so much easier," I whisper.

"I've thought that many times, baby girl," he says, his voice raspy with sleep. "But it would be the easy way out, and you know it."

"I know. Ready to go?"

"Yeah. Let me hit the head."

"Okay." I rest my lips where my fingers were moments ago. "Promise me we'll always be friends."

"I promise." He pulls me to him, and we lie like that, hiding from the bad things we know are coming.

On the drive into the city, he's looking more like himself, and I twist in my seat. "What *is* the next big thing to attend in Bridgeport?"

"The huge fundraiser for the Bridgeport Women's Reproductive Health and Resources Center. You really have been distracted. Variant is their biggest supporter. It's always held at the end of June."

"Oh, I remember now. I didn't go while Jack was dating Veronica, that's why."

As Jack's PA, I'd been issued an invitation for both years, but I couldn't bear to watch Jack and Veronica together. I skipped, claiming other obligations. Raff understood and didn't pressure me to be his date. It won't be out of the ordinary for me not to attend this year, either.

"It's the perfect event to show Bridgeport that Jack might have knocked her down, but she's not out of the fight. Everyone in the city will expect her to avoid it. Thank you for the idea, Em."

"It's not a big deal. I don't know Veronica well, but she doesn't deserve the professional backlash. Her personal life is no one's business." I pause. "I wonder if they support the medical center because of Zoey's daughter, Paige."

"Possibly. More than likely, Ron closed his eyes and pointed at a list of charities. The man doesn't seem like he cares about anything except making money. Does he have a heart? At dinner, did you hear it beating?"

"He cares more than anyone would ever guess. This surrogacy agreement disappointed him on a level that surprised me. I didn't think he'd have an opinion one way or another, but you know what? He told me not to do it."

We idle at a red light, and Raff flicks a glance at me. "Maybe he's thinking of the legality of it. You signed a contract, but Jack should have gone through an agency. The last thing Ron needs for Variant is for this to blow up in court."

"Yeah, maybe," I agree, but Raff didn't see Ron's face when Jack announced it, didn't see the slump of his shoulders when he walked out of the dining room.

"You don't think so?"

I shrug. "He said he wanted better for Jack's and Claire's children. This all has to do with their mother leaving, and what they were fighting about that day. What Jack heard before she disappeared in that taxi for good. No one knows except Ron what really happened."

"Then maybe you should ask. It might shed some light on why Jack keeps saying he'll never marry."

"The reason his mother left them won't matter, it's that she did it at all. Jack's scared his children's mother will abandon them like his mother abandoned him. People get divorced, hell, they die. Mom was gutted when my father passed away. You can't avoid marriage and falling in love because you're afraid of what could happen. Every day children lose a parent. What he doesn't understand is, what would our daughter do if he died? She'd have no one."

"No, the reason will still matter. If you found out, you could at least promise that it wouldn't happen between you two. He wouldn't believe it, but you'd have a stronger argument than what you have now. Maybe she was cheating on him and he found out, or, I don't know. She fell in love with another man, Ron told her she would never see her kids again, and she regretted saying anything. Maybe she did something illegal, and he wanted no part in it. Maybe *he* did something, and she couldn't live with it."

Raff turns onto my street, and I lean back in my seat.

Claire didn't want to make her father cry, and she stopped asking. Maybe Jack asked, but Ron wouldn't say anything.

What would Ron do if I asked? I doubt he would cry in front of me . . . if he talks to me at all.

Raff parks in front of my apartment door. "You're going over there."

"Maybe I wouldn't have the guts if we hadn't gone for dinner last night, but I think I might."

Raff squeezes my hand. "Be careful. People hide a lot of skeletons. If you're going to find out, ask yourself if you can still love Jack and marry him once you know. It could be that terrible you don't want anything to do with the Durands ever again."

"I wouldn't punish Jack and Claire for what their parents did."

"You're talking about having babies. You could already be pregnant if you were doing what I think you were doing all weekend. Ron will be that child's grandfather, and he's got the money to do whatever he damned well pleases and so does Jack. They say you shouldn't bring a knife to a gunfight, but baby girl, you can't fight a billionaire unless you're one, too."

I swallow.

Ron and Jack have the money to do whatever they want, but I've never been a quitter, or else I would have quit my job at Variant a long time ago. "I'll be careful."

"Okay. Call if you need me. I don't think Ron will hurt you, but he'll protect Jack and Claire. He's a father, so don't underestimate him."

"I won't."

Inside, I change into something more appropriate, wondering if I'm making the biggest mistake of my life. If it is, I can add it to the list of the dumb things I've already done.

During the entire drive to Jack's childhood home, I'm tempted to turn around. I idle in the driveway, and I want nothing more than to back up and go home. My finger hovers over the little lit circle of the doorbell, and I think I should forget the whole thing.

I press it before I chicken out.

Things need to change.

Irene answers the door. "Emma, how nice to see you. Did you leave something behind yesterday?"

"No, but thank you for asking. I'd like to speak to Mr. Durand, if that's all right."

"Let me see if he's accepting visitors. Can you wait a moment?"

"Yes, thank you."

She shuts the door, leaving me standing on the small brick landing. There isn't a porch, no rocking chairs. Nothing to indicate that anyone has wanted to sit outside, sip lemonade, and watch the world go by.

Irene returns a moment later. "He says that's fine. I'll show you to the library."

"Thanks."

I don't remember the way, and I'm relieved she doesn't let me fend for myself. I follow her through rooms and down a hallway that's not familiar to me, but the library where Claire, Jack, and I met Ron for drinks before dinner is the same. Ron isn't though, dressed down in a way I would never have seen if I hadn't gotten involved with Jack.

Ron turns from the window wearing black lounging pants, a t-shirt, and a thin cardigan. His face is lined with wrinkles, and his eyes are sad. They brighten for a moment when I step into the room, but the second Irene disappears and slides the two wooden doors closed, the spark dies.

"Emma. Is Jack okay?"

"As far as I know," I say cautiously. "He was this morning, at least."

He nods. "More baby-making last night, I presume."

I stand and blink. Ron might be my future child's grandfather, but I won't discuss my sex life with my boss.

"Right, right. Sit down. I don't suppose you want a drink."

"No, but thank you."

"Becky called me earlier this afternoon, distraught. She told me about your request to trade places with Nancy. You don't want to work under Jack anymore."

I slide onto a leather couch, and Ron sits across from me, setting a lowball glass onto the coffee table between us.

"This is a little more complicated than I thought it would be, Mr. Durand."

He meets my eyes when I call him that. Jack and I aren't together. I'm not his daughter-in-law and I won't ever be.

"All Jack's life, and Claire's too, I told them marriage was a fool's game. That a piece of paper couldn't make anyone stay, and that they should learn to find happiness alone. Claire couldn't accept that. Maybe it's the way girls are brought up, shoving a baby doll into their arms when they're still babies themselves. Dollhouses and little strollers, bottles filled with fake milk. Girls are taught to want weddings and white picket fences. After each divorce, I said, 'I told you so,' and after her second, she told me she'd never marry again. That's not a point of pride with me, Emma. I don't like seeing my children hurt more than they already are."

"Marriage is more than a piece of paper. That's why Jack struggles. When we were talking about his party and I told him Veronica expected a proposal, I pointed out if it didn't work, he could divorce her, but he doesn't want to begin a marriage already thinking about the end. I'm sure you didn't marry Elizabeth thinking about the end, either. Marriage is work. It involves understanding, flexibility, compromise, and you have to trust each other. Jack doesn't think he'll find a woman who will sign up for the long haul because he believes his mother bailed when times were tough. You led him to that conclusion, but that's not what happened, is it?"

"You know a lot about my family." He scowls.

I try to smile and relax. Jack's dad won't hurt me, but he has all the power in the world to do so. "You said I was sharp. At the time it sounded like an insult, and it still does."

"Thinking for yourself is never an insult. You knew enough to stop listening to rumors and come straight to the source. I admire your courage and intelligence in doing that. I loved Elizabeth. She was going to school to be a nurse and she had the kindness and compassion to be a good one. From the second I met her, I couldn't get her out of my mind. Much like you were with Jack. I remember the morning that airhead from HR introduced you to him. I watched you fall right then and there, and you never climbed out."

"Maybe that was my mistake," I whisper.

"Maybe it was. I didn't have a choice with Bess. I couldn't leave her side. But you do stupid things when you're in love." He glances at me. "As I'm sure you know. Stupid things that you can't compensate for, no matter how hard you try. You apologize, grovel, beg, plead, promise to do anything, and it's not enough. What you did can't be erased. Bess had every right to leave me, and in retaliation, I kept the kids from her. It's my fault Bess left. It's my fault Jack and Claire grew up without her, and I did the only thing I could. I raised them to avoid marriage so they couldn't make the same mistakes I did and end up alone."

"They are alone, Mr. Durand. Claire's miserable and is still in love with her first husband. Jack wants a family so badly he's willing to buy a baby. You need to tell them what really happened and be brave enough to realize they might hate you for what you did."

"You'd defend me, wouldn't you, Emma? To Jack? For your child's sake?"

I reach over and grip his hand. "Jack and I aren't going to end up together. You know that, don't you? He'll never trust me to give him my life as a wife and a mother to our children.

I asked for the transfer because I like working at Variant, but I need to find a new job and I don't want to work with Jack while I do. I should have cut ties and quit a long time ago. Everyone told me to, but you don't listen when you're in love."

"No, you certainly don't. What about the contract?"

"I'll honor it if I'm pregnant, and I hope you'll see to it she's raised in a loving family. If I'm not, I'd rather not see Jack again. I have to move on. I love him so much, but I'm not enough." I wipe the tears off my cheeks. "I gave him three years of my life. I can't give him anymore."

"I'll do what I can, Emma, but there's so much damage done that I'm afraid nothing can fix it. You have my absolute promise that if you go through with that contract, I will do whatever I can to ensure that baby has a bright future, and if you change your mind, I'll give you the resources you need to fight it in court, if it comes to that. I don't agree with it, and I'll tell the judge that, too."

I stand, lean over, and kiss his cheek. "Thank you. I miss my own father very much. He died a few years ago, and it would have been nice to be part of your family. Thank you for approving the transfer. The office will be uncomfortable until I can leave, but it's what I need right now."

"I understand. I didn't like that Chapman woman, but I would have been honored if you'd ended up my daughter-in-law. You have smarts and spunk. Can you find your way out?"

"Yeah. See you in the morning."

"Goodnight, Emma."

I walk back through the house the way I came, but I don't bump into Irene. I pause on their little landing and look over their yard. This house would have been a lovely place to grow up, but it's not where home is, it's who you build your life with that counts. I don't know what Ron did to Elizabeth that she left and refused to come back after an apology, and it's probably better I don't.

I drive home, my heart heavy. If I had any doubts I was doing the right thing, after Ron's confession, I know I am now. Ron will tell Jack and Claire what he did, and not only will they not have a mother, but they'll feel like they don't have a father, either.

Some things you can't forgive.

I said I would honor the contract, but if Jack forces me and walks away with our baby, that will be one of them.

CHAPTER NINETEEN

Jack

As I wake, I search for her, my hand smoothing over the cool sheets, but I know she's not here. I've relived Emma dodging my kiss a million times, and I'm scared of what I'm going to find at the office today. Dad texted me last night saying we needed to talk this evening, and the fact he didn't call to get whatever it is off his mind before bed only adds to my suspicions it's about Emma.

Bright and early Heath texts me, asking if we're running after work. I respond with a *yes*, drop my cell onto the nightstand, and cover my head with a pillow. I haven't been awake for ten minutes and my day is already shit.

Coffee, shower, dress for work. Every movement drags me down. It didn't used to be like this. When my relationship with my father wasn't strained, when I didn't mind dating Veronica, when Emma was simply my PA, not a woman I'm in love with.

Christ, who am I kidding? I've always had a thing for the way she dresses, her glittery blue eyes, her soft hair brushing my hand if we were working together and I sat too close. No, not too close. Just right. Believing she was with Clark wasn't an excuse not to do anything about how I felt about her. They've always looked cozier than friends, and if you have a high-profile gig like Clark, I don't blame him for keeping his personal business off the gossip sites. They've never admitted to a relationship, but they've never denied one, either. I kept my distance, and then I started dating Veronica and it seemed a moot point. But I just had to go and carry Emma out of the Bridgeport Hotel and everyone saw my feelings for her in that goddamned picture.

You think I didn't know people were talking about it? I knew, and I knew what we looked like. I'm not a heartless asshole. I printed it, and I'll never admit that again.

Veronica wasn't completely accurate when she accused me of trapping Emma in a contract because I don't have the guts to admit how I feel and ask her if she'd, fuck, I don't know. Date me? Marry me? I don't even know if she *likes* me. I do want children—I didn't make that up—but I don't want them with anyone but Emma.

I tap my foot all the way to the office, the driver from the car service looking nervously into his rearview mirror, concerned to the point he almost rear-ends someone at a red light.

Relieved I arrive at the Variant building in one piece, I jump out at the corner and dodge pedestrians on their way to work, my briefcase gripped tightly in my hand, my tie fluttering in the spring breeze.

I wonder what Clark and Emma did at her mother's? Did he fall asleep on her couch?

Christ. I have to stop thinking Emma rescinding her invitation was a slight. It wasn't a slight. It was practical. There's no reason on God's green earth why I need to meet her mother. I haven't thought about it once in the three years she's worked for me. I can stop thinking about it now.

I walk through security and say good morning to the guard (I don't care about the Yankees game yesterday afternoon) as he x-rays the contents of my briefcase.

Impatiently, I run for the elevator and cram myself into a full one. I couldn't care less about the dirty looks. I own this fucking building.

My heart starts to pound, sweats slides down my back, and I feel like I'm having a full-blown panic attack by the time I reach my office. I don't see Emma, and all the nervous energy I carried all morning multiplies. I drop my suitcase onto my desk and wake up my computer. There isn't the usual cup of coffee sitting by my keyboard.

I rush into the hallway.

Nancy slides behind Emma's desk, and I barely keep myself from falling to my knees. "What are you doing?" I snap.

Her eyes widen. "Emma and I traded places for the time being. Mr. Durand, your father, approved it. I read the email this morning in the taxi on the way here. I'm not familiar with how Emma handles your workload, but I assume she empties your email. Would you like me to do that, or do you have something else you need me to do instead?"

"Don't touch anything," I say.

Her hands sit limply in her lap.

Emma's settling in at Nancy's desk, my father's office door wide open. He's sitting behind his computer but not jabbing at his keyboard looking his usual sour and unhappy self, instead, he's staring forlornly out the window as if the clouds can solve all of his problems.

"What do you think you're doing?" I snarl, grabbing her arm and hauling her to her feet.

Her irises are like deep blue pools, and I fall in. My fingers sink into her soft skin, and tears fill her eyes. There's nothing I want to do more than pull her close and beg her to stay with me for the rest of her life.

"I can't keep doing this. I can't. I thought I could. I thought I was strong enough, but I'm not." Her breath shudders with a sob. "I'll honor the contract if I'm pregnant, but if I'm not, I can't try again. It hurts too much."

My father walks to his office door and leans against the doorjamb watching us.

"I don't understand. You were fine with it before," I say, my heart sinking.

"I was never fine with it, Jack." A tear drips down her cheek.

I want to wipe it away, tell her not to cry, that I'll fix anything if she would only ask, but I don't know what there is to fix. "Then why did you say you would? Why did you sign the contract?"

She steps closer, brushes her fingers over my tie. "Because I love you. I've been in love with you since the day we met. Do you remember what you said to me? The morning I was assigned to be your PA?"

I shake my head, thrown off. Out of anything she could have said to me, that she loves me wouldn't have crossed my mind, even if I admitted it's what I wanted to hear.

"'I drink my coffee black.'" She laughs a little. "That's all you said and you walked away and slammed your office door in my face. I told Mia and Haisley and they thought I was crazy, but they didn't see your eyes, the shape of your lips, the whiskers along your jaw, the crisp cut of your suit. I fell hard that day, and I thought, when you offered me that deal, if we spent time together, if we—" Her gaze flicks to my father who is still standing there watching us— "made love, that I could get you to fall in love with me too."

"That's why you wanted to go to Heath and Zoey's," I say, suddenly understanding. "And dinner at Dad's. It wasn't so I could see that I would need help raising our daughter alone. You wanted to spend time with me. Emma, why didn't you say something?"

She tries to smile. "What good would it have done? Sitting in Heath and Zoey's backyard with your arms wrapped around me, that was the happiest I've ever been. We felt like a couple. For three years, it's all I ever wanted."

Tears run in rivers down her cheeks, but I'm frozen, remembering the feel of her body in my lap, her soft laughter. We sat surrounded by friends near the warm glow of the fire. It was the happiest I'd ever been, too.

"When you started dating Veronica, I told myself it was okay. For two years I loved you knowing that one day you would ask her to marry you. The afternoon she told me to enter an appointment with a jeweler into your planner, I almost died. I couldn't watch you ask her, and you stepped onto the dais at your party . . ."

"You were drunk that night," I rasp.

"Because I couldn't," she chokes, and she tries again, "I couldn't, but then you didn't, and even though everyone said to forget you, to leave it alone, I thought I had a chance, only I didn't, and I never will. I'll never be enough. I could promise you my heart, body, and soul for all of eternity, and it would never be enough because you don't love me back."

"Emma—" I want to say yes, I do, I love you too, but my Dad is there and forty-one years of knowing that a marriage certificate doesn't mean forever.

"It's okay. You can't force someone to love you. It's what Raff was trying to get me to see all along. You don't love me, you've never been interested in me that way, and it's my fault I'm in this mess. I can't give you a baby—you'll be taking my heart and my future with her if I do." She lifts her chin. "I'll honor the contract—you'll sue me if I don't, and I know that, too—but I can't keep trying if what we did this weekend didn't work. I'm sorry." She pulls her purse out of the bottom drawer of her desk. "I'm sorry, Mr. Durand. I need a sick day."

Emma doesn't wait for my father to respond, only darts around me and hurries down the hallway, her heels clicking a desperate staccato away from me. She disappears around the corner and a moment later the elevator dings, announcing its arrival on our floor.

"Did you know about this?" I ask my dad. "You approved the transfer."

"She told me she's going to quit, and she didn't want to be your PA while she looks for a different position. It's better if you let her go."

I nod. I might love her, but I can't give her what she needs to be happy.

Wait. Yes, I can. After what she told me, I can do the right thing.

"Don't forget I want to see you and Claire at the house tonight. I have a few things I need to say."

"About Mom?"

Dad doesn't respond, only frowns and silently closes the door leaving me standing by Nancy's desk alone in the hallway.

———

I can't look at Nancy sitting in Emma's place, and I tell her to go back to her own desk. She does with a sigh of relief. If Emma comes in to work tomorrow, I'll tell her we're friends, nothing has changed, and to do her job until her two weeks' notice is up. I can be an adult about this.

I'll have to be. I have three hundred emails in my inbox and don't know how to throw the ones I don't need into the trash.

For all the work I get done, I should have gone home with Emma. Well, not with her, but you know what I mean.

Five o'clock finally rolls around, and I make a quick getaway. Whenever Dad asks us to stop by the house, we usually meet about seven, and Claire will be her usual late self. That means I have more than enough time to run with Heath at the gym.

In the locker room, I quickly change out of my suit and into shorts and a tank top. The workout area is busy, but today people prefer the ellipticals and Heath's and my treadmills are free. I set up mine the way I like it, and annoyed, I fiddle with the TV attached to the display, wanting to turn off one of Clark's *Talk of the Town* commercials. I'm really not in the mood. Clark was telling Emma to stay away from me for an entirely different reason than what I would have guessed.

Heath hops onto the treadmill next to me and drops a bottle of water into the cupholder.

I don't give him time to set the incline. "Emma's in love with me," I announce like I'm a little kid bursting at the seams with news.

"Color me amazed," he says, rolling his eyes. "Everyone knew but you." He cuts me a glance. "How did you find out?"

"She told me. And what do you mean, everyone knew?"

"I do see Emma, sometimes, Jack, and I've never seen her as blissed out as when you were holding her at our party. It was pretty fucking evident." He punches up the incline and starts to jog as he ups the speed. "And what do *you* mean, she told you?"

"At work this morning. She's quitting, and I'm breaking our contract." That was the only thing I did today. Revising the contract giving her complete rights as our baby's mother if she's pregnant. I can't keep her baby after what she told me. The only condition is that she move to a different city. I can't live in Bridgeport with her knowing we'll never be together.

"Good. I hope that means you're going to marry her and have a family the right way."

"No. Nothing's changed." That's the whole gist of it, isn't it? It doesn't matter who loves whom. Nothing's changed.

Heath clenches his jaw, his feet violently pounding the tread. He runs for half a mile before he says, "You're an idiot, you know that? Can you at least admit you love her too? For my own satisfaction?"

"I love her, but I didn't understand what I was feeling until yesterday. She said she changed her mind and didn't want to introduce me to her mother. It hurt and that confused the hell out of me."

He laughs, incredulous. "What did you think she was going to say? 'Mom, this is Jack Durand. He's been fucking me all weekend to get me pregnant so he can buy the baby from me.' Classy. I told you this whole thing was a terrible idea."

"Well, it's over." I focus all my energy on the run. I try to fend off glimpses and impressions of lying in bed holding Emma . . . her quiet sighs, her warm kisses . . . but it doesn't work. By mile ten, I'm drenched in sweat, my legs aching as much as my heart.

We slow our machines and do a cool down. Heath's too angry to look at me, and he doesn't say anything until we're stretching. "Why does it have to be over? If you love her, tell her. You don't have to get married, you don't have to have babies. Enjoy spending time together and be grateful she hung in there until you pulled your head out of your ass."

I look away. I'm reflected in the mirrors that line the walls, and I resemble my father, tired and worn out. I resemble how

Claire looked at lunch, sad and at a loss as to how to keep living a life alone. "I can't."

"If that's how you really feel, I'm glad she's leaving Variant. I hope she meets a man who falls head over heels in love with her and treats her the way she deserves to be treated. You know what? I'm petty enough to say I wish she and Clark would get together after all, and that you have to watch him living the life with her you could have had if you weren't such a dick. I get your mother hurt you, but instead of taking it out on Emma, talk to a therapist and move past it. You're forty-five, one of the richest, most powerful men in the country, but you're still that little boy watching his mother ride away in a taxi. Grow the fuck up, Jack."

He heaves himself off the mat and trudges toward the locker room. Didn't ask if I wanted to go for a beer like we usually do after a run. Not only have I lost Emma, but eventually I'm going to lose Heath's friendship, too.

I won't have Emma. I won't have Heath and Zoey or their children in my life. I won't go to the latest hotspot and hang out with Veronica, Clark, and Haisley and Mia. My personal life is crumbling because I can't get past listening to my mother crying and my father kicking her out.

I *am* that lost little boy, and for just a second, I thought Emma could save me.

But she won't. She *can't.*

One day, she'll leave, too.

———

"Twice in one month, I don't know what I'm going to do with myself," Claire says, meeting me in the middle of the driveway.

I usually drive myself anywhere I want to go, but Claire always uses her car and driver. She says it's to keep the paparazzi from hounding her, but the more I get to know the adult she is, the more I realize she uses her driver as company. Someone, anyone, who will occupy the lonely space around her. I hug her to me and press my lips against the top of her head.

"Gross, stop it," she says, laughing. "You look like shit."

"Feel like it, too," I say, tangling my fingers with hers and leading her up the walk to the side door that confused Emma at dinner.

"What's wrong? Are you and Emma fighting? Didn't get enough over the weekend?"

"We broke the contract. If she's pregnant, she's keeping it."

She pauses in the hallway. "I don't understand."

"Honestly, Claire, I don't either. I'm too tired to deal with it all, okay?"

"Yeah, sure, but she loves you. Why would she back out?"

"Because she *does* love me and wants better for herself."

"I don't think that sounds the way you meant it to sound."

"It's exactly what I wanted to say. Hi, Irene." I greet my father's housekeeper who has a worried frown on her face. The day keeps getting better. "Is he in the library?"

"Not today. He's in the backyard."

"Christ, he's dying," Claire says, rushing from the kitchen toward the back of the house.

It's my turn to frown. "Has he been to the doctor?"

"You would know more on that front," she says, and I tip my head. Maybe I would. He would go during business hours, but he didn't leave the building today. "He requested drinks on the patio. I'll bring them out in a moment."

"Thank you."

I follow Claire at a much more leisurely pace.

Dad's walking the yard, and she's watching, mystified. "He's lost his mind," she murmurs.

Dad sees I've joined them. "Do you know you kids never had a swing set out here? No sandbox. When you were small, you didn't play out here at all," he says, his voice carrying over the rich green grass.

"The nanny would force us to walk to the park," I mumble to my sister.

"Because she wanted us to nap all afternoon," she mutters back.

"What does that matter now?" I ask.

He shuffles through the grass toward us. "It matters to this old man."

Irene chooses that moment to serve us margaritas on the rocks. The pitcher and glasses, their rims dipped in salt, shove a ball of fire down my throat. I fight back the heartache I would tear up over something so simple, so simply *summertime* because it's such a fucking normal thing we never, ever, did.

"I want to talk to you, and I know that after I say what I have to say, you won't want anything more to do with me. I've accepted that."

I meet Claire's eyes. "Dad."

His words scare me. I can't lose anyone else in my life.

Claire and I sit on the top step of the patio, and Dad paces the immaculate weed-free grass, his gaze never meeting ours.

"I met your mom in college. She was going to nursing school on one side of the campus to be an obstetric nurse, I was earning my business degree on the opposite side. I fell hard the second I met her, and it doesn't matter what happened between us, I love her as much now, this very second, as I did back then."

I clutch Claire's hand. I've waited for this day my entire life, but I don't want anything now but to get into my truck, drive to Emma's, carry her to bed, and block all this out.

"We married after graduation, and I started working at the company with your grandfather. He was raking in the big bucks by then, and the paparazzi were like flies over a carcass. I hired a private investigator turned bodyguard to protect your mother, and she accepted it as the life she would lead married to a Durand. Things were good. We had you, Jack, and Christ, when you came along, Claire, we were so happy. I didn't think it was possible to feel such joy. It was around that time the only abortion clinic in the state closed its doors. I didn't keep track of why, and I admit, I didn't care. Women's health issues weren't interesting to me. I was trying to help your grandfather build Variant, and I wasn't thinking about much else."

I nod. I'm not up to date on abortion laws, either. I couldn't tell you if there are abortion clinics in Minnesota.

"Your mother started disappearing. Sometimes in the middle of the night, sometimes asking for a raincheck if I asked her to have lunch with me. I didn't notice it at first. I was busy, and when I wasn't at work, I was playing with you kids. You're too young to remember, but back then on the evenings and weekends, we were that stereotypical young, happy family. That happiness started crumbling. She'd come home late after a shift or ask me to finish bath time for you kids, saying she had book club or wanted to meet a friend for drinks."

It's easy to assume my mother started cheating, but Dad's not angry, only sad, and Claire and I let him speak.

"I grew suspicious and ordered her bodyguard to report to me. I wish I could say it was because I was worried about her, because I cared about her safety, but you two have brains between your ears and you know me asking him to follow her wasn't out of the kindness of my heart." Dad steps up onto the patio and pulls a file from a chair I didn't see when I came outside. He slides out a grainy black and white photograph and hands it to Claire. I look at it, too.

"That's Mom?" I ask, though I know it is. Claire inherited every one of her features.

"It is. What do you see?"

She's leaning into a man who's kissing her cheek, tears streaming down both their faces, the wet glinting in the sunlight. They're outside, a shitty motel blurry in the background. At first glance, anyone would think they're in love, meeting for an affair, but I know love now that I've let myself fall in love with Emma, and what's in the man's embrace isn't love, isn't passion.

It's gratitude.

"He's thanking her for something," Claire says, drawing the same conclusion I did.

Dad points at her. "He was, and I couldn't see it through a cloud of anger and jealousy."

"What was he thanking her for?" she asks. "It was something serious for both of them to be crying."

He leans against the railing and rubs his eyes. "The clinic in Bridgeport closed, and illegal abortions grew in number. Women without financial means couldn't leave the state to seek services elsewhere. Your mother, along with a group of other nurses and an OB/GYN from their office, banded together and started treating those women who were hurt because they were desperate enough to go underground. She didn't tell me what she was doing. She didn't tell anyone. She didn't want to risk her own license, but she didn't want to risk the licenses of the other nurses and the doctor helping them."

"She helped saved this man's wife," Claire murmurs, trailing her finger over the photo.

"She was his daughter, and yes, your mother saved her life. I didn't find out until years later, but that day, I confronted her." His eyes meet mine. "That's the fight you heard, Jack. I accused her of cheating on me with him. She denied it. She tried to get me to understand, but she wouldn't tell me where she was disappearing. I didn't have evidence she wasn't cheating, and she didn't give me a real explanation. I didn't believe what little she told me, and I called a taxi and threw her out."

"You never heard from her again," I say.

He shakes his head. "A year later, a new clinic opened in Bridgeport. The number of underground abortions went down, and a reporter for the paper did an exposé detailing how many women died due to the lack of proper medical care. The article alluded that some of the medical staff at Bridgeport Mercy Hospital may have been illegally assisting women who were victims of botched basement abortions. I read the article and put two and two together. I found her and apologized. I wanted her back."

"But by then, she didn't want you, did she?" I say bitterly. I know the ending of the story. He doesn't have to say anymore.

"No. She didn't forgive me for not trusting her, for not having faith in our marriage. She asked me for a divorce. I was hurt, angry, and more than anything, I felt guilty I tore our marriage apart over something so . . . I destroyed our marriage for the same exact reason I married her. Because she was kind and generous. She cared about people and always wanted to do the right thing. In a rage, I gave her the divorce, but I told her she would never see her children again, and if she tried, I would report her and her nursing co-workers to the authorities."

"She gave us up to protect her friends." Claire's voice is flat.

"Yes, she did. I didn't give her a choice. She didn't want to lose her license, either. I didn't give her a penny in the divorce, and nursing was the only way she had to support herself. She told me I broke her heart twice. Once when I wouldn't believe her and again when I stole her children away from her. She knew she couldn't fight me and didn't try. I kept track of her, and a few months later she found a position in a small family practice and moved to a little town about two hours from here.

She retired and she still lives there. I never remarried. I didn't deserve to start over."

Calmly, Claire stands and holds out the photo. Dad only stares, and she drops it. It flutters to the patio planks, and she quietly steps into the house.

I sit, stunned. "All this time, I blamed Mom. I blamed her for not trying hard enough, for not fighting for her family. You never once spoke about why she left us, and the only thing I had all these years were my own nightmares."

"I was ashamed and I twisted what happened until I believed my own lies."

"But why now? Why come out and say it now?"

"Because of Emma. I don't want you to throw away what you could have with her because of what I did."

Angrily, I stand. "Claire's been married and divorced, *twice*, and you didn't bother to say anything then? The truth could have prevented her from leaving Roman. She loved him, and she still left him. She didn't believe he could love her if her own mother didn't. You could have stopped that, Dad. So, why now?"

He sighs. "I didn't want Claire to need my help, and I was too big of a coward to step up, be the father she needed me to be. I hoped to God you wouldn't fall in love. You never dated seriously, and when you were with that Chapman woman, I thought I was safe. I knew you didn't love her. If you had just married her, viewed marriage as a business partnership the way I was trying to get you to all along so you wouldn't get hurt, I would have left well enough alone. But, no. You had to come up with that crazy scheme to get Emma pregnant, and then you fell in love with her. Don't push her away because of the lies I let you believe."

"I shaped my entire life around Mom's sobs and denials, around watching her shaking in the backseat of that taxi, her hand pressed to the glass. She saw me. Did I ever tell you that? She saw me that day and waved goodbye. She knew she would never see me again, just like I knew, when I was only four fucking years old. Claire grew up without a mother because of you. I might have turned out okay if you'd been a father, but you left with her. Claire and I grew up without parents and no one cared. Poor little rich kids, no parents, but look at all their money." I step toward the patio doors. "You know, I can't even hate you. You've lived with what you did for forty years. Now all you are is a sad old man with nothing but three billion dollars behind his name."

"You'll end up like me if you don't change."

"Why should that bother you? It's what you've always wanted."

I leave him sitting there staring at the photo laying on the pristine white wood.

———

I don't have anywhere to go. At one time, I could have called Heath, but he'd have no sympathy for me now. God knows where Claire is. She could have booked the jet and is halfway to Paris. If she is, I wish she would have taken me with her. Veronica won't talk to me (not that I would to talk to her about this), and Emma is out of the question. She would have received the new contract this afternoon. I paid my attorney triple his fees for the turnaround and had it sent to her before five.

I gave up everything and promised her anything she needed ensuring she could raise our child the way children are meant to be raised.

I don't have anywhere I can go, so I go home, grab a beer out of the fridge, flip on the replay of a baseball game, and sit.

CHAPTER TWENTY

Emma

Do you know how humiliating it is to tell someone you love them, knowing they won't say it back? Knowing you're laying your heart and soul in front of them only so they can smash them into millions of pieces as if they weren't broken enough already?

All Jack saw me as is a woman who would sell him a baby, not a woman he would risk his heart for.

I lie in bed most of the day, having spent only a half an hour at the Variant offices. I was there long enough to speak to Nancy, bring Ron a cup of coffee (a habit I won't be able to stop no matter whom I work for), and boot up Nancy's computer.

After speaking with Ron, I knew breaking it off was for the best. I didn't have to hear the entire story, all the gory details, to know that Jack and Claire will never get over what Ron did. Ron tore his family apart and didn't put it back together. I won't be able to, either.

I avoid social media. Raff is too in-tune with my online

habits and would know if I'm home and not working. Then he would want to know why and ask to come over, but he has his hands full and I don't want to be a burden. I wouldn't be in this situation at all if I would have found a new job after Jack and Veronica started dating.

Around three o'clock, and after a bucket of tears have soaked into my pillow, the doorbell rings. I want it to be Jack, but I have to stop wishing for that. It will never be Jack. Mia and Haisley, maybe. Raff, despite my best efforts to keep him from knowing I left work sick.

A man dressed in a local courier service uniform is standing on my stoop holding a manila envelope.

"Can I help you?" I ask through the crack between the door and the doorjamb. I'm wearing a robe and a flimsy nightgown under it.

"I have a delivery for Emma Cox."

"That's me."

"Sign here, please."

He offers me a tablet and stylus, and propping the door open with my foot, I scrawl my name onto the scratched screen. "Thank you," he says, pressing a button to accept my signature and passing the envelope to me. "Have a nice day."

"Thanks. You, too."

The name of Jack's attorney glares at me from the upper left corner, and my name and address are printed on a sticker pressed to the center of the envelope.

I don't want to open it. Maybe Jack terminated my employment and this is my severance package. I want to leave Variant on my own terms, and if he pushes me out . . . I don't know if I can live through him hurting me any more than he already has.

Taking a deep, fortifying breath, I grab a butter knife, slice it through the glue, and pull out two pieces of paper.

I skim the cover letter. "I wish you the best, I'm sorry I

thought this would work . . ." I push it aside. I don't want any more of his apologies. I want him to *do something*. I want him to love me, dammit.

He does love me. I felt it when we made love, I felt it when we were at Heath and Zoey's. I even felt it at his dad's. Everything he's done to me, to us, has been out of fear, but there is nothing I can do that I haven't tried. I'm out of options.

The second piece of paper is a new contract and nothing I have to sign. "All rights belong to you . . . financially provided for . . . residence in another city . . ." He's granting me full custody of the baby if I'm pregnant. Tears fill my eyes. He's giving me full parental rights on the contingency I relocate. Now he knows how difficult it would be to live near the people you love most in the world and not be able to hug them, kiss them. Not be able to go home to them after a long day.

He'd be living his mother's life.

I shower and eat a small dinner.

Maybe if I hang in there, he'll admit he loves me and wants a life with me. I've already given him three years. I *did* build a foundation. I was waiting for Jack and building a future with the only man I've ever loved. We need to talk—I'm not going to cut him out of his child's life. That would hurt him more than losing me, and I would give him custody before I did that. He's been hurt enough by the people who say they love him.

The next morning I put on my prettiest dress (I slip on a blazer to look professional), brush my hair until it shines, and carefully apply my makeup.

Tentatively, I step onto the executive floor, but Jack isn't here. That's not new—I always arrive at the office first. I set a cup of steaming hot coffee on his desk, and sitting at mine, open his email inbox. Yesterday, Nancy messaged me in a tizzy saying Jack told her to go back to her own desk, and she didn't want me upset. I don't mind—I didn't want to share Jack with her anyway—and I prepared to clean up a lot of damage my absence created. He needs me in more than just his personal life. I wouldn't mind helping Jack run Variant after Ron retires.

The minutes tick by and I wait for Jack to come in, each second feeling like a day. His coffee grows cold, and at ten to ten, Ron shuffles down the hallway toward my desk.

"Jack's not here yet," I say, not knowing if he told his father he would be late.

"He's not coming in today, or this week for that matter." Ron stops at my desk.

"You talked to him. To Claire, too?"

Ron nods, his skin sagging and grey.

"It didn't go well."

"It was what I expected, and what you expected, too, I imagine. No one can hold on to a forty-year-old secret and not expect some kind of repercussion."

"Not a secret like that," I point out.

"No, not a secret like that." He pauses. "We have a meeting in ten minutes. Would you be interested in sitting in on Jack's behalf? You know about the Lippman acquisition?"

I wince. "Some. Jack stayed late to work on it last week, but he was avoiding me and didn't include me."

"You know enough to listen and give me your opinion afterward. Grab your things. I'll see you in the conference room in five minutes. Don't worry about coffee. Nancy will handle it."

"Why? Why do you want me there?"

"I don't have many years left, Emma. I want this company settled and in good hands before I die. Claire was never interested, and Jack can't do it alone. Now, my son and his wife . . ."

My heart stutters. "You think there's hope for us? Even after you told him the truth? Claire said he was a lost cause, and that was before you told them what really happened with Elizabeth."

"It doesn't matter what I think, does it?"

I sit back, surprised. Jack's probably so angry at Ron he won't want to speak to his father ever again. Ron's blessing won't go anywhere with Jack. "No, I guess not." It doesn't matter what anyone thinks. It's what Jack and I do, and that's between us.

"If you want to attend, there will be a place for you at the table."

Ron walks away, and I waste no time gathering my tablet and stylus and the files off Jack's desk.

The only way I'll prove to Jack that I'm not going anywhere is by not going anywhere.

———

Ron involves me for the rest of the week. I miss Jack, and I hate looking at his empty office. By Friday afternoon, I'm concerned. I asked Raff if anyone had seen Jack or Claire around Bridgeport, and even Claire has disappeared off the society pages. On Mondays, Wednesdays, and Fridays, some junior paparazzo always snaps a picture of Heath and Jack walking the ten feet from their gym to the Irish pub next door thinking he was getting the chance of a lifetime, not knowing it's their regular routine after work. Those pictures have dried up, too, and I would hate to hear Heath stopped talking to Jack in my defense. I hope they stopped running together because Jack is hiding, not because Heath's fed up with Jack's stubbornness.

It's nearly time to go home for the day and I knock on Ron's open door and peek my head inside his office. "I'm going to check on him. He's had enough time to think about things."

Ron looks away from his computer. Without Jack coming into the office, Ron's been arriving early and staying late. "I would be in your debt if you did, Emma. He won't answer my calls or return my texts. Will you let me know how he is? If you see him."

"Yes, I will. Thank you for this week."

He nods. "You do good work. Thanks for the time you put in on the Lippman acquisition."

"You're welcome."

The intimidation I used to feel talking to him is gone. Ron might be rich, but his money can't fix what he did to his family. It's sad to think that on my salary with my meagre nest egg, I have more in life than Ronald Durand, one of the wealthiest men in the country. I have family and friends who love and care about me, and that's worth more than any account balance.

I don't stop at home to change. If I did, it would be too tempting not to go. Jack will be livid I'm sticking my nose into his business. I'm not scared . . . well, maybe a little, but the worst he can do is not let me up to the penthouse. If he does, it means he wants to see me, and we can spend the weekend talking—after he's done yelling at me.

I have to park in a parking ramp a few blocks away from his building. I've never been there but for the night of his birthday party, and the entrance of the luxury highrise resembles the Bridgeport Hotel's lobby. The marble floor gleams, beautiful furniture is arranged in small conversational areas, and an elegant chandelier hangs from the vaulted ceiling. There's even a check-in desk, and a man with beady eyes glares at me until I approach. "I'm here to see Mr. Durand."

It's strange to call him that—I'll always think of Jack's dad. After Jack told me how he liked his coffee, he apologized for being short with me and said he preferred to go by Jack, and only *jackass* when the situation called for it. I knew then that we would get along, and he's only been a jackass a handful of times since I started as his PA and fewer times than that I've had to call him on it.

"What is your name, please?"

"Emma Cox."

He opens a leather-bound notebook and runs his finger down a printed page. "You're on his list of visitors, Miss Cox."

I blink. "I am?"

"Yes. He added your name two weeks ago."

About the time I said I would surrogate.

"There's no reason for me to call ahead." The expression on his face thaws. "Do you know the way?"

"No, I'm sorry, I don't." I can't say I was paying attention when Jack carried me in from the limo.

"The elevators are to the rear of the building. Press P—" He looks at me for affirmation I understand P means penthouse— "and enter the code 1020 into the keypad. It will give you access to Mr. Durand's floor."

"Okay," I say faintly. October twentieth is my birthday.

The ride to the top lasts forever, despite no one riding in the car with me and there are no extra stops. The doors glide open revealing a huge entryway, black and white marble gleaming on the floor. I step farther inside, curiously looking around. Flashes from the night Jack carried me here flicker as I see everything again in the light.

The living room is a mess, clothes everywhere, unread newspapers, dirty coffee cups. He hasn't let a cleaning service in here, and no one has touched the kitchen. The sink is piled high with crusted dishes, and though there are coffee cups around, he hasn't used his coffeemaker in some time, if the grey film congealed on what's left in the current carafe is anything to go by.

Kicking off my heels, I call, "Jack?" but he doesn't answer.

The man at the front desk would have told me if he wasn't here, and I walk down a long, carpeted hallway, peering into each room until I reach the master suite at the end of the hall.

Though it's too early for bed, he's lying in a heap of rumpled sheets, his t-shirt and shorts twisted around his body, his sexy scruff resembling more of a beard, and his hair flopping over his forehead. He's sleeping, and he looks exhausted. I pad over to him, but I don't touch. I don't want to disturb him if he's finally able to get some sleep. His phone is laying on the nightstand next to an empty box of tissues. I hope the box is empty because it's been sitting there for a long time and not because he's been crying. I couldn't bear to see him cry.

Silently, I pick up his phone. He's missed (or ignored) over a hundred text messages and as many phone calls. My poor baby, hiding from the world. I give in and caress his cheek. I love him so much, I would do anything to take away his pain.

He stirs, and I drop my hand. I drift back into the living room and begin to clean up the large space. I gather old newspapers into a pile, toss his clothes into another. I set the grimy coffee mugs into the sink and fill the other side with soapy water. Something smells. The garbage will have to go out, but I don't know how he does that from here. I collect mine in a bin and wheel it to the curb on Friday mornings. I don't think Jack has ever done that in his life and couldn't regardless.

I wash his dishes and put them in the strainer to dry. I don't know where anything goes and don't want to invade his privacy. I scrub his coffee carafe with the hottest water I can stand, and using a cleaning spray I find under the sink, wipe the counters down. I put on a fresh pot of coffee, the grounds easy to find in the fridge, and I search for a vacuum cleaner. I find one in a linen closet in the hallway. Hoping it doesn't bother him, I run it over the carpet and pick up a week's worth of dust and crumbs.

His living room and kitchen look a lot better, and I carry all his dirty clothes to his bedroom. He must have a hamper somewhere, and a washing machine and dryer for that matter, but he didn't invite me here, and I don't want to press my luck. He may not appreciate me washing his dirty pajamas.

I dump them in front of his walk-in closet. He can figure out what to do with them later.

The enticing scent of dark roast wafts from the kitchen down the hallway, and maybe if I wake him now with the promise of some fresh coffee in a clean mug, he won't be mad.

I sit on the edge of the bed and scrub my fingers over his jaw. "Hey."

His eyes blink open. "Emma?"

"Or someone who looks exactly like me," I tease. "Are you okay?"

"What are you doing here?" He rubs at his face and props himself up onto an elbow.

"I was worried about you, and by the looks of it, I had every right to be. Have you gone anywhere since you talked with your dad?"

He drops onto his pillow and stares at the ceiling. "No."

"It was that bad?"

Jack meets my eyes, and he wiggles over, inviting me to lie next to him. I do, and we share his pillow.

"Yeah. Yeah, it was."

"I'm sorry."

"Me, too." He pauses. "What you said, at the office on Monday. You meant it?"

I scoot closer until our noses are almost touching. After not seeing him for a week, it's like a dream lying in his bed with him, even more so than when we made love at my apartment. There's an intimacy between us that wasn't present before. We're talking, and we're both listening. "Yeah, I did. I wouldn't have said it if I didn't mean it."

He blows out a breath, and I try not to wince. He needs to brush his teeth. "Did you get the new contract?"

"Yeah, but Jack, can't we figure this out? Why does there have to be a contract? Why can't you admit you love me too? You do, don't you? All of this wasn't for nothing."

His eyes soften, and that scares me more than if he would have gotten mad, spitting denial like a volcano spews lava and ash. "Is that what you want to hear? That I love you? What would you do with it, Emma? What would you do if I said, yes, I love you too, that I have for a long time and didn't want to admit it? That I never wanted to be in a relationship with anyone who mattered after watching my mom leave Claire and me behind? What would it change if you knew?" He brushes my cheek with his fingertips.

I capture his wrist and kiss his fingers. "It would change everything for me. I thought you loved Veronica enough to ask her to marry you, and you don't understand how devastating that was for me. She was going to have everything I ever wanted. If you could tell me, these three years I've waited for you would be worth it. I love you, and all I've ever wanted is for you to love me back."

"Emma," he whispers. "What have you waited for? You haven't waited for the words, you've waited for the actions behind them, and those actions are something that I can never give you. You want to get married and have babies, and you deserve those things, with a man who's not afraid to give them to you. If we were together, I would always be waiting for the day you leave me, and I can't live my life that way."

Every word that comes out of his mouth drops me lower. I thought if he could admit he loved me, it would tear down the wall he's built around himself, but it won't. Hearing him say he loves me but won't do anything about it is worse than hearing him deny it. With a denial, I could pretend to walk away unscathed, but now that I know, now that he's admitted it, he's trapped me in a life of waiting for him. I'll grow old, like Ron and Elizabeth, alone, waiting for something that will never happen.

"Then what do you want?" I ask, my voice steady. I won't cry until I leave.

A ghost of a smile plays with his mouth. "We can be friends. I've been out of the office all week and I bet Dad's been primping you, taking advantage of the time to do it behind my back. We can work together. We've worked together for the past three years, and if you want to stay with Variant, another thirty. If you're pregnant—"

"We'll raise her together—"

Jack opens his mouth to protest.

"—but separately, like any unmarried parents would. We'll split her fifty/fifty down the middle, and it will have to be enough because we were the idiots who created the situation in the first place."

"Emma, I don't want—"

"I don't care what you want and what you don't." I sit up. "You were the dummy who came up with the bright idea to ask me rather than go to an agency like a smart person would, and I was the fool who said yes thinking I could turn the surrogacy into something more. It won't ever be more, and that's both our faults. Our child won't pay for your stupidity or my silly dreams."

His eyes harden, and he sits up, too, his shirt wrinkled and stained with sweat. "They weren't silly, but I can't give you what you want."

"No, you can't, and for as many people who told me that, I should have listened. You should have married Veronica. You both could have gotten what you wanted. Why didn't you?"

"I don't want to get married, and after what Dad told me, after what he told me he did, I will never put myself in a position like that."

"A position like what?"

"Where I love someone so desperately, that I . . ."

I wait for him to finish, but he doesn't.

"I'm glad you were able to avoid it because I sure as hell haven't. I'm sorry, Jack. I'm sorry you didn't deal with your childhood trauma, and I'm sorry that I'll be the one to suffer." I lean over the bed and press my lips to his, his scruff scratching at my skin. "I'm sorry I ever loved you. I won't work at Variant with you. I should have done this a long time ago. I quit."

I do what I should have done the second I knew I fell in love with Jack Durand.

I slip on my heels and walk out of his life.

CHAPTER TWENTY-ONE

Jack

I stumble into the hallway as the elevator doors bump shut. She didn't see me, didn't see my chest heaving, my hands clenched into fists at my sides. She didn't see the beggar she turned me into when she kissed me goodbye.

The scent of my favorite dark roast clears the angry, desperate haze from my eyes. She cleaned my kitchen, straightened and vacuumed the living room, and put on fresh coffee. She checked on me when no one else did. She knows how to show someone she loves them. She will find someone she loves, and someone who will show her in return.

I pour a cup of coffee in a mug from the strainer and carry it with me to the shower. I can't live in limbo anymore. I can't live like maybe one day Emma and I will have a life. Maybe we could have before Dad told me what really happened. Maybe we could have if I had been left with the impression it was Mom's fault their marriage fell apart, but it was Dad's weakness and that same weakness is inside me.

I shower and drink another cup of coffee. I don't feel as foggy as I have all week, and I dress in jeans and a t-shirt. I don't have plans to go out, but there's something I have to do. I drive to Dad's. I don't bother to call ahead. Unless there's a fundraiser or a dinner for work, he stays home, and there's nothing like that scheduled for tonight.

I park in the driveway and let myself in. If Claire thought it was amazing to visit Dad twice in a month, she'd have a heart attack at three times, all three in the same two weeks no less. She'll never come back to this house. She'll never speak to our father again, and I'll say goodbye on her behalf.

He's sitting in the library in his favorite chair, and without saying a word, I sit on the leather couch across from him.

Scowling, he says, "Come to bitch me out? Tell me you don't want to work with me anymore? Don't consider me your father? I would deserve all those things, so say what you need to say." He's tired. Revealing the dark secret he's carried hasn't given him peace, and some, like my sister, would argue he doesn't deserve it.

Maybe he doesn't.

Maybe no one does.

"No. I've done a lot of thinking this past week."

"I'll retire and leave Variant to you and Emma," he says. "Whether you hate me or not, you won't want to work with me, and I should have retired a long time ago."

Angrily, I shake my head. "That's not gonna fly. I talked to Emma today, and she quit. If you retire, we'll need to promote from within. I've been stupid about a lot of things lately, but I won't try to run Variant alone."

Dad rears back, his lips parting in surprise. "Jack—"

"I can't give her what she wants."

"If this is because of what I did to your mother—"

"Of course it is." I stand, walk to the bar, and pour a drink. I haven't been drinking as much as you'd think. I've only laid in bed, turning over in my mind what I would have done had I been my father all those years ago. "But not in the way you think."

Dad twists in his chair watching me. I stare outside into the yard, but I can feel his gaze boring through my back. Maybe he has hope we can repair our relationship, or at the very least, I can understand why he did what he did and if not forgive him, accept it.

I lean against the window. "Ever since Emma started working for me, I've hated Rafferty Clark. I always thought it was because he liked to write shit about me, until one night we were at a fundraiser. This was, I don't know, six months after Emma started working for us. She'd gotten under my skin, you know? Coffee on my desk, wouldn't back down if I was in a mood. Always looking so damned good in those swishy skirts she likes to wear. And her eyes, I can't describe what it's like looking into her eyes. There's nothing like it. I brushed all that aside. She was my PA, but I made excuses to spend time with her. Inviting her down to The Menagerie for an extra hour of work. Asking her to stay at the office through the weekends. Then Veronica and I started dating, and it was almost a relief. Emma faded a little bit, and I could breathe. But it was at a fundraiser, and they were there. Clark had his arm around her, and he was whispering into her ear. She was laughing, and I have never, ever, hated anyone with such a passion as I hated Clark that night."

I've never told anyone that, not even Heath.

"She's full of fire, determination, and grit. She reminds me a lot of your mother," Dad says, and if he was hoping to encourage me to go after her, it's exactly the wrong thing to say.

"I started sleeping with Veronica, hoping to get the need for Emma out of my mind, but I should have broken it off. I was only using her, and after the party, she called me out on it fast enough. Emma signed the contract, but when she spent time with Clark, it ate at me. After we, you know, for the first time . . ." I scratch my neck. Dad and I aren't close, and we sure as hell aren't talking about me fucking Emma to make a baby. "All I could think about was him being with her that way, and I hurt her, Dad. I marked her, and that's when I knew how serious this all was. I hurt her because I was jealous."

"There are a lot of ways to hurt someone," he says calmly, studying me.

"Yeah, there are." I sip my drink, remembering the feel of Emma's pulse under my palm, the bruises she had to hide with a scarf. "I've thought a lot about it, and I don't hate you. Maybe I would have if you had confessed before I met Emma, but I don't now. Not now that I know how it feels to be in love with someone so completely. If I'd been in your shoes, married to the love of my life, kids at home, and Emma started disappearing like that, no explanations, I would have done the same thing. I can't hate you for doing what I would have done too. I can't be with her feeling the that way. I will always be waiting for her to leave me."

"Your mother didn't leave me. If I would have trusted her, accepted she wasn't cheating on her word alone, I would have said, 'Okay, I love you. Tell me when you're ready.' It wasn't long after that everything came out. But I didn't, and that's been on me for forty years."

"You went back for her. She wouldn't come home."

Dad sighs. "Jack. When you grabbed Emma, what did she do? She didn't sit there whimpering like a scared little kid. She told you to back off and to fuck off, didn't she?"

I scoff, but I smile. "Yeah, she did. But she kissed me first."

"She understood where that anger came from. Your mother understood it too, but she didn't want anything to do with me because of it. She didn't let me bully her, and as much as I hated her for it, I respected her. Maybe not everyone would agree with what she did—relationships will always need compromise and you kids suffered—but I do. It took a lot for me to get there, but I do. You think about Emma leaving, and you think about her running off with another man, maybe even Rafferty Clark. But she could die. A car accident. An illness. Will you stand over her grave hating her for something she couldn't stop? Your mother left because I didn't give her a choice. I would rather you hate me and go after Emma than sit here and agree with me and grow old alone."

"I thought I had proof, too," I say, referring to the photo Mom's bodyguard gave to Dad. "They're always together and he sleeps at her apartment."

"Then maybe it's better that she quit and you let her go. She's not going to live on the defensive for the rest of her life dreading what you'll accuse her of next. It's why your mother didn't come back. She wasn't going to listen to me accuse her of cheating every time she went out with her friends, and the bodyguard excuse would have only carried me so far before she got tired of being watched. I loved your mother, Jack, and I didn't deserve her."

Dad sags into the chair's cushion.

I still empathize, even if our situations are different. If I apologized to Emma today, tonight, and asked her to marry me, I think she would say yes, but we'd start building on a foundation of mistrust and if I couldn't control my jealousy, our relationship, our marriage, would wither and die.

"If she had come back home, would you have? Watched her?" I ask, carrying the decanter to the coffee table and adding an inch to my father's empty glass.

"I don't know. I'd lived without her for a year by that point, missing her so much but at the same time, hating her just as much. Maybe I would have. Maybe knowing the truth and having her back wouldn't have been enough for me to put those jealousies aside. I do know with the way I was feeling, we wouldn't have lasted even if she had forgiven me. You have to believe that when a woman loves you, you deserve that love, and after what I did, I knew I didn't. You grew up to be good man, Jack. I'm proud of you, and any woman would be lucky to have you."

"Maybe." I pause. "Claire will never forgive you." I sit on the edge of the cushion and swirl the scotch around my glass. "Even if our situations aren't similar, I can relate to what you were feeling. Claire won't."

"It's what I expected, and you were right when you said I should have told you sooner. I should have told you when you were kids. After the anger and resentment faded and I could accept the blame. I should have given your mother access to you, but as time went by, it was harder and harder for me to admit what I'd done. You grew into adults and didn't ask about her, and I thought maybe I wouldn't have to. It's too late for Claire, but not for you. If you learn anything from this, it's that right now, you're showing Emma the kind of person you are under the suits and the money. Once you teach her that, you won't be able to change her mind. Do you understand what I'm saying?"

"You showed Mom the kind of person you really were, and she didn't want you after that."

"No, she didn't." He chuckles, but there's no humor in the sound. "I always told her how smart she was. Bit me in the ass."

I heave to my feet. "I should go."

Dad follows me to the laundry room, and we stop near the door. "Thank you for talking with me. I hope you find what you need with Emma. If that's not a relationship with her, then friendship. I don't want her to quit. She worked with me on the

Lippman acquisition all week. She's a valuable asset to the company."

"It's not up to me. She might stay if she knows she won't have to see me or work with me, but that's setting the office up in a way that won't be sustainable long-term."

"Then you're not going to try to fix it." It's not a question.

"People don't change. What I am under the suits and the money is what I am. If you're serious about retiring, on Monday we'll start looking for promotion candidates. I know Emma well enough to guess she won't leave without notice, and she'll let HR know I need a new PA. She's smart, too, smart enough to walk away from me. Okay, Dad?"

He grips my hand in a strong handshake. "As long as you're making the choice for you and not because of my mistakes."

"No. I'm making the choice because of mine."

———

I don't often spend Friday nights alone, but without Veronica, that's the way things will be. I do more of the cleaning that Emma didn't when was here, throwing clothes into the washer and shoving the garbage down the trash chute. My cleaning service doesn't come on the weekends, and I've lived in squalor for long enough. My food delivery is still set for Monday morning, and I'll survive on what little food I have left after spending all week at home.

I text Claire and ask if she's okay.

She replies she's fine, but the quick response is to keep me from worrying. I will, but if she wants to be left alone, I won't bother her. Claire won't be impressed I spoke to Dad and I may end up on her shitlist if she finds out I said I understood where he was coming from. I'm still ashamed of the bruises that wrapped around Emma's neck, and the kiss she pressed to my cheek and her promise she would always be mine for as long as I wanted her humbles me. But humility isn't enough on which to build a relationship.

With the TV playing ESPN, I drop onto the couch with my phone.

In Bridgeport, there's always something going on, a place to see and be seen, and the foundation and charities director at Variant is going to start bugging me about the Bridgeport's Women's Reproductive Health and Resources Center yearly fundraiser. We always give millions of dollars, and the motivation behind Dad's need to support the cause is evident now. He does it in honor of Mom, the work she did, and the sacrifices she made for her patients and colleagues.

I search Emma's name in my browser, and of course she hits on *Talk of the Town*'s website. I pay for the premium access, though I would never admit it to anyone.

The piece that includes Emma is free, and I don't need to sign in to scroll through the pictures of her hanging out with Haisley, Mia, and Clark. They're at a showing, life-sized marble sculptures dotting a gleaming black floor. In one photo, they're standing in front of a sculpture of a woman with her hands secured behind her back. I don't know what the piece is supposed to represent, and I don't study it long enough to guess. I can't take my eyes off Emma dressed in a midnight blue cocktail dress, holding a glass of wine. Clark is staring at her, a hand pressed to her cheek and a look of utter adoration in his eyes. It's no wonder they've been mistaken for a couple, but after what I saw in the photo of my mother and the man holding onto her as he cried, I recognize gratitude. She did something for him, and he pledged his friendship and devotion to her as a thank you. He loves her, but only as a friend.

I can see that now, whereas before, I was as blind as everyone else.

But there will always be other men, and maybe my father knew that, too.

There will always be a risk she'll leave, but Emma's already proven her commitment to our daughter, and she's not even pregnant yet.

She can't leave if she's already gone.

The mantra used to justify my superficial relationship with Veronica, my cowardly unwillingness to commit, but all it did was tell everyone what an asshole I am.

I click off my phone.

There is one thing I'm going to have to deal with if I want Emma in my life, and it's this: Rafferty Clark will always be her friend. He'll be there at our wedding, perhaps part of the wedding party, he'll be there when our children are born, Emma will invite him to every party and get-together we ever throw. I can either accept that or let it bother me to the point I can't have a relationship with her.

I'll need to chew on it and be adult enough to admit if it's going to bother me, not to pursue her. It will only hurt both of us if I think I can handle it, and in the end, it turns out I can't.

You'd think it would be easy to accept, and maybe for anyone else if their significant other had a good friend of the opposite sex, it wouldn't be a problem, but my father destroyed a happy marriage out of jealousy, and Claire and I suffered. I can't throw forty-one years of a mindset into the trash.

That requires a lot of work, and I've barely begun to scratch the surface of what Emma would need to be happy with me for the rest of her life.

CHAPTER TWENTY-TWO

Emma

I walk through the gallery showing in a haze of loss. I haven't felt like this since my dad died and I would visit my mom. I would expect him to walk around every corner, his boisterous laugh reaching us before he did. I would open my mouth to say something to him, catch my mother's eye, and we'd share a sad smile. I feel like that now. A gallery showing would be such a normal thing for Jack and me to attend together, and so many times I turn to point out something to him, only it's Raff pretending everything is normal. He can't hide he wants to be somewhere else.

Reporters amble around, hoping for gossip, taking pictures, desperate to hit it big with their headlines tomorrow morning. They think sneaking pictures of Raff and me together will cause problems between Jack and me. I want to tell them there is no Jack and me. He won't let himself care, and I can do whatever I want.

I was proud of myself for walking out. It's more than I could have done a year ago.

"You didn't quit yet, did you?" Raff asks, distracted.

I think he's waiting for Veronica to show up, but I haven't seen her anywhere except work. She's still a chipper co-host on *Rise and Shine, Bridgeport!,* offering sincere opinions on their self-care suggestions during the when-a-relationship-runs-its-course segments. Maybe she's using the ideas their so-called experts come up with. Hell, maybe I should be taking notes. I still think it's cruel her personal life is put on display, and I hope she and Raff cause a big splash at the fundraiser in a couple of weeks. She deserves it for all the crap she's been through.

Mia and Haisley are around here somewhere, and even Heath and Zoey stopped in, Heath saying they've been a fan of this artist's work for a long time and didn't want to miss the opportunity to see it in person. They made Jack's absence even more pronounced, and I was glad they said goodbye and went their own way. The six of us hanging out without Jack would have been too much.

"No. I'll do it Monday morning. I need to put in my two weeks. That will give me time to get my period and find a new job. Nothing like a completely clean slate, huh?" I try to smile. Never mind that when those two things happen, any future I've been hoping for will be gone.

"After the past three years, Em, I think it would do you a world of good. Working at Variant has been hell for you, and I'm tired of watching you pretend to be happy."

I glance at him, and he cups my cheek, staring into my eyes. A photographer chooses that second to snap our picture and I scowl.

Maybe one thing I won't miss is attending events like this. I came along as a favor to Raff, but if he and Veronica started going out, I could stay home more often. I can work somewhere more low-key, and the invitations I receive because of my position as Jack's assistant will dry up. I can go back to being Emma Cox, a schoolteacher's daughter.

"I'm not miserable."

Raff chuckles. "Yes, you are, and I wish you would have done something about it a long time ago. Anyway, it will give you a chance to meet someone new. Someone who's emotionally available. Someone who doesn't hate me."

"Jack doesn't hate you."

"Yes, he does, and I've been okay with it. It's a natural response if someone envies you for something you have, but it's bewildering that what he wanted, he could have reached out and taken. He never told you what really happened between Ron and his mother?"

"Nope, and I didn't ask. By then it wouldn't have made a difference. I thought the only way I could prove I wouldn't leave him would be not to leave him, but how long would I have to hang around before he realizes I meant it? He should believe it when I say it. It's how normal couples work."

"Jack's not normal and never has been."

I scoff. "If we're talking family money, you're not normal either. In fact, I may be the only normal one here."

"I think Zoey was poor before Heath struck it rich."

"Great. I'm going to find her so we can be poor in the ladies' restroom together."

"You just went. Besides, he never said anything to you about money, did he?"

"Jack, you mean?"

"Yeah."

"The closest we ever came to talking about money was Ron saying he wanted to promote me. I think my salary would have shot up a thousand percent."

"I'm sure he would have been happier than a pig in you know what if you and Jack had gotten married, made little Durand babies, and ran Variant together."

Sadly, I quirk my lips, my dreams so flippantly coming out of Raff's mouth. "Well, we can't always have what we want, can we?"

"Don't you mean, be careful what you wish for, you just might get it? There's still a chance you could be pregnant. Talking like you aren't won't make it so."

"The odds were twenty-five percent at best, and besides, Jack doesn't want her, so even if I am, he won't care."

Raff stops me with a hand to my arm. "He said that?"

"I talked to him earlier this afternoon, and he fought me on partial custody. He doesn't want her, and he especially doesn't want to raise her with me. I tore up the stupid contract he sent over on Monday. I'm not leaving Bridgeport, and I don't need his money. I make enough to support a baby, and with Mom retired now, I can ask her if she'll help with daycare. She'll be thrilled not to spend her days alone anymore."

"It will be better than a nanny," Raff agrees.

I sniff. "I wouldn't know."

"You wouldn't know until little Jacqueline grew up like Auntie Claire."

"That's a terrible name. Besides, I decided we're having a boy."

"JJ?" Raff asks.

Wrinkling my nose, I ask, "What does that stand for?"

Raff leads me toward the doors. "Jack Junior, of course."

Setting my wineglass on an empty table, I say, "JJ sounds like a dog's name."

"That's what I've been saying all along. Jack should have adopted a dog. All of this could have been avoided."

"And that," I say as he opens the door for me and we step into the cool spring air, "is God's honest truth."

———

After the showing, we met Mia and Haisley at a little jazz bar down the street. One of the guys on Raff's team live streamed us walking, his arm wrapped around my shoulders. Later, I watched the video online and it looked like we were filming a love scene in a movie.

That will be stopping, too. There's something going on between him and Veronica, and she'll like me spending time with Raff about as much as Jack did. We've been leaning on each other, but if they start dating, he'll prefer to spend all of his free time with her, and it's another reason I'm glad I had the courage to move on from Variant. I need to meet new people, make new friends. I'll always have Mia and Haisley, but Heath and Zoey will fade off—they were Jack's friends first and that's what happens. I don't have much free time outside of work, but one day I'd like to meet someone. Not only to have babies as Raff teasingly implied, but I'm lonely and tired of going to bed alone. I want to share my life with someone, and I've had three years to learn that someone won't be Jack.

Raff and I didn't plan anything for tomorrow, and I'll catch up on a show I'm streaming and do laundry. I can sleep in, and later, start looking for a new job. Mia and Haisley might invite me to go somewhere. Maybe I'll go, maybe I won't. A day where I have absolutely nothing to do is an anomaly I fully plan on enjoying. I'll spend Sunday with Mom, and Raff may or may not go with me. Things are changing, and I can either try to embrace it or be unsettled by it.

Missing Jack will be in the back of my mind and heart for a long time—his kind eyes, his amused smile, all the scruff, his long fingers and short, buffed nails as he would type on his keyboard. The suits. The next man I fall in love with will need to wear suits and ties. I've lost a lot of time fantasizing about unknotting Jack's.

I go to bed, but I lie awake for hours. I still wake up at seven, my weekday schedule engrained into my weekend habits. I putter around the apartment, make coffee, skim the paper. Shower. Scroll social media and scan the career websites for jobs. I bookmark a few that look promising and closer to my apartment. I'll apply when I officially give my two weeks' notice. I'm going to miss Variant. Nancy and Ron, LouAnne, the receptionist on the executive floor. I don't know everyone in the entire building, but I've worked there long enough that almost everyone recognizes me as Jack's PA. The camaraderie will be difficult to replace.

Not in the mood to eat but knowing I should, I dig around in my fridge and look for ham and cheese to fix a sandwich. My cell phone chimes, interrupting me. Zoey's name pops up, and I hope she's inviting me to lunch. I'll have to talk about Jack, but I feel down enough I would trade that for someone to chat with.

"Hey, Zoey, what's up?"

She sobs into the phone.

Alarmed, I say, "Zoey?"

"C-can you come over? Paige is missing and we need help looking for her."

Her words are barely intelligible through her tears.

"Oh, God. I'll be right there."

I disconnect the call, grab my purse, and run for my car.

There aren't any parking spaces available on their block, and I park two streets away. I sprint down the sidewalk toward Heath and Zoey's brownstone. Jack is just stepping out of a taxi, the driver double parked and waiting for him to get out. His eyes meet mine, but I look away. I'm not here for him.

Heath and Zoey's door is cracked open, and I push inside without knocking, Jack on my heels.

Mia and Haisley are standing in the kitchen with a few other people I recognize from the party last week.

Zoey's crying against Heath's chest, his tank top soaked with sweat, his arms wrapped around her.

"What happened?" Jack asks.

Heath speaks over Zoey's head. "Gracie and Hil are at summer music camp. I was out for a run, and Zoey and Paige were playing hide and seek. Sheila usually has the weekends off unless we have plans."

Zoey tries to push away. "It's my fault. It's all my fault she's gone."

Heath holds her against him, one strong hand splayed over her back, the other tangled in her hair. "It is not. Don't think that."

She struggles, trying to free herself, and a cross between a scream and a moan screeches from her throat. "It is. I wasn't watching her—"

"Stop it," Heath says firmly, trapping her in a tight embrace, not allowing her an inch of room. "Stop it. I don't blame you."

Zoey lets go and sobs, and only Heath's arms keep her from falling to the floor. "I don't blame you, Zoey. I love you and we are going to find her." He steadies her and grips her sticky cheeks in his hands. Forcing her to meet his eyes, he says, "I love you, and this is not your fault. Do you hear what I'm saying?"

She nods but her gaze slides away from his. She doesn't believe him. He hugs her, and she starts crying again. Closing his eyes and blocking out everything but his wife, he kisses the top of her head.

That's what I want. Someone who will be strong enough to hold me up if something goes wrong. Someone who will support me when accidents and emergencies happen. Even if something is my fault. Especially if something is my fault. I don't want to be with anyone who would judge and punish me because I made a mistake. Heath could be angry, blame Zoey as much as she's blaming herself, but he loves her and instead of pushing all the guilt onto her, he shares it. They're a family in every way, and I want that. I want it desperately.

"How long has she been missing?" Jack asks, watching Heath hold his wife.

"About a half an hour. Zoey called my cell, and I was close to the house. Paige isn't here. We searched every room."

"Have you called the police?" Jack says at the same time I ask, "Where do you want us to look? Outside?"

"We haven't reported it yet. Can you knock on doors? Ask the neighbors if they've seen her or if she went inside somewhere to play? I made a couple of calls, but we were busy looking for her here."

"Okay. I'll head east," I say, stepping toward the front door.

"I'll go with you," Jack says.

I don't want him searching with me. I can't be around him . . . it hurts too much. "We'll cover more ground if we split up." I cling to the excuse we don't question the neighbors together.

Tersely, he nods. "Fine. I'll go west."

"We'll search the park and the playground," Haisley says, gripping Mia's hand.

Squeezing Zoey's shoulder, I ask her, "What was she wearing? Zoey? Can you tell me what she was wearing?"

She turns in Heath's arms and draws in a staggering breath.

Her skin is red from crying, and tears fill her eyes. "Sh-shorts. Denim shorts and a yellow t-shirt. Pink and white sandals if she put them on."

"Okay. I have my cell, keep in touch."

Jack follows me out of the brownstone, and we pause on the sidewalk. His eyes shimmer with longing, but for what, I don't know. I've offered myself to him so many times, in so many ways, and he won't have me, doesn't want me. "You don't have to be sorry, Jack. I'll be okay." I turn and jog away from him. This isn't the time or place for my personal problems.

Everyone on Heath and Zoey's street knows who they are, and all their neighbors are familiar with Paige. On my cell, I pull up a photo I took of her at the party in case I bump into anyone who doesn't know what she looks like. The pink glasses and her smile are memorable, and the picture would trigger even a stranger's recollection.

For an hour, I zig zag back and forth from one side of the street to the other, asking mothers where a little four-year-old girl could have run off to, if their children have seen her. They were playing hide and seek, and Paige could have thought to hide anywhere.

Mia and Haisley send a group text saying they searched the playground and the park two blocks from Heath and Zoey's brownstone, with no luck. I don't know Paige very well, and I don't know the behaviors of a four year old, but Paige wandering alone to a playground wouldn't be like her, even to find a smart hiding place. Heath and Zoey spend a ton of time with their kids—Paige would have asked her mother if they could go to the playground together.

I respond to the text letting everyone know which street I'm on.

Jack also sends an update, and he was able to search a few more streets and houses than I have so far.

Heath and Zoey's other friends report back, and I sink to the sidewalk in dread. No one has found her after an hour of searching. My stomach rolls in fear. Where could Paige have gone? I won't start thinking the worst.

If it were my child, I couldn't bear to hear one negative scenario. Zoey must be out of her mind.

Heath responds to the group text and asks us to return to the house, but I'm reluctant to stop searching. I doubt Paige would have gotten this far, but it feels wrong to give up.

I reach Heath and Zoey's a lot faster than when I was knocking on every door and questioning the neighbors, but I'm still the last one to step inside the kitchen. Jack's rubbing his eyes, and Zoey's sitting at the table, her head cradled in her arms. Mia and Haisley are looking at a map of the neighborhood, and Heath is on the phone with the police.

"Two hours," he says, his voice cracking. "She's not in the house, and we've searched our block." He meets my eyes for confirmation, and I nod.

Heath focuses his attention back to the officer, and I head toward the coffeemaker. I need to do something with my hands. I busy myself with the mundane task and wait for further instructions from the police who will take over the search.

CHAPTER TWENTY-THREE

Jack

Heath called, chagrined and embarrassed, asking if I would be willing to help look for Paige even though he gave me the cold shoulder all week. If I could have, I would have punched him. Something like that, when he's so clearly in the right in the first place, would never have stopped me from searching for their daughter. Heath was already in enough pain, and I walked into the kitchen with Emma and didn't say goddamned thing other than ask him what he wanted us to do.

I was disappointed Emma didn't want to search with me—I didn't want to look for Paige alone. I saw the hurt pinch her face before an excuse flew from her mouth in a relieved jumble. That she had a point didn't soothe the sting any, and with every door I knocked on and every person I asked who said they hadn't seen Paige, my heart beat a little faster and I sweated a little more.

Heath sent out a group text asking us to go back to the

brownstone to regroup, but I was reluctant to backtrack. In a message to only me, he said he would be contacting the police and that he wanted their friends with Zoey.

It was the only thing he could have said that would have made me stop.

Emma's presence in the kitchen grounds me. Heath and Zoey needed her and she came, even knowing she would see me here.

I love her so much.

She shuffles to the coffeemaker and stands motionless, her hand on the carafe.

Heath is mumbling into the phone, Zoey shaking even more violently at the table with every second that passes by.

Succumbing to the need to touch her, I crowd Emma against the counter and kiss the top of her head. She stiffens but doesn't pull away. "Give me a second," I plea, a sinner asking for redemption and knowing he won't be granted it. "I need this."

"Jack," she whispers, and my name sounds hopeless on her lips. She turns around and rests her head on my chest.

Mia squeezes Emma's shoulder, but she looks at me and her eyes harden.

Haisley tugs Mia away.

I wrap my arms around Emma, and tears sting my eyes.

I think I imagine it when a little voice says, "I fell asleep."

―――――

We all whip toward Paige's voice. Her hair is tousled, and her pink glasses are askew on her face. She's pulling a *Frozen* blanket behind her, and she blinks sleepily, noting the very crowded kitchen.

With a cry, Zoey shoots from the table and pulls her daughter into her arms. She sobs into the little girl's neck.

"We found her, thank you so much," Heath chokes into the phone. "She's okay." He disconnects, his hands shaking so terribly he has to try twice.

Paige stands there, bewildered. "Is Mommy crying because she lost?"

Heath rubs his cheeks. "Yeah, baby, that's why. Christ. Where did you hide, sweetheart?"

"In Gracie's room," Paige says proudly. "In her closet. I hid under a coat, but I fell asleep." Her bottom lip trembles. "Am I in trouble?"

"No," Zoey says, pulling away. "No. I was a little worried, that's all. I didn't know where you were. I called for help, and we looked everywhere. You found a good hiding place."

"Sorry, Mommy," Paige says, but she grins. "Don't feel bad. Are we having another party? Is there cake?"

Heath drops to the floor near his wife and daughter. Wrapping them in his arms, he says, "Yeah, we're having another party, and there's cake."

Zoey presses her face into Heath's chest, and he lifts her head with a finger under her chin. "I love you. This could have had a million different outcomes and I wouldn't have loved you any less. You are my heart, always."

Paige dances out of Heath's embrace. "Let's order pizza!"

Zoey snuggles in Heath's lap, and she pulls their daughter into hers. They sit in a pile of love, and my arms tighten around Emma.

"I want that," I say, my lips close to her ear.

She looks into my face, and hers is empty of any emotion. "So do I, but I know it won't be with you. You've made that very clear, and I'm finally listening."

My arms drop to my sides, and she steps away from me. I

watch her kiss Paige's cheek and say goodbye to Heath and Zoey.

Heath looks like he wants to say something, opening his mouth and drawing in a breath, but he lets her go with only a, "Thank you for your help" and she disappears out of the kitchen.

———

Heath orders pizza, and Zoey opens bottles of wine. Paige glows, high off her nap and the winner of hide and seek. Everyone wants to touch her, to feel for themselves she's okay.

Mia and Haisley linger, both of them shooting me dirty looks.

Zoey's exhausted, but she plays the generous hostess. She's crashing and needs to lie down, but she and Heath are too polite to kick us out. It's their nature to want to pay us back for searching, but I don't want to be in their way. Heath's alone outside, and I join him on the patio, intending to say a quick goodbye. Our friendship isn't back to normal, and it may never be. I hurt Emma, and Heath warned me he wouldn't tolerate it. He chose sides, but I'm glad he's on Emma's.

"Hey, I need to get going," I say, closing the glass doors. The chatter in the kitchen quiets behind me.

The sun is shining, the clouds drift by. I wonder what Emma is going to do with the rest of her day. Sit outside on her little slab of concrete and read a book? Dinner plans with Clark, more than likely, a quiet meal as she relays the afternoon. He would have been here, had Zoey and Heath asked for his help. I've needed too much time to realize that Rafferty Clark is a good guy. Or maybe she'll hang out with Mia and Haisley, and they'll tell her how proud they are of her for walking away from me today. Or maybe tonight she'll watch

TV and look for a different job. Monday she'll put in her notice, and I'll have to change offices. I won't be able to look at her desk and not picture her sitting in her chair typing up meeting notes.

Heath blows out a sigh. Fatigue weighs heavy on his face, too. He was strong for himself, but he was stronger for Zoey. She needed him, and he didn't let her down. "I'm sorry about this week," he says, leaning against the railing. "I don't agree with what you're doing, but I shouldn't have taken it out on you. It's none of my business what you and Emma do."

I shrug. "It's okay. You were right. It didn't end well, and we're not even speaking. You warned me it would happen, and it did. You can say I told you so."

"I don't want to say I told you so," he says angrily, swiping a hand through his hair. "I want you to understand what you're losing because you can't stop—"

He could say a hundred things. Because I can't stop being an asshole. Because I can't stop not wanting to turn into my father. Because I can't stop living my life in fear.

"I know. I'm glad things turned out okay." I rub my chest and chuckle. "She gave me a heart attack."

"Christ. You and me both." He pauses. "Zoey, you saw her. She wouldn't have been okay. If something happened to Paige, we wouldn't have been okay. You understand that, don't you, Jack? That families, no matter how much you love each other, they're not indestructible? Zoey would have blamed herself forever, and our family wouldn't have survived it."

My answer is quick. "I don't believe that."

"If it were Gracie or Hilary—" he pulls a face— "God, how morbid is it to think that way? Maybe we would get through it. Maybe. But Paige has always been the chink in our armor. Her birth and the time in the NICU. She wasn't planned. She was conceived after my vasectomy, but we didn't wait long enough and things happen."

I sit on a patio chair and hitch my ankle onto my knee. I might not be as tired as Heath and Zoey, but this afternoon drained me, too. "You always made it sound like she was."

He smiles faintly. "Hilary was hard on Zoey, but she wanted another baby. I convinced her it wasn't worth it. We had two, there was no reason for more, especially since I was happy with the girls and didn't want to try for a boy. It would have been better for Zoey if we hadn't had a third, but she was ecstatic, didn't matter how difficult the pregnancy was. What's funny is after Paige was born too early, I blamed myself for knocking Zoey up, and she blamed herself for not being strong enough to carry to term. Paige is our hard-earned little angel, and all that we went through to have her, if she would have disappeared without a trace, nope. Our marriage couldn't have survived it."

"I don't think you give yourself enough credit. If something like that were to happen, Zoey would need you, and you wouldn't leave her to deal with it on her own. I remember the day you met her. She was bartending at that crappy bar we stopped in that night after, Christ, what were we doing? Celebrating you getting that shitty entry-level position, weren't we?" I muse, trying to think back to the little jerks we were when we were barely more than kids celebrating graduation, though we both would go on to earn our MBAs.

Heath chuckles. "Something like that. She gave me her number, and I thought I won the lottery."

I jut my chin out at him. "You did."

"Yeah," he says softly, "I did."

Paige chooses that moment to slide the doors open carrying two bottles of beer. "Mommy said you need this for your nerves," she says, giving one to Heath and one to me.

"Mommy knows me too well," he says, snaking his arm around his daughter and giving her a smack on the cheek. "I'm glad you're safe. I love you very much."

Paige crawls into his lap and rests her head against his shoulder.

I came up with the surrogacy idea thinking that's what I wanted. A child who would love me, but what I didn't understand was that I wanted Heath's whole package. The house, the wife who sends their daughter out to the patio with a beer, the friends who would drop everything to help find a little girl sleeping in a closet.

Heath twists the cap off the bottle and guzzles half of it. "You know when I knew you had a thing for Emma?"

I shift my gaze from Paige's content face to meet Heath's eyes. "No. Was I that obvious?"

"No, not to anyone who doesn't know you, but we've been good friends for years, and I knew. I'm not sure how long Emma had been your PA. Three months? Four? We went for a run after work and we were pounding the pavement. You said you came back from lunch and were getting ready for a meeting. Emma stepped into your office and said you had crumbs on your lips. She brushed them off with her fingers, and you said—"

"That she reminded me of my mother. She would clean my face that way after a meal."

"Yeah. You hardly ever talk about your mother, and for Emma to remind you of her . . . and for you to say it out loud? That was big. You admitted that, and I knew you'd feel a lot of shit working with her, but I didn't know how far it would go. Now I do, and I'm asking you as my best friend. Leave her alone. There was a lot going on this afternoon, but I saw her face. Stay away from her and let her get on with living without you."

Paige wiggles in Heath's lap. "I like Emma, Uncle Jack. You make her sad."

"Why do you think that?" I ask around a ball of misery in my throat.

"I told her I was going to marry a prince when I grew up. Gracie said it was stupid, but Emma said I could marry whoever I wanted. I asked her if she wanted to marry a prince too, and she said you make her feel like a princess but you didn't want to marry her. I felt bad I made her cry and to cheer her up I painted her fingernails. She liked the pink heart stickers the best. She let me fall asleep in her lap." She scoots off Heath's leg and wrinkles her nose. "You're stinky. Mommy said pizza would be here soon. I'm gonna go check."

Paige rushes inside, closing the glass doors behind her, and Heath says, "You should have married Veronica and been done with the whole thing."

I stiffen and sigh. "I don't want . . ." I need to stop saying I don't want to get married. It's not true. I do want to get married and I do want a family, and I only want that with Emma. Setting my unopened beer bottle on the patio table I say, "I need to go."

"What are you going to do?" There's a warning in Heath's voice, but I can't let other people dictate how I live my life. What my father did to my mother guided me in a direction I don't want to go anymore, and if I lose Heath's friendship, so be it. It's time I start living how I want, reaching out to take what I want, and stop being scared of something that might not even happen.

"What I should have done long before this." I hold out my hand, and Heath shakes it, his eyes narrowed.

In the kitchen, Zoey's sitting at the table. She stands shakily to her feet and wraps her arms around me. "Thank you for being here for us."

I grasp her shoulders. "I will always be here for you and your family. You have my absolute word that whatever you and your girls need, I will do my damnedest to make sure you have it."

She rests her hands on my biceps and her eyes search mine. "You're going after her."

Mia and Haisley glare at me from the table.

I say what I should have admitted a long time ago. "I love her and I let too much time go by. The minute I knew, I should have told her."

Paige hops up from coloring at the coffee table in the living room. "Wait!" she yells at me and runs up the stairs.

Zoey shakes her head in amused confusion.

Paige's bare feet slap against the wooden staircase, and she scrambles down as quickly as she went up, bright pieces of paper clutched in her hand. "Here! If you make her sad again, give her these. They'll cheer her up." She jabs a handful of sheets covered in stickers at me. "She likes the pink hearts best."

"I remember. Thank you."

"She wants to be a princess and wear pretty dresses and crowns. If you tell her that she can, she'll say yes."

I drop to my haunches and ask, "Do you want to be in our wedding?"

Comically, Paige slaps her hands to her cheeks. "Can I?"

"Oh, God," Zoey says. "What the hell have you started?"

"If your mom and dad say it's okay."

"He still has to do the asking," Heath says from the glass doors, his arms crossed over his chest. "And that might require a lot of groveling on his part. She might say no. Don't get your hopes up, Paige."

"I'll do whatever I have to do." I stand, Paige's stickers gripped in my hand.

Zoey squeezes my arm. "Good luck. You're perfect for each other."

"Zoey," Heath says, his voice low.

"We're all allowed to make mistakes. It's up to Emma if she's going to forgive Jack for his."

I stand on the sidewalk, Zoey's words echoing in my heart. I've fucked up, and I'm not the only one who's suffered. I know what I need to do next, but I don't know where to go from here. I text Claire—I hope she'll have the information I need.

She responds quickly, and I silently thank her for not asking why I want it. I send a text to the number she sends me. *Where are you?*

Who the fuck is this? I read in response. I'm not surprised he doesn't know. We've never swapped numbers. Had no reason to, but after today, Emma's friends are my friends.

Durand.

Fuck. I'm at my office.

I'll be there in fifteen. We need to talk.

Of course we do.

I can't decide if he's being sarcastic or serious. I've never needed to talk to him about anything, always keeping my distance or I'd smash a fist into his face.

His suite of offices is located near Variant, and I impatiently sit in the back of the car I ordered, the driver competently navigating traffic. Rafferty Clark can afford the prime real estate—his e-zine and smartphone app bring in millions of dollars a year. I would never tell him, but the amount of hard work he's put into his business impresses me. He's built a media empire reporting the truth and proving rumors either true or false. Readers flock to his website and download his app in the hundreds of thousands. They know what they find won't be clickbait full of lies. Reporting with integrity, he's beat out the competition by a landslide, and never once has he been tempted to risk that reputation on a shady story for the hits.

The building is open despite it being Saturday, and I'm quickly waved through security. Clark must have called down to approve my visit—the guard ushers me through with a grin and quick directions.

Talk of the Town's offices are spread over an entire floor, and I walk through a maze of desks resembling a newspaper's bullpen.

Colored all in black, Clark's office is sleek, but I wouldn't have expected anything less. It's similar to mine—a metal three-tiered cart parked by the windows serves as a bar, the bottles gleaming in the sun, and a massive black lacquered desk is positioned in one corner. His office is larger, but my only excuse is I took mine over when my grandfather died and I didn't care about size and still don't.

His desk is a jumble of keyboards and computer screens, and he leans away from the one in the center to watch me walk through his open door.

There are bloggers sitting at some of the desks behind me, clicking away at their keyboards, writing up events like the sculpture showing Friday night and a charity lunch earlier this afternoon benefitting domestic violence victims.

If we had still been together, Veronica and I would have attended the charity luncheon—things like that were her go-to to promote her job and the show. I don't know if the producers of *Rise and Shine, Bridgeport!* forced her to go today, and if she did, if she went alone or found someone else to go with. I've been too preoccupied to care what she's doing now, and that's another shitty thing Heath could have called me on.

I doubt Clark will let the opportunity pass him by.

He's dressed in navy slacks, a pristine white dress shirt, a crisp, well-cut vest, and a matching navy and yellow tie is knotted neatly at his throat. I feel dirty and unkept wearing a t-shirt and jeans, Paige's stickers shoved into my back pocket, and ornery I'm on his turf and he's one upped me with his suit, my first instinct is to insult him. *Prissy.* I have to tamp down the knee-jerk reaction.

"Are you done staring? What do you want?" he asks, scowling.

"I'm going to ask Emma to marry me," I say, watching for the jealousy that would have been plain on my face had he been the one to say that to me. Jealousy, hell. A statement like that coming from Clark about Emma would have fueled a rage unlike anything I have ever felt before.

He scoffs. "Good for you. Good luck getting her to say yes."

Angry he knows more about her than I do, I ask in frustration, "*Who is she to you?*"

"You asked me that at your party. Wasn't my answer enough? We're friends, and if you can't accept that, don't ask her to marry you. She'll need more than seeing your sorry ass all the time, and I won't let you isolate her because of some sick idea she's going to cheat on you like your father thought your mother did."

I swallow. "You know about that? Did you say anything to Emma?"

"I know everything that goes on in this fucking city, and no, I didn't tell Emma. I can keep my nose out of piles of shit if it doesn't belong there, and your family issues aren't my problem. I figured if you wanted Emma to know, you'd tell her yourself."

"How long have you known?"

He shakes his head. "Not long. I didn't find out for myself. Your sister asked me to do a little snooping, and I did as a favor. Eventually, Emma will be Claire's sister-in-law and I do what I can to help the people I consider family."

There's a lot to unpack there, and I stand in the center of his office not knowing what to say first.

"Christ. Sit down, have a drink, say what you need to say, and get the hell out of my office." He slides out of his desk chair, steps over to the bar, and pours a drink into a lowball glass that has *Talk of the Town* etched into the side.

It's not so gracious, but I accept his invitation and sit in a conversational area on the opposite side of the room. The leather couch is warm to the touch, the sun shining into the window exactly right as it sinks into the horizon.

Clark passes me the glass, and I knock it back, letting the heat run through me. It's been a helluva day.

"Is Paige okay?" he asks.

Figures Emma would tell him what happened earlier this afternoon. Another thing I'll have to get used to. Clark knowing most of our business. Mia and Haisley too, for that matter. Claire. She's my sister and I tell her everything, and I never keep much from Heath. When you have a group of friends as close as we are, it's natural to share.

Instead of being resentful he knows, I remind myself to be thankful he cares enough to ask. "Little stinker. I don't think she understood the panic she caused. Yeah, she's fine."

"Good." At the bar, he pours himself a drink. He carries the decanter to the couch and adds more to my empty glass. Setting it on the table for easy access, he sits facing me on a matching couch's armrest. "Kids. I have to say, not sure I want them."

"You have time to decide. You're what? Emma's age?"

"Yeah." He sips his whiskey. "Do you really want to know about Emma and me?"

Leaning forward, I brace my elbows on my knees. "I really do."

I wait for a story that starts with, "I've been in love with her for a long time . . ." but what he really says is, "When I was a kid, I was a punk, and my parents didn't know what to do with me. I wasn't born in Bridgeport—my parents are from Boston. The year I turned twelve, the all-boys school my parents shoved me into hoping to make me grow up kicked me out. That was my fifth school in as many years." He glances at me. "You grew up rich. It's not easy."

"No, no it's not." Traditions. Expectations. Scrutiny.

"My parents were, *are,* good people, but they were at a loss with what to do with me, so they sent me here, to my Aunt Caro's. Caroline is my mother's younger sister, and she gave up the family fortune for love, or so the story goes. She doesn't live far from Emma's mother. When they did that, I knew I'd reached my parents' last resort. If I didn't behave, I'd have nowhere else to go." Clark sets his empty glass near the decanter, stands, and shoves his hands into his pockets.

"Let me guess, you met Emma."

He smiles wistfully, back to twelve years old. "Yeah. My first day at school. I tried to act tough, you know, but what I really wanted was to belong. I think that was what was missing in those other schools. I couldn't make friends. I couldn't find the connections I needed to feel like a person and not just a wad of my parents' cash."

I nod. School wasn't that tough for me. I always had Heath and my sister.

"I was standing with my tray in the cafeteria trying to find a place to sit. God, I interview rockstars, *royalty,* for fuck's sake, and there is fucking nothing scarier than facing a room packed full of kids who don't give a fuck who you are, and don't want to know, either. Emma walked up beside me with her own tray." He circles his hand in front of his face. "Her eyes, you know? You think she's gorgeous now, you should have seen her at twelve. Even the principal ate out of her hand. She said, 'You're new.' I expected her to make fun of my moppy hair or my clothes, but she didn't. 'Come sit with us,' she said, and I don't think I could have stopped my feet from following her even if I had wanted to." His eyes crinkle with the memory. "She led me to a table with a bunch of other kids, including Mia and Haisley."

"They've been friends for that long?" I ask, surprised.

Clark chuckles. "Oh, yeah. Mia and Haisley lived in the same school district as Emma and they've been friends since Kindergarten. They were all friends long before Mia and Haisley started dating and got married. Sometimes I wonder what that would be like—attached to the same person for your whole life. Anyway, some other kids were there, and Emma introduced me around. Not one kid made fun of my accent, and I don't think I've ever felt that . . . settled."

"It should have been natural then, for you two to hook up." I don't say it out of jealousy, I'm too enthralled with this little piece of Emma's history I didn't know.

Clark tilts his head in acknowledgement. "You'd think that. We were attached at the hip since lunch that day. We walked home together, did homework together. If Emma was around, so was I."

I scoff. Exactly how I've thought of them, too.

"It went on for years. We went to school dances together. Proms. But there wasn't a spark between us. One afternoon, I think it was tenth grade or so, we were walking out of the high school to go home and some kids started razzing me, calling me gay, a fag, the usual. I suppose our friendship was weird, especially since Emma's beautiful. I got so sick of them saying shitty things about me that I grabbed her and kissed her. Tongue and everything. I think, if there had been anything between us, we would have felt it that day. I kissed her until those assholes left. I pulled away, and she wiped her mouth with the back of her hand and said, 'I hope they leave you alone now.' And that was it. We never talked about it again."

"What did you do after graduation?"

"I didn't want high school to end. It was a safe haven for me, with Emma standing watch. I told her where I came from, what my family wanted me to do. The thought of leaving Emma to go to college was the scariest fucking thing—after the ceremony, I cried. She found me sitting in a dark hallway behind the auditorium bawling my eyes out. She promised everything would be okay, but how could I believe that?" He glances at me from the window. "You know what she did?"

I shake my head.

"She asked Aunt Caro for my mom's phone number. I'd been caught up at the school, I don't even know for what now, a missing assignment, I think, and she called my mom. She asked if she would let me go to the University of Minnesota with her, and my mom said yes. I couldn't believe it. We both majored in English, and she minored in business. After that, I was scared, but in a better place. She moved back here, and I went on to Harvard to get my law degree."

"You're a lawyer?"

He lifts a shoulder. "Not exactly. Law's a family tradition, and let's just say . . . I haven't fulfilled my legacy. Not doing what I'm doing." He waves his hand to encompass his office. "I thought our friendship would crumble with the distance, but I should have known Emma wouldn't let that happen. I moved back to Bridgeport to be near my aunt, and we picked up right where we left off. She helped me find some office space and *Talk of the Town* was born. I wanted to be an investigative reporter, work for a newspaper, but my parents wouldn't let me. I thought since they let me follow Emma to the U of M, I could compromise. I don't hate law, but it wasn't my first choice. And now you're all caught up. The day she started working at Variant and met you, I knew I'd lose her. She dated here and there, but you were different. When you started dating Veronica, it broke her heart. Then those rumors started you were going to ask her to marry you, and I think it took every ounce of energy Emma had in her body to get out of bed every morning."

"I didn't want to admit I had feelings for her. I told myself I didn't want my children growing up without a mother if my wife ever left me, but that was only part of the shit I believed to protect myself. Dad told me happened between him and my mom was due to his jealousy and to not let it affect what I wanted with Emma. I struggled with that—I've been envious of your relationship with her for years. If this is going to work, I have to put my bias against you aside. You will always be Emma's friend and she would never let me cut you out of her life. I can accept it or lose her."

"Durand, if Emma and I had something, I would have married her ten years ago. Fifteen. Hell, I would have begged her the minute we were both legal. There were times we talked about it, and I think if you would have married Veronica, she would have been receptive. But she doesn't want less than to marry for love, and I don't either. We all deserve that. She watched you date Veronica for two years, and this surrogacy situation on top of that hurt her. I told her you didn't have it in you to give her what she wants, and I still think that's true. If you dangle a ring in front of her, you can't hate her for wanting it and all that goes with it. She's not going to let you fuck around. Be the husband she'll need you to be or let her go. She said she's going to put her two weeks' notice in on Monday morning. If you can't stand behind your vows, let her do it."

I get up from the couch. I could let Clark's words scare me, but they only harden my resolve. What my dad did to my mom had nothing to do with me. Even if it had been my mother's choice to leave us, it still wouldn't have had anything to do with me or the kind of wife the woman I marry will turn out to be. Emma needs me to love her unconditionally, without reservations, and I will because I already do.

"Will you be one of my groomsmen? I can't offer you the top spot—I owe that to Heath—but it would mean a lot if you were there, standing up with us," I say, holding out my hand.

"Aren't you getting a little ahead of yourself?" He shakes it firmly.

"I already landed us a flower girl, I didn't think it would hurt to ask."

"All I want is for Emma to be happy. Maybe I would have turned out okay without her, but maybe I wouldn't have. If she says yes, you'll be one lucky son of a bitch."

"I know, trust me, I know. I'm going to go talk to her. At Heath and Zoey's she said she didn't want . . . but I can't let her go."

"Good luck. I mean that."

I turn toward his office door, the bloggers still cranking out their words.

"Hey, can I ask you something?" Clark asks.

"Yeah, sure." I owe him for the hour he gave me, the honesty, the . . . friendship.

"You and Veronica are done, done? Did she love you?"

"I . . . don't know. She never said she did, and I never said it to her. We didn't spend much time together. If we—" I grimace. I want to talk to Clark about my sex life with Veronica about as much as I wanted to talk to my dad about my sex life with Emma. "—I rarely spent the night. She pushed me into that proposal, and I was too angry to ask her why."

"But it wasn't because she's in love with you."

"No, I don't believe that was why."

Clark nods. "Okay. You don't have any claim on her then."

I wouldn't stress about Emma's friendship with Clark if he was dating someone, but that's not why I say, "She has a wall up. Against what, I don't know. I was a jackass and didn't ask because I didn't care enough to know. If you're asking what I think you're asking, you'll need to knock it down or you won't have even a ghost of a chance with her."

"When we were doing damage control, I felt it, but I thought it was the situation—or you."

"No. It's always been there."

He searches my face. "Okay. Thanks."

"Yeah, and to you, too."

I turn to leave, and this time he lets me go.

I don't know what I'm going to say to Emma, don't know what I *can* say that would make up for the past three years, and I mean all three years. If I would have just admitted how I felt, all this could have been avoided.

It's time to stop hiding.

Emma showed me her courage and strength, telling me she loved me and still walking away.

It's only right I tell her I love her too and be brave enough to let her go if I'm too late to fix the damage I caused.

CHAPTER TWENTY-FOUR

Emma

I'm exhausted, and the second I step inside my apartment, I shower and crawl into bed. Pulling out of Jack's embrace was the hardest thing I've ever done. It's right where I've always wanted to be, a united front against the terrors of the world, but after what he told me yesterday, I know it wouldn't last. He said he loves me, but if he's not willing to give me everything that goes with it, that's not love then, is it? It's fancy wrapping paper taped around an empty box.

Haisley texts and asks if I'm home and okay.

I respond yes to both, but I'm not okay. I haven't been okay since my first day at Variant, and I don't have anyone to blame but myself.

Speaking of that, my two weeks' notice will go by quickly, and I'll need to have something lined up. I can't rely on my retirement savings, and I can't count on a pregnancy to keep me afloat. I'm more than capable of making my own money, and I don't want to live off Jack's. I'm not in the mood for it, but I drag my laptop into bed with me and go over the job postings I bookmarked last night after Jack turned my already shattered dreams to dust.

I update my résumé, adding my job duties at Variant. Ron asking me to sit in on meetings is a nice addition, even if it didn't last long, and I try to think of how to describe the new responsibilities that weren't part of my everyday tasks.

Someone knocks on my door, and I save my progress. I haven't heard from Raff today, or maybe Haisley and Mia didn't believe I'm doing okay. It could even be my mom stopping by to see how I am. I'd like to ignore it and stay tucked in bed, but I don't want anyone to worry.

Sighing, I crawl from beneath the warm comforter and secure my robe a little tighter around my body.

I know before I open the door who's on the other side, and I don't want to deal with it. "What do you want?"

Jack's still wearing the clothes he wore to Heath and Zoey's, his t-shirt smeared with dirt. "I want to talk, that's all. If you don't like what I have to say, I'll let you go. I mean it."

I wish it were that simple. I could run to the other side of the world, and it still wouldn't be far enough to slip out of his grasp.

I cross my arms over my chest.

"Please," he says. His eyes are pinched, lines frame his mouth, and scruff covers his jaw.

I've always been a sucker for that scruff. I open the door wider and stepping aside, let him come in. "Fine."

"Thank you."

Reluctantly, I lead him into the living room and sit on the corner of my couch expecting him to sit on the opposite side, but he sits near me, his hard thigh brushing my leg. Scowling, I lean away.

"I've been a prick," he says, reaching for my hand. I try to yank it back, but he holds on. "To you, to Veronica. To Clark."

I tug again, and he grips harder. "What does Raff have to do with this?" I ask.

"Actually, a lot. I didn't know how much until my dad told Claire and me what happened between him and Mom that day."

I stop struggling. "What *did* happen, Jack? Why didn't you tell me yesterday?"

"I was scared. I've never been in love before, and I didn't know what to do with it. I've *avoided* it all my life because I never wanted to be vulnerable and at the mercy of another human being like my dad was with my mom. I talk about reliving the day Mom rode away in that taxi, but I don't talk about what that turned Dad into. Anger fueled him, but he lost the love of his life."

"Claire told me she asked him why she didn't have a mother and it made him cry."

Jack rubs his thumb over my knuckles. "He cried a lot, Emma. Started drinking. He was never violent, but he stopped living. He stopped being a dad. You said I had childhood trauma, but you will probably never guess just how much Dad kicking Mom out fucked me up."

"Tell me from the beginning," I say, and I can't help it. I tangle my fingers with his, giving him something to hold on to, and he finally unloads his little four-year-old heart.

He talks me through Elizabeth disappearing at all hours of the day and night, his father hiring a private investigator to spy on her. He doesn't say it that way, but I weigh everything he tells me as if one day I'll be wearing her shoes. Ron threw her out, and the truth about the clinic and what she'd allegedly been doing came to light. The humiliation, anger, and blame he felt when she wouldn't come home. And his retaliation to force her to buckle, though she never did.

"My father was jealous, and after he told me that, I saw so many parallels. Parallels I didn't want to admit to. I thought you were more to Clark than what you are—"

I open my mouth to object. I was always honest with him, but he accepts the blame before I can speak.

"—I know, but that's what I'm trying to say. I didn't want to believe it. I was *safe* if I didn't believe it. I owe Veronica an apology. I didn't want to love you and I shoved her between you and me, but I couldn't stop. Then I came up with that stupid contract, and I thought maybe *that* would put some space between us and still allow me to be near you, but after we made love for the first time, all it did was throw me into a tailspin. I thought you were sleeping with Clark, and I hurt you." He brushes his fingers over my throat. "That was the last thing I wanted to do, and I tried to stay away."

I pull my hand free, and he lets me. I stand from the couch. "I don't know what you want. I'll never stop being friends with Raff."

"I talked to him this afternoon, before I came here. He told me how you met, that you'd been friends for most of your lives. I'll do my best not to interfere. If I tried, that would mean I didn't trust you, and I do."

"No, you don't. You went to talk to him? Why?"

"I needed to know once and for all that you two are only friends."

"*I* told you that. That should have been enough."

"Well, it wasn't. Not the way you hang on each other, not the way you dance so closely someone can't even slip a piece of paper between your bodies. Everywhere you go, he's there too, whispering into your ear, making you laugh. Do you know how torturous it is to watch him skim his fingers over your skin? It's a habit he has, it doesn't matter where, Emma. Your arm, your back. Your thigh if you're both sitting down and you're wearing a dress. He's *always* fucking touching you, then you try to tell me you're only friends. You say one thing, and you act another. How am I supposed to believe that?" He pushes off the couch and onto his feet, his body tense, his jaw clenched. Waiting for me to argue or justify what Raff and I have. Excuses. Lies. Standing in front of me, he frames my face with his hands. "You act like lovers. How was I supposed to believe you're only friends?"

Sucking in a breath, I step out of his grasp, and he drops his hands to his sides.

I see what he sees, and I say, "You're right. Years of loneliness will do that to you. I dated some in college, but I could never find what I was looking for. Raff and I have always blown off the rumors. We've heard them since we were kids, but we've never felt that way about each other."

"I know that now, it was just a lot to process."

"Then what do you want to do?"

"I want to mar—" He stops and rubs his face.

We're far from marriage, but it stings he can't say the word.

"I don't want you to quit. I want to work with you every day. I want to do everything you wanted to do when you signed that stupid contract. Hang out with family—I'm working on forgiving my dad. Spend time with friends. Spend time with each other. I want to sleep with you at night. Wake up to you in the morning and bring you coffee in bed. What I'd really like is if you moved into the penthouse with me, but if you think we're not ready for that then let me sleep here, and when you—" he chokes— "get tired of me, you can kick me out. But more than anything, I'm going to ask, and only ask, that you and Clark don't see each other as much as you have been. I love you, Emma, and I want you to give me your time, not him."

"You want me to move into your penthouse?" I ask faintly. "Raff said you don't invite women up there."

"I don't. Heath thought I never wanted to have to do what Dad did to Mom, but that's not true. I was just waiting for the right woman. The night I brought you up after my party, you looked good on my bed. You looked like you belonged there, and that's where I want to keep you. One day we'll move. You said our daughter should have a yard to play in, and she will."

"Our daughter?" He's saying everything I want him to say, and I want to trust it, God, do I want to trust it.

"I want children with you. I want everything with you. I want to ask you to marry me, but I can't do it here."

I don't know what he means . . . I'd say yes if he asked me anywhere.

"For now, we take it slow. Don't quit unless you think it would be uncomfortable working together. Think about moving in with me. And tell me, please, Emma, that you still love me."

I search his face, but all I see is truth, honesty, and a little fear that maybe after all he's said, I would still turn him away.

"Tell me again," I whisper.

"I love you. I'm sorry you thought I was going to propose to Veronica. It's why you looked so sick, wasn't it?"

I nod.

"Fuck. I am so sorry about that. At The Menagerie, you said you were in love with someone who was getting married. You were talking about me, weren't you?"

"Yeah. I didn't want you to know."

"I was never going to marry Veronica, and I didn't put two and two together. I had no idea you were talking about me. I can't say things would have been easier. I had a lot to work through to get to where I'm standing, literally, but I'm sorry it had to be so hard."

I pause for a moment, but there's nothing on his face except hope. I rush toward him and jump into his arms. He catches me, strong and sure, and crushes me to his chest, burying his face in my hair.

"I love you, and I am so sorry," he mumbles.

Leaning away, I frame his scruffy cheeks in my hands. "I am, too. I love you, Jack, and I have for years."

"Then I am one lucky bastard," he says, walking toward my bedroom, my legs wrapped around his waist. He sets me down, and slowly, gently, he pushes the robe from my shoulders. "Is this okay?"

"Yeah," I murmur. It flutters to the floor, and I shove my hands up his t-shirt.

"You had no idea how scared I was I blew it," he says, tugging his shirt over his head and throwing it onto the floor near my robe.

"What changed your mind?" I unbutton his jeans and encircle my hand around his cock. It surges under my touch. There's still a small chance we could make a baby today, and I want to, so much.

"Heath and Zoey, mostly. There wasn't one second he wasn't what she needed him to be, and that was when I realized my relationship with you, our marriage, will be whatever I want it to be. It won't have anything to do with anyone but us. God, that feels good. You have too many clothes on."

"Get undressed," I say, stepping away and sliding my nightgown down my body.

Jack tosses his wallet onto the nightstand and shucks his jeans.

We meet in the middle of my bed, and I don't wait a second before I'm in his arms, his warm body everything I need. His fingers open me, finding me wet and so ready for him, and I press my face against the strong curve of his shoulder.

Needing to be closer, I rest my leg over his hip, the tip of his cock positioned just right.

"Emma, no. Wait."

I still. "What?"

"Stop." He reaches for his wallet and pulls out a condom. Meeting my eyes in the dusky room, he says, "If you're pregnant, I will love our baby with everything I have, but if you're not, we'll decide when to have children together."

Stunned, I lower onto my pillow. "You'd really wait? I thought you wanted a baby more than anything."

"Not more than you." He brushes my hair away from my face, the look in his eyes so earnest it brings tears to mine. "I was so proud of myself for coming up with that whole damned scheme, but I didn't want a baby. I wanted you."

"That's sweet, but . . ." I pull the condom packet from his fingers and tap it against my mouth. "What if that's what I want? I'll be thirty-five this year, and the whole reason you started this was because of your age. If you want two kids, it would be nice if we could before I turned forty."

"Yeah?" He smiles.

"Yeah."

"Okay, but only if you're sure."

I wrap my arms around his neck, encouraging him to move his body over mine. "I've never been surer about anything in my life."

We make love, the condom packet glittering on my comforter. He comes, but I don't feel like this is the end the way I used to. It's the beginning of our life together.

He cuddles me to him, his lips pressed to my temple. He drifts, rung out from searching for Paige. Snuggled tightly in his embrace, I think about what he said on the couch, what Ron did to Elizabeth. Jack might have been scared he'd do the same to me, but communication works both ways. "Jack."

"Hmmm."

"Why didn't your mother tell Ron what she was doing?"

He stiffens, not used to talking about his parents. "She didn't want to put her colleagues at risk." His voice is hard, still blaming his father for not trusting his wife.

"I understand that, but he wouldn't have said anything. He might have even helped, right? Your grandfather founded Variant and your family was well-off by then, weren't you?"

"Yeah, but I don't understand what you're getting at, Emma. She needed to keep it a secret."

"Maybe she did, but from your dad? What was he going to do, run up to the hospital and tattle on her? He loved her and he could have helped somehow. Bought them supplies, even opened a non-affiliated, low-income clinic. Your mother didn't need her job at the hospital, she wanted it. Ron could have employed her and all of her colleagues, let her run her own women's resources center."

"Are you saying my mom didn't trust my dad?" He props his head on his hand and looks down at me. He's not angry. We're having a conversation, and if we can always talk about things like this, we'll never have a misunderstanding.

"I'm saying that maybe they weren't accustomed to trusting another person and sharing important information. I don't know how long they were married before they had you, and I'm only suggesting that maybe their relationship was new enough that they *both* made mistakes."

"Maybe you're right, but I doubt I'll ever know without hearing her side of the story. I don't know if I want to find her. Would you think poorly of me?"

I brush my fingers over his jaw. "You need to do whatever

you need to do to be okay. I'll support you with whatever you need. If that means letting it go, it does."

He blows out a breath. "Thank you."

Pushing him onto his back, I ask, "Can we make love again?"

With his hands to my waist, Jack positions me over him. "Emma, honey, I love you so much, I'll always give you whatever you want," he says as he slips inside me.

I rock my hips, taking all of him as deeply as I can. "Good. Then can we sleep at the penthouse? You need a shower and you don't have anything here."

He cups my breasts in his hands, pinching my nipples. The sensation shoots straight to my core and I moan.

"Christ, you are so sexy. Yeah, we can sleep at the penthouse, but why do I need a shower?"

Lowering myself against his chest, I rub my lips over his mouth. "Because it's time you met my mother."

CHAPTER TWENTY-FIVE

Jack

A week after I meet Marti Cox, Emma sits on the bed in our room at the bed and breakfast licking blueberry jam from her fingers and perusing the paper. A sheet is tucked around her torso, and her hair is mussed from us making love as the sun rose.

She's the most beautiful thing I have ever seen.

We drove to the B&B yesterday morning. She has no idea why we're staying at the little inn sitting on the outskirts of Bridgeport, a shallow creek running through the backyard. She asked, but all I said was I wanted a couple of days alone with her. She didn't point out that we could have had them at her place or mine simply by not answering phone calls or texts or that we could have rented a room at the Bridgeport Hotel.

It was important I do this here, and I wasn't going to wait until winter.

We've spent the last week between her apartment and my penthouse. My father was ecstatic she and I worked it out, kissing her cheek and welcoming her to both the Durand family and Variant.

I told Claire over text since she still hasn't surfaced, and now that Emma and I are straightened out, I need to go see her. I've been putting myself first and that has to stop. She's my sister, and no matter how strong she pretends to be, I want to be there for her while we figure out Dad's mess together.

"Hey, did you want breakfast? These biscuits are fantastic. Do you think Evelyn will give me the recipe if I asked? You need to have at least one, or I'm going to eat them all and I'll look pregnant even if I'm not." Emma looks up from the newspaper, her eyes crinkling with amusement.

Christ, I don't know how I can love one person so much.

I have to clear my throat before I answer. With that stupid surrogacy contract, I could have royally fucked us up and no amount of money or power would have been able to fix it. I would have learned Dad's lesson after all.

"I need to talk to you for a second," I say, moving the tray from the bed to a table near the window that looks over the creek.

She frowns. "Is everything okay?"

Sometimes she gets a little nervous, her smile trembling when she looks at me. I know this whole thing feels too good to be true, and I feel that way, too. Clark took our announcement in stride, kissing her cheek, shaking my hand, and inviting us out for a celebratory dinner. The paparazzi swarmed us, wanting to know our wedding date. Everyone assumes we're engaged, but I haven't asked and she hasn't brought it up. We're still finding our footing, but I would prefer we did with a ring on her finger.

I settle onto the bed, pushing the newspaper aside. I kept the box in the truck—I didn't want her to accidentally find it. I dressed in lounging pants and a t-shirt to run outside, but we have the B&B to ourselves. I reserved every room for the weekend, and we always will. I bought it. I don't want someone else staying in this room. It's too important to me and will hold too much sentimental value in the years to come.

"Yeah, yeah. You're happy?" I ask, smoothing my fingers down her cheek.

Tears fill her eyes. "I never thought you'd be mine. That you would ever love me back."

"I can't apologize enough for the past three years. The second I felt something, I should have told you, whether I thought you and Clark were a couple or not. If I would have asked you out on a date instead of hiding, maybe we could have done this years ago."

A tear drips down her cheek. "I love you, Jack."

"I hope you never stop." I pull the box out of my pocket, flip the lid, and set it on her knee. The square princess cut diamond sitting on a platinum band blinks at us. Holding her face in my hands, I say, "I know it's not winter. There's no fire in the fireplace, and I'm not making love to you on the floor when there's a perfectly good bed right here."

A smile quivers on her mouth, and she presses the back of her hand to her lips to hold in a sob.

"But, Emma, I'm never happier than when I'm with you. Grow old with me and let me love you for the rest of our lives. Will you marry me?"

"You remembered." She falls against my chest in a puddle of tears and laughter.

Wrapping my arms around her, I say, "I could never forget, but I'm sorry it's not snowing."

She sits up. "That's okay. I forgive you."

I wiggle the ring from the slit in the box and hold her left hand. "You didn't say yes."

She meets my eyes, curling her fingers away from me. "You said you didn't want to marry anyone."

"I didn't want to marry *just* anyone. I want to marry you. I love you, Emma. Be my wife."

Her hand shakes. "Yeah, I will."

My breath rushes out of me. She straightens out her hand, and I slip the ring onto her finger. I've been such an asshole, that could have been hit or miss, but I'm lucky Emma loves me and is willing to risk her heart.

"I won't let you down. I promise. I might not have had a very good role model growing up, but we'll carve out our own path, you and me and our children." I pause. "Emma, will you promise me something?"

Tilting her hand back and forth, letting the sun catch the diamond, she asks, "What?"

"If you are *ever* unhappy, will you tell me?"

Rising onto her knees, she rests her arms on my shoulders. She scrapes her fingernails along the nape of my neck, and it sends shivers over my skin. "Maybe Ron wasn't what you needed him to be, but my parents were everything I needed to understand how a healthy marriage should work. I know I'm going to have to adjust to certain things, seeing Raff less being one of them, but for every tiny thing I give up, I will gain a million more. If I ever do anything to make you unhappy, you have to tell me, too. Don't be afraid to talk to me. I will never leave you. I've wanted this for too long to throw it away."

We lie in bed for the rest of the day, talking, laughing, unearthing each other's secrets. I catch a glimpse of what the rest of my life will be like, and the mantra I used to tell myself dissipates.

There are no guarantees in this life.

People grow, people change. Sometimes they do it together, and sometimes they do it apart.

We make mistakes and regret them.

All I can do is learn from the mistakes my father made and promise with the ring on Emma's finger not to repeat them.

She loves me and will give me the chance.

I love her and I'll try my best, and as I fall into her eyes brimming with my future, I know that will be enough.

CHAPTER TWENTY-SIX

Rafferty

I knew it would happen. That the day Emma met Durand my world would eventually come undone. Sitting at my desk, sipping a whiskey, I know it's not as bad as that. She'll still be my best friend, albeit time spent with her relegated to dinner parties and fundraisers, texts and phone calls if she's not puking her guts out. Durand won't waste a second knocking her up.

But that's as it should be.

I'm happy for her, and I'll die on that hill.

The floor is empty and I'm alone in my office. I don't have much going on without plans with Emma every second I'm not at *Talk of the Town* verifying gossip and interviewing the celebs who trickle through Bridgeport for one thing or another.

My phone chimes, and Nic's name pops.

Her job is hanging by a shoestring, and I'm still pissed Durand left her high and dry. I don't know why she wanted to marry the fucker so bad. He might be a good looking asshole, but he has manners like he was born in a barn, and no offense to Jesus, either.

"Hey, dollface."

I don't know if the nickname pisses her off or turns her on.

"Raff, c-can you come over here?"

I lean forward in my chair. I've talked with Nic a lot over the past couple of weeks since Durand's public display of insensitivity, and I've never heard her sound like this.

"I'll be right there. Lock your doors."

I don't know why I said the last. A woman like Nic, she knows how to take care of herself.

She lives in an older part of Bridgeport—the kind of building where the hardwood floors are real, claw-foot bathtubs sit in the bathrooms waiting for a drop-dead gorgeous woman to fill them with bubbles, and tenants who use the fire escapes to climb onto the roof to count stars through the milky haze of light pollution. I order a car—I'll never find a parking space on the street this late at night.

The elegant elevator doesn't hurry to the tenth floor, and I stand impatiently in the stuffy car. Under my suit, sweat drips down my back.

Nic's apartment is a corner unit and I jog down the hallway. Someone is watching TV, the jingle of a popular sitcom carrying to me over the floorboards squeaking under my weight. I rap my knuckles against her door twenty minutes after she called me.

She checks the peephole, releases the security chain, and turns the deadbolt.

I push the door open and step inside, unsure of what I'm going to find. I turn the lock, and the *snick* itches under my skin.

Nic stands in the living room, and Bridgeport's glow through the large picture window lights her up like a movie star. Her skin is alabaster, her silver hair sparkles. My dick stirs, but I tell him to calm down. Jack Durand had her first, and I don't want sloppy seconds, even if they belong to a billionaire.

"What is it?" I ask, my throat dry.

"I need help, but I don't know who I can trust."

I step forward, but she stiffens and I stop. "What are you talking about?"

She lifts her arm, and a piece of paper flutters from her fingers.

It settles at my feet, and I pick it up and and skim the black words gouged into the white.

Nic sinks to the floor and covers her face with her hands.

"What does this mean? Who sent you this?"

I wait for an answer that doesn't come.

She's crying too hard to speak.

———

Raff and Veronica's story, *Lost & Found*, is available now on Kindle, in Kindle Unlimited, and Paperback.

Want to keep up with news, special sales, and giveaways? Sign up for my newsletter and have exclusive access to that and a free full-length ugly-duckling billionaire romance novel, *My Biggest Mistake*. Sign up here: https://vmrheault.com/subscribe/

ACKNOWLEDGMENTS

It's lonely work writing a book. Never mind that writing is work in itself, but it's worse when you don't have people to share that time with. Some writers have a fabulous support system in their spouses and other family members, and some writers go at it completely alone, from the moment they open a new document until they press publish, however they go about it.

I'm fortunate I've found some lovely people online to share my passion of writing with. They offer support and advice, and I hope I do the same for them in return.

But I have found that after I publish a book, the best way to celebrate is to pour a glass of wine and toast myself for never giving up. I could have dropped out of this game a long time ago, but I'm sure my characters are relieved because since I didn't, they exist.

Thanks to everyone in my life who has made this possible.

(And if you're looking for a good wine, Barefoot Cranberry is definitely the way to go.)

ALSO BY VM RHEAULT

Captivated by Her (Cedar Hill Duet Book One)

Addicted to Her (Cedar Hill Duet Book Two)

———

Rescue Me

———

Give & Take (The Lost & Found Trilogy Book One)

Lost & Found (The Lost & Found Trilogy Book Two)

Safe & Sound (The Lost & Found Trilogy Book Three)

———

Faking Forever

———

Twisted Alibis (Ghost Town Trilogy Book One)

Twisted Lullabies (Ghost Town Trilogy Book Two)

Twisted Lies (Ghost Town Trilogy Book Three)

———

A Heartache for Christmas

ABOUT THE AUTHOR

VM Rheault writes billionaire romance and contemporary romance under Vania Rheault.

She lives in Minnesota with her two children. When she's not writing, she's working her day job, sleeping, or enjoying the four seasons with a hot cup of coffee in hand.

Find her at vmrheault.com.

www.ingramcontent.com/pod-product-compliance
Lightning Source LLC
Chambersburg PA
CBHW061534210726
48287CB00006B/1956